The Toll of the Bush

BY

WILLIAM SATCHELL

ISBN 978-0-473-53642-8

Cover Photo: Broadwood Saddle, Hokianga, from the Northwood Collection, courtesy Alexander Turnbull Library, New Zealand.

Table of Contents

Geoffrey Hernshaw has left the high life in London to help his brother Robert with a scrub farm in Wairangi. Despite the difficulties the new world provides, Geoffrey finds friendship with Eve Milford, the daughter of the town's store keeper. Their similar interests and provocative conversations on evolution and religion has Geoffrey hoping for more than just friendship. Eve however, has another more aggressive suitor in Mr. Fletcher, the local clergyman and Geoffrey has an enemy, one with a secret that promises to be his undoing. Satchell's second novel *A Toll in the Bush* gives intrigue, scandal, drama and romance set against the striking backdrop of the Hokianga.

FOREWORD

William Satchell is known as the first major New Zealand pre-World War I poet and novelist. Most of his novels describe the stunning New Zealand landscape and the struggles that both colonizers and Maori faced. Some would consider him a romance novelist as relationships are important to his plots.

Satchell was born in London, England on 1 February 1860 to Thomas and Hannah Satchell. Thomas Satchell influenced his son with his love of books, editing and publishing. Thomas Satchell occasionally contributed to what is now known as the Oxford English Dictionary and became Surveyor-General before his death in 1887.

William Satchell went to St. John's College, Hurstpier point in Brighton and in 1877, he attended Heidelberg University in Germany. By 1879 however, he was back in England working with his father at his publishing company W. Satchell and Co., which published various art books and two periodicals. Satchell also tried his hand at writing.

There were no profits in the publishing company and disappointed with his writing, having no occupation and being in poor health, Satchell decided to emigrate to New Zealand. He advertised for a hired man and on 21 May 1886 Satchell sailed with Elmer J. Brown on the *Arawa*. His brother and cousin followed a year later and was financially supported by Satchell.

He spent time looking for land in the Waikato and Whangarei districts, but influenced by John Lundon of Rawene, Satchell settled in Waima in the Hokianga region in November 1887. He purchased 300-400 acres of land and actively turned it into fields of orchards and built a double storyhouse and outbuildings. He was well-known in Waima as Satchell founded a cricket club and helped build a hall there. He was still every bit an English patriot at this time. This added to his bearing, shyness, and mannerisms earned him the nickname "The Little Duke".

On 15th of November in 1889, Satchell married Susan Bryers, the grand-daughter of Joseph Bryers and Kohu Whareumu. This marriage would quietly influence Satchell's writing as he learned more about Maori culture and community. This only begins to appear in his novels

A Toll in the Bush and finally in *The Greenstone Door* more than twenty years later. His daughter Edith was born in 1890. Three more daughters and five sons would follow.

In 1891, Satchell discovered that he did not own his land as the person who sold it to him was not the sole owner. He was refused a refund and after receiving legal advice, Satchell was forced to give up the land and work as a local storekeeper. The store closed and in 1893, Satchell left to find work in Auckland, leaving his family behind in the care of his wife's aunt.

Satchell began to write again. He earned money through clerical work and journalism. In the years that followed, he was published in the *New Zealand Graphic*, *Auckland Star*, *New Zealand Herald* and Sydney *Bulletin*. He wrote under various pen names such as Samuel Cliall White, Warwick Simpson, William J. Stewart, William Sage and William Scott. Satchell became known as a minor colonial poet.

He was reunited with his family and because of his investments in the *Auckland Free Stock and Mining Exchange*as well as his work, he could afford to buy a home on Grange Street in Mount Roskill. His first published book *Patriotic and other poems* released in 1900 and was well received.

In 1901 Satchell started the weekly magazine *The Maorilander* which he solely wrote, edited, collected advertisements and supervised its circulation. It was short-lived and survived for only two months. The magazine showed Satchell's interest in literature from New Zealand and by New Zealanders. Though it was only briefly published, it is often cited as one of Satchell's major accomplishments.

Satchell began to write novels and in 1902 *The Land of the Lost* was published, followed by *The Toll of the Bush*in 1905 and *The Elixir of Life*in 1907. Bad investments caused Satchell to sell his Grange Street home and move to Birkenhead. He settled in Northcote on 5 acres of orchard.

Satchell worked in horticulture and poultry farming and became the part-time secretary to the Auckland Horticultural Society in 1909. He continued to write and published *The Greenstone Door* 1914. It was not well received due to the impending war. This disappointed Satchell so much that he never wrote another novel.

Instead he found work as an accountant for the Robert P. Gibbons Timber Company first in Kopu, Thames and then in Auckland until 1936. His novel the *The Greenstone Door* became popular and it was reprinted in 1935. *The Land of the Lost* was reprinted in 1938 a year after Satchell's wife, Susan, died.

Satchell lived in semi-retirement in Mount Roskill until he was awarded a Civil list pension for his contribution to New Zealand literature. He accepted it due to his poor royalties. He did care a great deal about his family and "never took up his pen to write without a feeling of guilt." He died on 21ˢᵗ October 1942. The *Bulletin* wrote "he was one of his adopted countries best novelists, if not with his *The Greenstone Door* the very best."

Satchell drew upon his early years in New Zealand when writing *The Toll of the Bush*. The settings are beautifully and accurately described and even though Geoffrey hates this land, he can't help but admire its beauty.

The Toll of the Bush tells us about the lives of a small group of pioneers. The protagonists Geoffrey and Robert Hernshaw have a scrub farm. Their lives entangle with many "lost" people including Mrs. Andersen, a woman dealing with a drunken bush husband and raising a large family on her own as well as her eldest daughter Lena who becomes Robert's love interest. We meet Sandy Milward whose father runs a store in town and his sister – Geoffrey's love interest – Eve. There is Mr. Fletcher the evangelical clergyman and Geoffrey's rival for Eve, Mr. and Mrs. Gird whom most people go to for advice and finally, Mr. Wickers who holds a secret which may be Geoffrey's undoing.

Geoffrey's character could be likened to Hamlet in the sense that he ponders more than he acts. He does not feel worthy enough to marry Eve and does not defend himself when he is implicated by Wickers. Because of his lack of action, Geoffrey loses Eve to Mr. Fletcher and they become engaged.

Geoffrey also gives Satchell the means to hold a debate between evolution and religion. As Geoffrey's principles are guided by Christianity but his scientific reasoning and belief in evolution is a direct contrast to Fletcher's blind belief in faith.

Maori characters play very minor parts in the novel, one of which is Pine, portrayed initially as lazy and a bit of a cheat as he is "caught out" by Robert for not ploughing as deep as when he is in sight of his bosses. Satchell describes Maori community in a similar fashion to the land "fertile but neglected". There are Maori that gather for service on the beach and Maori trackers later in the novel. They are little more than props and background in this book but richer characters in comparison to *The Land of the Lost*.

The interaction of these characters create a very intriguing and layered novel full of action and plot twists. Characters are stereotypes but complex ones and the plot is executed with precision and skill. This novel though set at the turn of last century is easy to read and absorbing. It could easily rival any popular novel written today.

CHAPTER I

ON THE ROAD TO THE SECTION

AT that point, and for the next fifty miles, the Great North Road was a sea of mud, but the travellers paid small attention to the fact, and it was only when their horses legs sank suddenly through a broken culvert that they made remarks uncomplimentary to the County Council and the Government. The horses said nothing, but there was a sufficient reason for that. They plodded along steadily, their noses down, their heels sucking at monotonous intervals out of the yellow clay. The track they followed was that of the horses which had gone before them, and it was churned up to the consistency, and much of the colour, of butter in summer-time. It led them sometimes into the middle of the road, sometimes—especially if there were a deep ditch there—along the extreme edge, and the only consistency it showed was in going to spots which the riders, for their part, would rather have avoided.

The men rode in single file, the man in front talking back over his shoulder to the one behind him. Now and then the nature of the road permitted them to range up alongside, but this was seldom. Behind them, on a neck of land jutting out into the broad tidal river, lay the township—a handful of white wooden buildings—shut in, save where cut by the roadway, by an impenetrable sea of scrub. A steamer lay alongside the wharf, the throb of a winch floating up through the chill an of the wintry afternoon. A few cows grazed outside the Court House. These were the sole evidences of activity. The steamer was an excitement which repeated itself—weather permitting—once a fortnight throughout the year, and affected the destinies of the people for fifty miles around. The cows were constant—except at milking-time, when they had to be sought for in the scrub, usually standing perfectly still until discovered by an irate owner and driven off recalcitrant to a half-starved calf.

The men were both young, the elder not more than twenty-eight, and the other scarcely yet come to manhood. There was a likeness between them which betrayed some relationship, though this was rather in indefinable characteristics than in actual resemblance, the elder brother's face possessing a beauty and restlessness of spirit which were lacking in the simpler, yet more forceful countenance of the younger. The face of the man in front was for the moment clouded and gloomy, while that of the younger brother wore an apologetic expression.

'Couldn't see his way?' said the elder brother, with a short laugh. 'He's like ourselves, then. What else did he say?'

'Said he'd got a lot of money out he never expected to see again. The natives had gone through him for four or five hundred, and that there was close on three hundred owing in the settlement alone. Said he'd put the wire in at a trifle over cost if we could manage to pay cash. He's not a bad sort, Geoffrey.'

Geoffrey was silent awhile. Then he said, 'I ought to have gone myself. You can't get credit without lying, and you're a poor hand at it, Robert.'

'I just said what you told me,' replied Robert slowly. 'Only when he came to talk back it looked different somehow, and—I'm not clever like you, Geoff.'

The words were simply spoken, and free from intent, but the elder brother laughed as though he saw something suggestive about them.

'We'll just have to go on blasting out rails,' he said presently. 'My God! how sick I am of the whole business. Is there any hope for the wretched country at all? Look at it!' he continued with a sudden angry scorn,—' clay and scrub and precipices, with here and there an acre of orchard, and all the plagues of Egypt domiciled in it. What's the good of going on?'

'I was looking at Thomas's place,' said Robert ponderingly, 'when I was up there with the cricket team last Christmas. It must have looked like this twenty years ago. It's green enough now.'

'And you can look forward twenty years? Yet after all, why not? It's better than looking back. They have electric railways in England now, but when Queen Elizabeth lived they were probably content with roads no better than this.'

'Is she dead?' asked Robert, relieved at the sudden change of subject.

Geoffrey started and laughed; then a flush deepened in his cheek, and he muttered, 'What a damned shame!' and thereafter jogged along in silence.

The road wound gradually upwards round the hillsides, presenting a clay bank on one hand, and a steep, scrub-covered slope on the other. Down in the hollow the river lay like a silver octopus, its tentacles stretching far into the black bush-covered lands. Here and there were clearings, dwarfed into insignificance by the immensity of the virgin landscape from which they had been hewn. Some were black from a recent burn, others vividly green with the newly sown grass; in their midst slab or weatherboard huts marked the abodes of the pioneers. The river itself was deserted—not a boat or sail was visible, and save for a pair of black swans drifting in with the tide there was no sign of moving life within the compass of the horizon.

Geoffrey's eye scanned the scene as he moved forward. 'Poor devils!' he said presently, 'working, their hearts out, and for what? What we want here is an army. Why are there not armies of peace as of war? Man's the most astonishing kind of fool, if you come to reflect upon his ways. He could land an army corps here, and for an amount no greater than it costs to keep the beggars in idleness, convert the wilderness into a garden where men could live contentedly.'

'Perhaps some day he will think of that,' said. Robert.

Reaching the brow of the hill, the tea-tree came to an end, and they began to descend through mixed bush, the road rapidly degenerating into a quagmire as they proceeded. Here and there fascines of tea-tree bridged the more rotten places, and for a chain or so at a dark turn of the road rough slabs took the place of the tea-tree and slush. At length the winding track turned suddenly out of the bush, and beneath them, at the bottom of a steep slope, lay a green valley bathed in sunlight. Low scrub-covered hills walled it in; beyond rose great bush-clad ranges, sharply outlined against the silvery sky.

Like pilgrims gazing on the Promised Land, the men scanned the scene, as their horses ploughed and floundered down the muddy slope. In the centre of the green plain was a group of white buildings, surrounded by a hedge of macrocarpa. Maori children were pouring out of a gate in the hedge and scattering themselves over the valley, the sound of their voices rising sharply through the still air. Large tracts of the green sward were unfenced, and over these strayed the cattle and horses of the native community. Along the sides of the road, and back in fenced paddocks, stood a number of unpainted weatherboard huts and rakish-looking whares,[1] the edges of their palm-thatched roofs torn into fibres by the wind. Here and there was a storehouse built on piles, or a steep palm roof rising from the ground, and probably sheltering

---

[1] 'Wharrey,' native hut.

the kumara or sweet-potato pits. The only signs of cultivation were the bleached maize stems of the previous season. Old fruit-trees—chiefly peach, quince, and fig—grouped themselves at various points. Cattle, horses, pigs, dogs, fowls, ducks roamed everywhere through the broken fences at their own sweet will.

'If one had a place like this now,' said Geoffrey, reining in his horse, 'it might be possible to do something. It seems to me that the only land worth having in this north country is in the hands of the natives.'

'They were here first, I suppose?' Robert said.

'Yes, that is a good argument so far as it goes, but meantime the white men are sitting round on the hills eating grass, and the country is at a standstill. If this sort of thing were happening just outside Wellington, it would not be tolerated for longer than was necessary for the framing of an Act to put an end to it, but the justice of the case is not affected by the fact that we are a long way from the seat of government and unable to make ourselves heard.'

'The rails will be better in the long run,' Robert said, reverting to the original subject of discussion. 'There's plenty of good timber, and it's only just the difference of a month or so in getting it out. Of course, if you're set on doing the fencing right off there is no trouble about it— Major Milward will give us all the credit we want, and—there is Uncle Geoffrey.'

Geoffrey's brows contracted and he shifted his seat in the saddle. 'We will get out the rails,' he said shortly.

At the foot of the hill the ground became unexpectedly solid, and the horses, pricking up their ears, scampered gleefully forward.

'Shall we see about the ploughing?' Robert shouted, as they galloped round the bend by the schoolhouse, and came abreast of a low Maori whare.

Geoffrey reined in his horse, and turning from the road, jumped the broken fence, and pulled up at the open doorway.

A young native girl, with dishevelled hair, came out at the sound of his approach and stood regarding them, rubbing the sandflies off one leg with the toes of the other.

'Pine[1] in?' Geoffrey asked.

---

[1] Pronounced 'Pinney.'

The girl turned and called to some one in the interior in a shrill voice. There was a rustling inside, and presently a native appeared, yawning and rubbing his eyes. He was an intensely ugly, good-humoured-looking man of some thirty years. His clothing consisted of a pair of tattered trousers and a faded and dirty singlet, which had long since parted company with its buttons. He looked at his visitors, said 'Hullo' in a sleepy voice, and leaned against the doorpost.

'Lazy beggar!' said Geoffrey, smiling. 'Why aren't you tilling the soil?'

'Too soon to tirr him yet,' replied Pine; 'nex' mont' prenty nuff time.'

'Now's the time for me. I want you to come over and plough up a few acres for the potatoes.'

'I tink dis time too soon for taters. More better by'm-by.'

'Well, we'll chance that. When can you come?'

Pine turned the question over in his mind. 'My burrock up te bush tese times,' he said at length, with a prodigious yawn. 'I not seen. P'r'aps tree days I find him. You got any prough up to your place?'

Geoffrey nodded and gathered up the reins. 'Well, l'11 look for you on Thursday then,' he said; 'and mind, no humbug. I want the thing done before you start working the bullocks to death on your own account.'

Pine laughed boisterously. 'How many acres you tink?' he asked.

'About three,' said Robert; 'it won't take you long.'

'All ri'; p'r'aps I come Wensday.' He pulled a pipe from his belt, thrust a finger into the interior, and then began to search his pockets, uttering little clicks of astonishment. Geoffrey threw him the remains of a plug of tobacco, which he caught dexterously and proceeded to cut up.

'New parson here little before time,' he said. 'Kapai dat chap mo te korero.[1] Ah, te pest!'[2]

'Good talker, is he?' asked Geoffrey, pausing on the point of wheeling his horse.

'All the same te saw-mill,' said Pine; 'very big soun'.' He laid his hand suddenly on the girl's head. 'Aha, my ch-eild! Poh! poh!'

---

[1] Good man for the talk.

[2] 'Te pest,' the best.

The girl ducked under his arm, and dived into the interior of the whare.

'He's like that, is he?' said Geoffrey. Then he smiled and added, 'Yes, I've heard of him.'

'Te big rangatira[1] that,' said Pine admiringly, taking a slow and stately step from one doorpost to the other. 'Poh! poh! I tink very soon now all the people go to church a good deal.'

'Shouldn't wonder,' said Geoffrey.

Pine filled his pipe and lit it. 'You tink dat ferra the big rangatira?' he asked, fixing his dark eyes on Geoffrey.

'All parsons are rangatiras, you know,' Geoffrey responded lightly.

Pine squatted down in the doorway and blew a fragrant tobacco cloud. 'Yes'day,' he said, 'I come roun' Major Milward's place up to Wairangi. I see te new parson on a beach, walk up an' down with Iwi, how you call Eve. I tink very soon dat te pair.'

Geoffrey was gazing moodily at some object across the valley, but he appeared to have heard. 'What makes you think so?' he asked idly.

Pine continued to watch him with undisguised curiosity. 'I come on a little way,' he continued. 'I see Sandy an' I say to him, "By'm-by your sister marry te pakeha?" "Oh, go to hell!" say Sandy. Dat why I tink.'

'Then because Sandy told you to go to hell you argue that his sister is about to marry a parson,' Geoffrey remarked with a wry smile.

'Dat why,' said Pine confidently. 'If Sandy laugh, den p'r'aps yes, p'r'aps no, but Sandy angry, I say to myself, "Aha!"'

Geoffrey lifted his eyebrows slightly, then with a curt good-night turned his horse for the road. Robert stayed a moment to renew the subject of the ploughing, then set out after his brother.

The sun was setting in the gap above the river, and the sky to the eastward showed signs of darkening. Geoffrey was already far ahead, flying along rapidly through the shifting shadows. Robert set his horse in motion, but it was not until he had left the confines of the valley and reached the muddy road that wound through the gap, that he again caught up with Geoffrey. The latter acknowledged his arrival by a glance over his shoulder, and they jogged along in silence in single file as be-

---

[1] 'Rangatira,' a chief.

fore. The road deteriorated rapidly as they descended the other side of the cutting, finally striking an un-bridged creek, where the flood waters roared up to the saddle flaps. From this point an ascent of half a mile brought them to the brow of the hill overlooking the river. There was still a glimmer of twilight, revealing dimly the slab huts of the settlers, the rigid arms of fire-blackened trees, extended as though in a sort of mad frenzy at the fate which had overtaken them, outlined here and there against the river.

There was a sound as of distant thunder that never died away—the roar of the surf on the bar at the river mouth.

CHAPTER II

THE BROTHERS

THE home of Geoffrey and Robert Hernshaw was a weatherboard shell, divided into three rooms by rough wooden partitions. It possessed a brick fireplace and chimney—one of the two contained in the settlement—and was further remarkable in having three windows and being floored throughout. The furniture was scanty, comprising nothing but the barest necessaries. There were two stretchers in the bedroom, a table, a few wooden chairs and some cooking utensils in the kitchen. The third room, which also contained a stretcher, appeared to be used for the storage of anything not immediately required in the other parts of the house. The main door opened direct into the kitchen, and the first thing likely to strike a visitor was the fact that the opening of the door caused the chimney to smoke violently.

The smell of recent cooking had not quite left the kitchen. A Rochester lamp stood on the table. Robert was seated on a box in a corner scraping a few pieces of gum, which had turned up in the process of digging a vegetable garden. Occasionally he looked thoughtfully at his brother, who was moving restlessly about the small room, giving vent now and then to a smothered exclamation as though his thoughts were too many for him.

'You never opened that last English paper, Geoff,' he said at last.

'Didn't I?' and Geoffrey coming to a standstill looked absently at his brother; then he resumed his restless movements.

'It's over there in the corner, under the oatmeal,' Robert said presently.

Geoffrey looked hazily in the direction indicated, then crossed over, pulled the paper from its resting-place, and tearing it open sat resolutely down at the table, and glared steadfastly at a picture purporting to portray a minor incident in the Boer war. He was still staring at it when, a quarter of an hour later, Robert, having finished his gum, came to look over his shoulder. Geoffrey turned a few pages hurriedly and found a fresh picture.

' "Re-inforcements leaving South-ampton," ' read Robert slowly. 'That's London, I suppose.'

Geoffrey paused before replying, and there was something of irritation in his voice as he answered: 'Your admiration for London rather carries you away, Robert. That city does not embrace the whole of England. If you could really grasp the fact that London is the capital of England and not *vice versa,* that would be a step towards the understanding of many things at present concealed from you. And, by the way, Elizabeth *is* dead.'

'Elizabeth?'

'You remember my alluding to Queen Elizabeth and your asking me whether she was dead. She has been dead, as a matter of fact, about three hundred years.'

Robert sat down. 'It's a good job there was no one about when I asked you,' he said, with an uneasy laugh. 'But it's not exactly my fault that I am so ignorant. I don't think that I ever really had time to learn things. There was always something: what with father being sick and that—and no money in the house most times, except the bit I was able to pick up.'

Geoffrey let his hand fall on his brother's. 'I am a brute,' he said, flushing. 'Every word you say is true and a thousand more. God forgive me, old chap; you are worth a hundred such wretches as I! I have had all the good things of life and made nothing of them, while you have had to remain content with the crumbs.' He rose and resumed his pacing of the room. 'If there were any way of escape,' he muttered. 'Is this to go on all our lives? For that's the devil of it—in a few years we shall cease to care, like every one else. Look at the beggars up in the township. A lot of young-old men, half of them bachelors, living a life of drift and satisfied. If I am to be content with such a life I should prefer to die now, while the lust for something better is gnawing my heart out. Are *you* content with the prospect?' he asked suddenly, facing his brother.

Robert looked ponderingly at the wall in front of him. 'I was telling you about Thomas's place,' he said slowly; 'but that's not the only one, and they all say the same thing. They stuck to it year after year, and the life was hard, there's no denying, but in the end *they—got—there.*'

'I see,' said Geoffrey, seating himself and watching his brother's face.

'There was Major Mil ward,' Robert resumed, in the same slow, calculating manner, as though possessed of an anxiety to say what was in his thoughts to the best of his ability; 'he used to tell me about it during the three years I was working for him before you came out. It was fifty years ago that he built his first whare on the sand-bank where he lives now. It is a long time, but in fifty years you would be no older than he is now. He didn't have a great deal of money—just a few hundreds. He got hold of things slowly—kauri[1] bushes and that, and every now and then he put in a few trees, and branded a few calves, and added a room or two to the house. He kept on growing, and it didn't take as long as I said—not by a generation; he's been a rich man longer'n we've been alive. Yes, and he's given away more'n we've ever owned besides. And he's lived well and had the best of everything up from Auckland—wine and that; and he's been home in England, and most of his family have been there, and I guess he's got enough left to do all our fencing at one pop, and the bank 'Id never notice he'd done it. Yet I'm not saying fifty years isn't a terrible time to look forward to,' he concluded a little lamely, turning an apologetic glance from the wall to the other's face.

Geoffrey sat watching him in a sort of fascination, and for awhile nothing was said.

Robert, if he had expected an outbreak, was perhaps agreeably surprised when Geoffrey's next remark showed his thoughts to have slipped into another channel.

'There's that box of books in the other room. It's a pity we can't put up a few shelves for them—or would it be better to wait till the place is lined?'

'The rain does leak through the walls some when the wind's blowing; but perhaps the corner by the fireplace would do as it is.'

Geoffrey rose, measured the corner with his eye, glanced at one or two other possible positions for the library, then lit a candle and went away into the storeroom.

The place was in great disorder, and bore the appearance of having had its contents pitched in through a doorway only sufficiently opened to effect that object, and Geoffrey's new-born enthusiasm was slightly damped by the spectacle. However, he set down the light, took off his coat, and looked resolutely about him. The box he was in search of stood in one corner, and had been used as a suitable spot on which to deposit such articles as a camp oven, a bag of staples, a couple of rusty ploughshares and other miscellaneous ironmongery. Geoffrey removed them one by one, and having returned to the outer room for a bunch of

---

[1] *Kauri Dammara australis,* the chief timber tree of the North Island.

keys, unlocked the box. Some stout oiled paper covered the top, and beneath were the books carefully packed away, as though by a hand that loved them. He remembered that it was almost exactly a year since he had placed the last volume in position, and the thought of the life that closed with the closing lid lay heavy on his heart as he gazed. But it was not a book, he now remembered, that was the last thing to be put away; it was this bundle of letters, some of them dating back nearly twenty years. He pulled one out at random and, still on his knees before the box, began to read.

He was busily reading when, over an hour later, Robert put his head in at the door to remind him of the necessity for sleep.

What Geoffrey saw in the letters may be more conveniently put before the reader in narrative form.

More than twenty years before Robert Hernshaw, senior, journalist, having come within measureable distance of grasping one of the plums of his profession—it seemed he had but to stretch out his hand to attain it—was brought up standing by the verdict of his family physician. The latter diagnosed lung trouble of a serious nature, and put before his patient the alternative of a short life in London, or restored health and a prospect of longevity in a kindlier climate. Hernshaw, when he had become convinced that the alternatives were real, left the solution of the problem to his wife, merely expressing his own preference for the present order of things at whatever cost. But Mrs. Hernshaw decided differently. And so it came about that husband and wife sailed for New Zealand, leaving their only child, Geoffrey, then a boy of seven, in the care of his paternal uncle, after whom he had been named. Shortly after reaching their new home their second son, Robert, was born to them.

Having relinquished the prospect of power and comparative affluence for the sake of an increase in years, Robert Hernshaw determined that it should not be through any action of his if the price of the relinquishment went unpaid. He had been told that an active outdoor life was demanded of him, and he was determined that the demand should be met. So when Mrs. Hernshaw proposed that they should make their home in a pleasant suburb of one of the larger towns, and that he should continue in the practice of his profession, Hernshaw at once vetoed the idea. Instead, he bought a piece of land in the Auckland district and settled down to make a living by the sweat of his brow. He had too lately emerged from the barren places of his profession to have accumulated much money, and his knowledge of his new pursuit would have been ludicrous if it had not been tragic in its inadequacy —the result was a foregone conclusion. All might yet have been well, even though his capital was exhausted, had his nature showed any signs of rooting itself in the new soil. But it was not so. The manual labour, the people with whom he was brought in contact, the very air and aspect of his adopted country, were alike repugnant to him. The scorn of his surroundings accompanied him throughout the days; and after some years the old malady, scotched for the time, again came to life, and added its torments to the general misery. Then the morbid brooding developed into a sort of madness. He was seized with a fierce resentment at destiny. He accused the heavens of treachery, as though his action in coming to New Zealand had been the result of a compact with God. In this persuasion he died miserably, supported towards the end by the efforts of the wife and child whom, in his self-absorption, he had neglected.

Robert at this time was fourteen years of age, and had been brought up almost entirely without schooling. His mother had taught him to read and write and solve simple problems in arithmetic, but beyond this the only knowledge he possessed had been derived haphazard from the conversation of those about him. For seven or eight months mother and son were dependent largely on the charity of Major Milward, the pioneer settler of the district, and then the woman, worn out by the long trouble, sickened and died. It is probable that the sufferings of the wife had been little if any less keen than those of the husband, but she made no sign—not even when she lay dying with her arms round the neck of her beloved boy. 'It will be better for you, my darling,' was the one tacit acknowledgment she made that life had been a failure. And though the boy did not believe it then or afterwards, it may be that she was right. Life did in fact improve for him immediately. Major Milward, who had entertained a sort of half-tolerant, half-contemptuous pity for the father, showed only pity for the son. He made an opening for him on the station, and when finally, at the age of nineteen, Robert left to join his brother, he carried nothing but good wishes with him.

Far removed from contact with this sordid drama, Geoffrey meanwhile had grown up into manhood. The change which meant so much to his parents affected him not at all. From the comforts of his own home he passed easily to those of his uncle's well-appointed house, in whose serene atmosphere he found none but the pleasant things of life. Though not exactly a wealthy man, Mr. Hernshaw was an extremely generous one. Having taken over the charge of the boy, he at once placed him on a footing of absolute equality with his own children, and so naturally was this accomplished that neither as a child nor a man could Geoffrey recall one instance of a distinction being made between him and his cousins. He received the same public-school training, the same holidays, the same allowance of pocket-money. His scholastic career, though showing no brilliance, was well above the average, and if the youth revealed no instinctive leaning towards any particular pursuit or profession, he at least showed a power of doing a number of very dissimilar things remarkably well. It was this very versatility that went against him in the end. His uncle, keeping a keen eye on his family, at once seized on any bent in his children which seemed to give a prospect of being profitably employed, but Geoffrey puzzled him. The youth, having visited a picture gallery, would come home full of the idea of painting a picture himself. With a liberal allowance of pocket-money, he was able to gratify any whim immediately on its occurrence, and he would set to work. In a space of time incredibly short, considering everything, he would have something to show the family, and whatever may have been its real merits, it was at least sufficient to convince Mr. Hernshaw that he had at last discovered his nephew's bent. But in the course of a month or so —or when, to speak precisely, Geoffrey had learned enough to know that his labours were only on the point of commencing—he would begin to lose ardour, and very shortly thereafter the implements of his art would find their way to the lumber-room. This was a course of things which repeated itself again and again.

'Do you think you would care to study painting?' his uncle would ask.

'It would take some time, sir, and cost a good deal of money.'

'Well, that's all right; you find the time and I'll find the money.'

'It's very good of you, sir,' Geoffrey would say, and promise to think the thing over. That was the end of it.

Whether it were that there was an ineradicable defect in the young man's nature, or merely that his character was slow in developing, was hard to say, but the years crept by and left the problem still unsolved. If he had any taste to which he returned more frequently than another it was for literature. From his boyhood he had been in the habit of scribbling verses and tales for his own amusement, and though there were long intervals between these fits the number of them had given him a certain facility with his pen. His uncle had suggested that he should follow the profession of his father, and Geoffrey consented to give the thing a trial; but this did not last long. He satisfied neither his employers nor himself. The things they wanted done rarely possessed any interest for him, and when his interest was not aroused he was, and felt himself to be, but a dull dog.

'I was talking to Humphreys,' his uncle said at last. 'He seems to think you are wasting your time.'

'I'm sure of it,' said Geoffrey.

'Ah, well, I suppose we had better give it up and try something else. Humphreys tells me he thinks you might succeed in light literature. How does the idea strike you?'

'I fancy it would be preferable to the heavy, if the heavy is what I have been attempting so far.'

His uncle looked serious, and after a moment got up and paced thoughtfully up and down the room. The nephew noticed that some haggard lines that had lately come into the elder man's face were more pronounced than usual. 'I am willing to give it a trial, sir,' he said.

'Yes, but what I am anxious to find out is not what you are willing to attempt to oblige me, but what you are desirous of doing yourself, because time is going on and the matter is—important.' He came to a standstill and looked down on his nephew, his face working under the stress of some inward emotion. 'I have tried, my boy,' he said, 'to obtain and deserve your confidence.'

'Oh, sir,' said Geoffrey, springing to his feet, deeply moved, 'all my life I have looked up to you as the best and most generous of men.'

'I have endeavoured to make no difference between you and your cousins. When I die you will find that what I have is divided equally amongst all of you. I had already made up my mind to that when I first undertook the charge of you, and the only thing which could have made me alter my intention was the chance of your father's success in New Zealand. I never thought he would succeed, and as a fact he did not. From what Robert tells us he appears to have left very little.' Mr. Hernshaw paused a moment and collected his thoughts. 'I have mentioned this for a reason you will see presently. Of late I have had losses; they have been long continued and severe, and though I believe I have weathered the worst and am now beginning to make headway again, yet, as a fact, I am a poorer man than I was fifteen or twenty years ago. At one time the fact of your having no occupation would perhaps not have greatly mattered, though to my mind every man is strengthened in character by making a living for himself; but now things are different, and though the means of subsistence are secured to you all, there is not, I am afraid, at this moment very much more.' Mr. Hernshaw concluded with an apologetic and anxious glance at his nephew.

Whatever Geoffrey's defects were, his heart at least was sound, and he was genuinely touched at the elder man's generosity and unselfishness, and could not but reflect that the losses so quietly referred to must have been a source of long-standing and wearing anxiety to his uncle. But the effect of the confidence was not what Mr. Hernshaw had expected or desired at the time it was made. The young man's placid acceptance of the existing order of things had in fact suffered disturbance, but the result was not apparently the creation of anxiety as to his own future, but the desire to relieve his uncle of the cost of his support.

It was at this juncture that a letter came to hand from Robert descriptive of his life at Major Milward's, and full of hopes and projects for the future. To Geoffrey it seemed like the opening of a direct path through a maze, and his resolve was quickly taken.

Then began a long and strenuous struggle with his uncle, his aunt, and his cousins. The girls promised him a Maori wife, and to arouse his aversion to such a lot appeared before him in petticoats, their hair dishevelled, whereat he was struck with admiration and expressed a still keener desire to be gone. The boys characterised the proceeding strongly as 'rotten,' and suggested all manner of harrowing and degrading occupations, which they feigned to believe were preferable to the abandonment of the land of his birth. Mrs. Hernshaw spoke of the grief he was causing his uncle, who, she said, suspected that Geoffrey had taken his confidence as an indirect way of saying he did not care to support him any longer.

Geoffrey fairly laughed at the idea. 'I should know myself an ungrateful scoundrel if such a thought had ever entered my mind,' he said. 'I want to go to New Zealand for my own personal gratification.'

'Is there nothing behind all this? If it were only for a short time! But you do not say that.'

'No, I do not say that; I don't know how that may be.'

That was as far as he would go towards the possibility of a return.

Mr. Hernshaw's objections were those of a man of the world. 'I have always believed,' he said once, 'that the people who succeed in colonial life are the people who would succeed anywhere.'

'Their opportunities may be greater there,' Geoffrey suggested.

'I should doubt it, except on special lines. The opportunities for a clever man in a city of four or five million inhabitants must be enormous. New Zealand has only the population of a London suburb.'

'A man's chances would therefore seem to be proportionately increased.'

'With respect to the area of the country, yes; and were you proposing to ship a few million labourers the argument would be sound; but how does the fact that there are large areas of imperfectly populated country affect your prospects?'

Geoffrey was unable to explain with any clearness. His ideas, it must be confessed, were vague, but there was no vagueness about his determination.

And so it came about that one summer afternoon he stood on the deck of an outward bound steamer and saw the coasts of England fade into the haze.

CHAPTER III

PLOUGHING THE LAND

IT was a cloudless August morning, warm in the sun and cold in the shade. The settlement was wide-awake, and a pleasant smell of wood-fires mingled with the fresh breath of the river. The sun had been above the horizon a considerable time, but Mrs. Gird's rooster still proclaimed the fact at intervals, the announcement being received with derision or silent contempt by the birds nearer the river. The Girds occupied the out-post, so to speak, of the little army of pioneers, their section being the far-thest from the water and the most densely timbered of any. The rooster might be excused, for there was hardly more than twilight there yet.

Robert had been fishing since daylight and was returning up the track, laden with a large bundle of schnappers. The track rose diagonal-ly through the settlement, cutting it into halves and affording an outlet to the settlers on both sides. It was in fact a continuation of the road followed by the brothers some days before, but though the trees had been cut away to the correct width, it had not yet been formed and—paradoxical as it may appear to the uninitiated—was consequently passable even to a pedestrian. Now the way would be merely a wide track through a dense jungle, again it would open out and disclose a fire-blackened landscape, covered with unsightly stumps, with perhaps a rude slab hut in the midst of it.

Robert's progress had been twice interrupted by morning greetings from neighbouring housewives, and fish being always an acceptable offering he reached the house somewhat more lightly burdened than when he had left the boat. Outside the fence was a team of bullocks in charge of a small native boy, whose striking likeness to Pine at once at-tested the ownership of the team. Pine himself was in the paddock with Geoffrey, looking at the land to be ploughed. Robert made his way to the door, where he found two persons seated on the doorstep, evidently waiting his arrival. The elder was a fair, blue-eyed girl, named Lena An-dersen, while the other, a child of three or four years, Robert judged to be one of her numerous brothers and sisters. The girl was dressed in a flour-bag, from which the brand had not entirely faded, and this, so far as could be judged, was the whole of her costume.

'Well, Lena,' said Robert, 'what's the trouble?'

'Please, Robert, mother says can you spare her some tea till father goes to the store?'

The request was not an isolated one, and the implied promise of return Robert knew to be problematical of fulfilment, but he said 'Yes' cheerfully and went for the tea.

'And mother says,' Lena went on quickly, 'if you could spare her some soap she would do her washing to-day while it's fine; but if not, it doesn't matter till father goes up the river.'

'That's all right, Lena,' Robert said. Then a thought struck him. 'What do you all do when your mother washes the clothes?' he asked.

The girl blushed furiously and backed out of the house. 'That's our business,' she retorted.

Robert seemed staggered at the result of his simple question and hastened to restore amicable relations by a gift of fish from his bundle. 'They're just out of the river,' he said; 'and here's the soap and tea, and I didn't mean to offend you.'

Lena, with downcast eyes, allowed herself to be burdened with the fish and other articles.

'You are sure you don't want any sugar or anything,' Robert asked anxiously, 'till—till your father comes back?'

'No, thank you,' said Lena.

Robert thought he detected a suspicion of a smile at the corner of the girl's mouth and became more cheerful. 'I haven't seen you going to school for the last week or two,' he said.

'I haven't been going,' replied Lena, looking up. 'I've left school—I've passed the sixth standard.'

Robert looked impressed, as he was intended to be. 'I suppose you've read Green's *Short?*' he asked tentatively.

Green's *Short History of the English People* was one of the volumes unearthed from the box of books, and Robert was already deep in the perusal of it. He spoke of it as Green's *Short,* not that he had any idea that there was a Green's Long, but to suggest lifelong familiarity with the work.

'No,' said Lena, puzzled.

Robert smiled a little to himself. 'It's real good,' he said. 'And couldn't they fight! That Black Prince was a good piece. I'll lend it you by and by.'

'Oh, it's history!' exclaimed Lena, curling her lip disdainfully. 'Of course I've learned that, but it wasn't Green's. I know all the kings and queens by heart and all the dates.'

It had never occurred to Robert that there might be more than one history of England, and the possibilities opened up by Lena's concluding words brought him rapidly to his bearings. Still he let himself down as gracefully as possible. 'It's good reading of an evening,' he said lightly. 'That Henry VIII. was a fair terror,' he added.

'He was Defender of the Faith,' said Lena.

Robert looked thoughtful. 'I suppose he was in a way,' he admitted; then he made a dart for firmer ground, 'but he had a terrible lot of wives.'

Lena had nothing to say to this, and Robert, feeling that he had scored a point, wisely changed the subject.

'Geoff's got a rare lot of books, Lena,' he said, following her to the fence. 'When you want something to read, you come to me and I'll find you a stunner.'

Lena made no reply, but when the slip-rail was reached she looked quickly at her companion. 'Thank you for these,' she said, indicating the articles she was carrying; 'but I have a good mind to give you the soap back.'

Robert could make nothing of this remark until considerably later in the day, and by that time Mrs. Andersen's washing was probably on the line.

Pine and Geoffrey were still discussing the ploughing. Pine, having had the piece pointed out to him, had cast his eyes about and found a spot easier of accomplishment, and he was now trying to persuade Geoffrey to select the easier site for the plantation.

'I tink much more betterer dis piece,' he said. 'Why for no?'

'That is the piece I want you to plough, Pine,' Geoffrey said with some exasperation for the fourth time; 'that and no other.'

'If you prough him, by'm-by rain come and wash taters down a hill.'

'No,' said Geoffrey, 'because we intend to nail them in.'

'I tink nail no good,' Pine replied doggedly; 'you want 'em screw.'

'Look here, you beggar, I'm not going to have you capping my jokes; take your bullocks and clear out.'

Pine groaned. 'Where your prough?' he asked.

The plough was got out from under the house, and Pine, after cluck-ing disparagingly around it for awhile, called to the boy to let down the slip-rails.

By the time the porridge was cooked and the fish ready for breakfast, Pine came down carrying the ploughshare. He looked heated, and his mouth was contorted from swearing at the bullocks, which, not having done any ploughing for twelve months, were inclined to disregard the necessity for following a straight line.

'Too many rust your prough,' he said; 'you want to put some more greases on him.'

'Have you had breakfast?' Geoffrey asked.

Pine chewed the cud of an early meal of potatoes, looked at the spread table, and replied in the negative.

'Put on your coat then and sit down. We'll see about the greases by and by.'

Pine did as he was bidden, and having discovered by watching the brothers that porridge was eaten with a spoon—this was after a mo-mentary aberration with a knife and fork—he fell to, first helping him-self liberally to sugar, pepper, and salt, the latter condiments being add-ed to show a perfect acquaintance with European customs.

'Seen any more of the Reverend Fletcher?' asked Robert.

'I not seen,' said Pine; 'but my mother's father she seen, and all the people up there very religiously now.'

'Where's that?' Robert asked.

'Up to Wairangi. You know the how-you-call 'Vation Army?'

'Salvation Army?'

'That te ferra. My mother's father's people all belonga him dis time. I tink a very good ting dat, p'r'aps not?' he asked.

Robert nodded. 'What do they do?' he asked.

'They sell all deir tings. No cow dere, no riwai,[1] no gum. All te people buy biggy drum and tombones and blow him up and down te beach. My mother's father she very ol' man — more'n one hund'ed years—he play te tombones too. When he come down to see us yes'day, he got

_____
[1] Potatoes.

tombones on his back an' he play all a time. Then by'm-by Kanara's bull he hear him and say, "Golly, I tink dat cow got belly ache; I go see"; an' when he see only tombones he very angry. Pshut! My mother's father she clear; Kanara's bull clear af'er him. Te ol' man make very quick time and get on top te kumara house. Then he play tombones more'n more an' say, "Praise Lord!" But Kanara's bull he walk roun' an' roun' an' say, "By gorry, I get you, I break your burry neck."'

'And how did it all end?'

'By'm-by,' said Pine, 'ol' man do the haka,[1] an' while he tance the roof bust up and he fall in the kumara pit. Then when Kanara's bull see, he say, "Aha! Goo' jhob!" and he go away.'

After breakfast the ploughing was resumed, the brothers meanwhile going on with their own work of digging up the vegetable garden. For the next couple of hours the only sounds to be heard were the cracking of the bullock whip and the cries of the driver.

'Cee Hernshaw! Get town, Fretchah! Come here, Mirward! *Come here!* (with rising inflection) Ah-h! (as the plough ran off). By clikey, Fretchah, you the bad burrock!' Half a minute of silence; then again: 'Cee Hernshaw! Cee Moblay! Get town, Tawperry! Ah-h, Fretchah! Damn! Bloomin'!!!'

A loud whistle from the direction of the road attracted the brothers' attention, and shading their eyes from the sun, they saw a young man on a big bay horse drawn up at their slip-rail.

'Sandy Milward,' said Robert, thrusting his spade into the ground and moving off.

The visitor was a young man of fair complexion, with gray-blue eyes and light moustache. The eyes were Full of observation and humour, but the cheeks and jaw seemed fixed in an inflexible solemnity. A dog was running at his horse's heels, and he had a gun across the saddle in front of him and a net of game swinging from his shoulder. Both he and his horse were a good deal mud-bespattered.

'What brings you to this benighted spot?' Geoffrey asked when they had shaken hands.

'I was in the neighbourhood,' Sandy said, his eyes roaming critically over the section,' so I thought I might as well look you up. Getting to be strangers a bit, ain't you?'

---

[1] Native dance; in this case the war dance of defiance.

'I don't know,' said Geoffrey slowly; 'but get off your horse and come in.'

Sandy looked meditatively at his dog, who was running in and out amongst the high fern on the margin of the road. 'I'm looking for a couple of our beasts,' he said. 'I'll go as far as the end of the settlement and then come back.'

There was a whir from the fern where the dog had disappeared, and two cock pheasants whirled up and sailed across the road. Sandy's horse quivered, then stood like a rock, and a couple of shots brought the birds to the ground.

'What's the matter, Geoff?' Sandy asked quickly, as Robert moved off after the dog.

'Matter?'

'Anything gone wrong with the boat? It's nearly two months since you were down the river.'

'The boat's all right, I think,' Geoffrey replied. 'I haven't seen it since we came back from Wairangi that time. We do all our travelling on the road.'

'How's that?' Sandy asked, standing up in his stirrups to get a better view of the ploughing.

Geoffrey laughed uneasily. 'All my life,' he said, 'I have had a tendency to go with the stream.'

'Well, it runs our way, you know.' Sandy took another good look at the ploughing and chuckled solemnly.

'What is it?' asked Geoffrey, preparing to feel amused.

'Oh, nothing. There's plenty of excitement down our way now,' he said. 'The new parson's making things' hum all right.'

'I heard something of it. How are the Major and Miss Milward?'

'Old man's tip-top, barring a bad leg. Eve's pretty well too.'

'Has she been unwell?'

'No,' said Sandy slowly; 'health's all right. 'Tisn't that. Well,'—he broke off, seeing Robert approaching—' I'll see you again directly'; and picking up the reins he rode towards the younger brother. Geoffrey watched him pull up and exchange a word or two with Robert, then they both gazed for a moment or two in the direction of the ploughing;

finally Robert came on, bringing the birds with him.

The point about the ploughing which had interested Sandy was the difference in time occupied by Pine in turning over the line on the side where, from the slope of the ground, he was out of sight, and the side where he was in full view of the brothers. The discrepancy seemed to need accounting for, and after Pine had got round the bend Robert ascended the hill to investigate. All along the front slope the bullocks had moved slowly, their heads down, their shoulders set hard into the yoke, but along the back stretch the ground was apparently easier and the team went forward with much greater celerity. Yet when Pine's quick eye caught sight of one of his employers it seemed that the ground was, after all, of a varying texture, for the bullocks all but came to a standstill under the increased strain. Geoffrey probably would have regarded this fact without suspicion, but Robert, not so easily hoodwinked, strolled over and kicked up the turf. Pine brought the team to a stand.

'How you look?' he asked, his eyes rolling.

'Going a bit light, aren't you?' Robert asked.

'That te good proughing,' said Pine confidently; 'if too deep then no good.'

'Then why are you ploughing it deeper the other side?'

'Where about?'

'Over the other side where we can see you.'

'That te other side te hill,' Pine explained.

'Yes, but____'

'Your prough no good dis side te hill, no good at all. Where you buy dis prough?'

'If you can plough deep over there you can plough deep here,' was Robert's comment.

Pine looked at the plough and reflected. 'You got some more greases down to your place?' he asked at length.

'Oh, gammon!' said Robert. 'You get along and plough it the same depth all over.'

CHAPTER IV

SANDY MILWARD MAKES AN OFFER

'AND how long will it all take?' asked Sandy.

'About a month, I suppose.'

'And after that?'

'Well, there's a good deal of fencing to be done, and then there's the hoeing—I don't know. It seems to go on.' Geoffrey looked absently out across the landscape.

It was late in the afternoon. The brown parallel lines of the ploughing were drawing close together and but a strip of green divided them. Robert was digging on methodically, changing his foot as he arrived at each end of the ground. At times he whistled melodiously like a bird; this was when he stopped to clean his spade. Sandy sat on the step, his back against the doorpost, tapping his boot with his whip and looking up at his companion, who leant against the wall of the house.

'It will if you let it,' he said.

'You can't prevent it. How can you? Every stroke of work on a place like this accumulates further work at compound interest. It's a true bill that the curse of God is on the tiller of the soil.'

'It's not your style, you know,' Sandy said after a pause. 'I wonder—but that's not the point. Shall we say this day month?'

Geoffrey gnawed his moustache, his face changing momentarily 'Yes,' he said at last.

'Then that's settled.' Sandy rose to his feet, stretched himself and glanced at his horse, who was dozing comfortably, his head over the slip-rail. 'By the way,' he said—and Geoffrey knew intuitively that the real object of Sandy Milward's visit was about to be disclosed—'Raymond is leaving us.'

'Oh,' said Geoffrey. 'Sudden?'

'Well, no. He and the old man never exactly hit it off together. It's been coming on for quite awhile, but Raymond, though he's a clever chap in his way, was too dense or too conceited to see it. You play chess, don't you?'

'A little.'

Sandy made a sound in his throat. 'Raymond plays more than a little, and he has no more tact than a bullock. The old man likes a game of chess of an evening, and he has been accustomed to win it. When he doesn't win it he likes two games, and if he wins the second all is well, but if not, then he wants three; also, he begins to get polite. Did you ever see the governor when he was polite?'

'He is always polite to me,' said Geoffrey.

'Of course, but that's not the sort. When he gets really polite the atmosphere kind of freezes. Most men when they are angry become coarse, but the old man takes on an Arctic refinement. But that ass Raymond has no sense of humour, and he's cold-blooded and unaffected by variations in the temperature; and things being a bit uncomfortable generally, I am going to put him out.'

'You have not done so yet then?'

'Not yet, but I have quite made up my mind. You see, the old man ought to be in bed by ten o'clock, then he's up in the morning fresh as a lark, and the place runs on wheels; but they've taken to burning the midnight oil, and everything's upsides in consequence.'

'Why not take it over yourself?'

'The chess? I can't make a good enough defence—that's the trouble; the old man plays too well for nine out of ten, only it happens he's struck the tenth.'

Geoffrey smiled.

'I suppose you would consider storekeeping *infra dig.*?' Sandy said suddenly.

'Does that mean you are offering me the job?'

'Raymond's a university man, you know—so he says.'

Geoffrey shrugged his shoulders and looked at Sandy with a slow smile. 'I have never suited my employers yet,' he said, 'and I have had two or three; but I should not be above trying again if I thought, on consideration, I could do both of us justice.'

'I'll take the risk if you will,' Sandy replied. 'There's no bullocking attached to the job; all that'll be done for you. Raymond keeps the books of the station and superintends the store. He seems to have plenty of time over without neglecting anything. The old man's a bit of a martinet, perhaps, but I never knew a decent chap that couldn't rub along with him. You see,' Sandy continued, lowering his voice confidentially, 'I've really got the reins in my own hands, but we practise a sort of innocent little formula up there. We consult him, and then he asks us what we think, and whatever it is he agrees to it. That's the system right through, and it acts like clock-work.'

'I see,' said Geoffrey; 'but you don't suppose that he doesn't see through your little artifice, I hope.'

Sandy winked solemnly. 'Of course he does,' he admitted, 'but that makes no difference. Bless you, he's as keen as a hawk, but he doesn't really want to be bothered with things; and so long as he has the semblance of authority, and everything goes forward smoothly, he is satisfied.'

Geoffrey stood lost in thought. The prospect was sufficiently attractive, but there were reasons why he should hesitate before accepting Sandy's offer. One of them was the section, though that was not the one that first occurred to him. It seemed hard to leave Robert to continue at a task which he himself found distasteful. But it was not distasteful to Robert. Then he would certainly save money, and thus be able to help with the fencing. That alone made it worth while—perhaps. But it was only three or four days since he had made up his mind to force an interest in the farm, and he had been working hard and was settling down a little more contentedly. It was a pity to go back now, and perhaps have to begin all over again by and by. He doubted if he could work up resolution to accept such a lot a second time. He caught a word in Sandy's remarks, and came out of his reverie with a start.

'The room opens on the side verandah, and has no door leading into the house, so the old man thought he would fix a bell to ring inside in case it might be wanted. He likes little jobs like that, and gets dreadfully interested in them. Well, he'd about got it fixed, when the rope of the step-ladder broke, and he fell and barked his shin.'

'Not badly, I hope.'

'Pretty bad; but it's a painful thing anyway, and it has made him irritable, because he's an active man and can't stand laying up. But would you believe it, that thundering brute Raymond wins two games out of three all the same. It has come to this: that when the old man crawls out on top, Eve and I want to rush outside and shout "Victory!"and when he gets beat, as he mostly does, I feel like taking Raymond down the beach and kicking him.'

'And why don't you do it?'

'Well, Raymond has the reputation of being a champion full-back, and though he must be a good deal out of practice now, still it's surprising how a knack like that clings to a man.'

'Have you really no better reason for wanting to get rid of him than his chess-playing abilities?' Geoffrey asked curiously.

Sandy shifted uneasily. 'What's the matter with that for a reason?' he asked.

'You might so easily give him a hint that would solve the trouble.'

'If I did that, and it came to the old man's ears, he would never forgive me,' Sandy replied. 'Then also I want a man I can get on with, and he's not that. I don't like him.'

Geoffrey nodded absently.

Sandy stood patiently by till the other came out of his reverie. 'Would a month hence be too late for you?' he was asked at length.

'No,' he replied, 'that would do.'

'Well, I will talk it over with Robert, and let you know as soon as we come to a decision.'

'Good,' said Sandy cheerfully. 'Well, I don't want to get caught in the dark. I'll just run over and shake hands with Robert, then I'm off. By the way, there's a note from Eve in the game bag, and help yourself to a couple of pigeons at the same time.'

Sandy crossed over to Robert, and stood talking earnestly for five or ten minutes, while Geoffrey went into the house, and turned the contents of the game bag out on to the table. The envelope was twisted at one end, and tied to the network, evidently that its delivery might not be overlooked. It was blood-stained, and a momentary anger at Sandy's carelessness stirred him as he cut the string. Suddenly, as he stood looking at his name with the blot of blood across it, there came on him one of those strange, fleeting aberrations which are said to be due to one hemisphere of the brain acting in advance of the other. Something of this had happened before. The impression was momentary, no more than a flash, but as a flash it was vivid. Geoffrey stood for awhile trying to reconstruct the experience, endeavouring to refer it to some parallel event in the past, but the more he concentrated his mind on its elucidation the more visionary it became. Finally he opened the letter. The blood had soaked through the envelope, and in accordance with the manner in which the paper was folded its effects were visible at the top and bottom of the sheet. The words came to him at a glance, but they did not occupy his mind, which was fixed on the faint yellowish stain, embracing himself and Eve Milward in a common fate. It was perhaps due to the moment which had preceded this discovery that its effect on Geoffrey was so pronounced. Though we laugh easily at the superstitious, no man is entirely exempt from the feeling that his own destiny is of special concern. He will readily admit otherwise as a matter of argument, but the feeling will crop out in crucial moments, reason notwithstanding. Geoffrey did not ask himself if he should take this as a warning or a direction of Providence as to his future conduct; the effect went deeper than that. As his mind had momentarily slipped from the present into a vague, unrecallable past, so now it slipped forward into an equally vague future, when the coincidence was to establish itself among realities. A sort of mental powerlessness seemed gradually to creep upon him. The room darkened, and took on a mysterious, impenetrable vastness and gloom. Involuntarily he threw out his arms, striving to thrust back a tangle as of network that threatened to enmesh him in its folds. The effect of the physical action was instantaneous—he was again back in the narrow room, with the afternoon sunlight streaming through the open doorway. This trick of the imagination was less real to Geoffrey than its relation in so many words might lead the reader to suppose. It was but as if he had closed his eyes and suffered a vivid fancy to play with the horror which the blood-stain had evoked. He smiled a little grimly as he again turned his eyes on the letter. The imagination he had sometimes tried to enslave in the cause of art remained unshackled and his master; that was all.

'DEAR MR. HERNSHAW—Some time ago you offered to lend me Darwin's *Origin of Species.* I did not express any eagerness then, because our household has always accepted evolution, much as we accept gravitation and other things we know perhaps equally little about, and one does not require proof of what one never hears questioned. I have a reason, however, for desiring to see the book now, if you are still able and willing to let me do so.

'Your name is frequently on Major Milward's lips, and we are hoping that it is not indisposition which is to blame for the fact that we have not seen you for such a time.

'I have laid particular injunctions on my brother as to the safeguarding of your book in transit.

'With kind regards to yourself and Robert, believe me, yours sincerely, Eve Milward.'

Geoffrey found the book, wrapped it up, and fastened it to the game bag; then he took the latter outside and hung it on a post by the patiently waiting horse. He did this so that there should be no need for Sandy to re-enter the house, and having accomplished it, he went into his bedroom and shut the door. He had ceased to notice the stains on the paper now, and his mind was occupied in an endeavour to arrive at the reasons which had dictated the writing of the letter itself.

'Dear Mr. Hernshaw,' — the word was conventional, of course—of course. 'One does not require proof of what one never hears questioned. I have a reason, however, for desiring to see the book now.' Then it has been questioned. By whom? She has a certain amount of belief in him, or she would not trouble to follow it up. The next paragraph is conventional again, put in to prevent the note appearing too one-sided; that's plain. Or is there something behind that too? No, we get back to the book—the book's the thing. 'Yours sincerely, Eve.' Suddenly he raised the letter passionately to his lips.

'What is the use of trying to deceive myself any longer? If I go it will be because of her, and for no other reason. I have let myself drift into this, fool that I am! There was but this folly left for me to commit, and now it also has come to pass. Of course they wonder at my absence; for months there was not a week but I blundered into the flame. If I went back to-morrow, not five minutes would pass before she would be more myself than I am. It is so now. I am her slave. There is no deceiving myself as to what going there means. It will be with my eyes open. It will be my last stake. Her father is a wealthy man; I have nothing. He is a successful man; I am a failure. Those are two business-like reasons why I should wish to marry her. Then if I go, it will be as her fathers hired man—that will always be a pleasing reflection. I foresee that I shall have a good time chewing that. Do I mean to go? It seems that I have never wanted anything in my life till now. Certainly no other woman,'— his thoughts checked themselves, and he frowned,—'not wealth, not rank. This is the one thing I have asked of Destiny, or shall ask. Nothing seemed to matter till now, but now I see how everything has mattered all the time. What chances I have had, and how I have fooled them away! Is this a chance, or what is it? And shall I fool it away, or what?'

His musing was interrupted by a sound without, and looking through the window he caught sight of Sandy disappearing down the road.

Putting on his hat and coat, Geoffrey left the house and crossed over to his brother. 'I shall not be long, Robert,' he said; 'I am going as far as Mrs. Gird's.'

CHAPTER V

THE BUSH ORACLE

THE river lay like a string of jewels in the crevasses of the hills. Away in the sun-haze to the west the sand dunes of Wairangi blazed like pyramids of gold.

Geoffrey paused on the summit of Bald Hill to gaze at the familiar scene. Eighteen or twenty miles away, but looking vastly nearer, rose a green hillock, cut into terraces, a Norfolk Island pine on its summit. He had once spent an afternoon with Eve beneath the shadow of that tree, and memory recalled easily the homestead in its sheltering plantation, nestling under the pa.[1] His mind's eye saw the flashing casements, the deep, cool verandahs, the sub-tropical flower-garden, the woods and orchards in which the house was embowered. Peace was there if anywhere in the world. It was in the pens, where were the prize-bred fowls in which Major Milward took such a deep interest; in the ducks diving in the creek; in the cows coming lazily down to the slip-rail for the evening's milking; in the flocks of sheep cropping the broad pastures over a score of hills; in—and his heart-beats quickened as he called up the figure of the young mistress, moving everywhere with her light step, like the spirit of Peace herself.

Wairangi— 'the heavenly waters.' Such a splendour of light lay over the scene that he might well have been gazing into Paradise itself. There were rest and content. The memory of the resplendent glories of summer came to him whispering that there also was delight. How could he hesitate? What was it that bade him pause, his feet on the threshold, his will fainting to be there? Was it pride that could not brook the thought of asking so much and offering so little? All his life he had eaten the bread of dependence, but love had sweetened it to his lips. Would it not continue to do so? Was it doubt as to how his advances would be received? Doubt was there, but if it influenced him at all it was towards its own elimination.

The Bald Hill was the highest point in the settlement. It was so named on account of the landslips which had denuded its summit of soil and left the white inhospitable clay exposed. The settler to whom it had

---

[1] 'Pah,' a fortified hill.

43

been allotted was supposed to be recompensed for its barrenness by an increased depth of soil in the hollows into which Geoffrey now descended, but there were no evidences of any attempt having been made to utilise this compensation—supposing it existed—beyond what were furnished by a hut roofed with kerosene tin and a small enclosure mainly choked with weeds. A slipshod youngish woman stood in the open doorway, watching him with the frank, sexless interest which is due to the presence of another human being of the same race. A sound of children screaming came from the interior of the hut. Geoffrey touched his hat and was passing when the woman called to him and came down to the fence.

'I hope you didn't mind my sending for the things this morning,' she said as Geoffrey approached.

She leant her arms wearily on the fence and looked steadily at him as though she derived pleasure from the act. Her face showed traces of good looks, prematurely faded; her eyes were tired and sullen. Through her imperfectly fastened bodice Geoffrey caught a glimpse of a black bruise staining her white skin.

'Not at all,' he said. 'We were only too glad to be able to help you— that is, I hope we were____' and Geoffrey looked at her inquiringly.

'I got what I sent for,' said Mrs. Andersen, nodding. 'I always do when I send to you. That's why I go to you last.'

Geoffrey laughed, and the woman smiled slowly in sympathy.

'I suppose we have got to live,' she said, with a return of gravity. 'At any rate we do,' she added, the first proposition encountering a bar of doubt in her mind.

'Of course,' Geoffrey agreed, as though there could be no doubt at all.

Mrs. Andersen looked at him and condensed the problem of the ages in one word—'Why?'

The answer—several of them—came out of the house ready-made and arrayed in flour-bags. Geoffrey noticed that the family patronised two brands of flour, 'Champion' and 'Snowdrift,' and there was also among the younger branches an attempt to advertise a special make of oatmeal from Tokomairiro.

'How is Mr. Andersen getting on?' he asked cheerfully, lifting one blue-eyed, tow-headed urchin of doubtful sex on to the rail beside him.

Mrs. Andersen shrugged her shoulders. 'I haven't seen him for the best part of a month— (Run away, kids, and don't bother)—I shouldn't care if I never saw him again,' she added, frowning.

There seemed no ready-made convention for a remark of this nature, and Geoffrey looked smilingly at the child.

'I suppose that shocks you,' the woman said bitterly. 'One thing, I don't often have the chance of saying what I think.'

'I'm sorry it's like that,' Geoffrey said, forced into saying something. 'You must have a hard time feeding and—looking after all these children.' He was going to say clothing, but, remembering the scantiness of their wardrobe, checked himself in time. 'If there is anything I or Robert could do to help you, I'm sure we should be very glad.'

Mrs. Andersen shook her head. 'What could you do?' she asked. And indeed Geoffrey was conscious as he spoke of the inadequacy of any assistance in his power to render. Short of the reformation, or in the alternative the death of her drunken husband, there seemed no help for her.

This contact with the troubles of another had turned his thoughts from the too intense brooding on the difficulties that beset himself, and he went on his way in a more reasonable frame of mind.

''Ook, mammy,'ook, the pretty sing man div me!'

Mrs. Andersen clutched the money as a drowning person clutches an oar, and for the same reason. 'There,' she said, as the child began to whimper,'don't cry. Mammy will get you some jam for tea. Run in, kids, and tell Lena to stir up the fire.' She turned on the threshold and waved her hand to the unconscious form of Geoffrey, whose back was just disappearing into the bush. There was a silent benediction in the act.

'I will ask Mrs. Gird's advice,' Geoffrey was saying to himself at that moment; 'and whatever she advises I will agree to.'

Many and very dissimilar people went to Mrs. Gird for advice, and she gave it to all with equal candour. Probably if it suited them they acted on it; but whether it suited them or no, she took care that they got what they came for. She was no witch whose elixirs were potent in the troubles of true love, yet the loves of the settlement were mostly confided to her. She rarely left her home on the section, yet everything that occurred for miles around was known to her almost on its happening. She knew when M'Clusky's bull had broken Finnerty's fence and eaten the tops off his apple trees, and she had a spirited account of the meeting of Finnerty and M'Clusky ready the same day for the amusement of her husband, who sat all day long in his invalid's chair following her with adoring eyes, but incapable either of speech or motion. She knew when Sven Andersen was in the lock-up for drunkenness, and whether or no Mrs. Andersen had gone into the township to pay his fine, and she called herself a lucky woman when she related the facts to that same listener. She knew when the girls got into trouble, as they sometimes did, and who was the responsible party, and what was the best course to take in the delicate operation of bringing the delinquent to book. But whatever she knew the poor cripple knew also, for on that understanding alone would she accept a confidence. 'You can speak out,' she would say, when her visitor showed a delicacy in beginning, 'because I shall tell him when you are gone, whether or no.'

He made a splendid wreck, this husband of hers, as he sat there day after day, dead up to the eyes, but alive from that point upwards. She had been told that when the light dimmed in his eyes then he would die; so she watched him hour by hour, week in week out, instilling, perhaps, some of her own superabundant vitality into the dying flame. She was a tall, strong woman, yet not so very long ago that poor cripple was in the habit of taking her up in his arms like an infant, and holding her there till a hearty tug at his hair effected her release. But there came a black and treacherous day when wife and children looked for him in vain as the twilight fell. Struck by a flying branch, he lay in the shadow of the woods that should never again have cause to tremble at his tread. That was the first tragedy of the settlement, and nothing of all the subsequent happenings had made such a strong and abiding impression on the minds of the settlers.

Every bushman knows the toll of blood demanded by the virgin forest. It is fixed and inexorable, and though skill in bush craft will carry a man far in the avoidance of accidents, it counts for nothing when the time comes for the bush to demand its price. There was a superstition in the settlement that so long as Mark Gird lived the woodman was safe, and many besides the devoted wife watched for the dying out of the flame.

Geoffrey heard the sound of an axe in the dimness ahead, and, smiling to himself, he left the track and made softly towards it. In a few minutes he reached the clearing.

'Geoffrey, you wretch,' said the lady, 'how dare you come creeping up like that?'

'Like which? I thought you always completed your sentences.'

'Good. Your sentence is to take hold of the other end of that saw.'

'Everything all right?' asked Geoffrey, laying his hand on the tree and looking up.

Mrs. Gird allowed him to walk round the barrel and examine the scarf. 'Well?' she asked.

'The fowl-house won't be there when we've done,' he remarked, taking off his coat.

'Rubbish!' said the lady. 'The fowl-house is fifty yards off.'

'Well, you'll see,' said Geoffrey, bringing the maul and wedges up to the tree and picking up the saw. 'Are you ready?'

Mrs. Gird tucked the sleeves higher up her fine arms, made a mysterious arrangement of her skirt which seemed to convert it into a sort of sublimated masculine garment on the spot, gripped the handle and started the saw.

'Tell me when you are tired,' said Geoffrey, smiling retiringly behind his side of the barrel.

'A likely thing,' said Mrs. Gird, 'that you should tire me.'

'I am rather nice,' the young man admitted.

'Heavens!' exclaimed the lady, with a laugh; 'what a gift of repartee. Why this abnormal cheerfulness? You are rather silent as a rule, Geoffrey.'

'That is so,' the young man admitted, and gave an instance. 'Spell oh!' he called presently. 'Time for a wedge.'

The wedge was inserted. Then came another spell of sawing, followed by more wedges; then more sawing and a vigorous driving with the maul, and presently down came the tree.

'Splendid!' Mrs. Gird exclaimed. 'Just where I wanted it to fall.'

'Beautiful!' agreed Geoffrey; 'but do you notice the undignified attitude of your fowl-house?'

'Well, I never!' said the lady, astonished.

'I did,' said Geoffrey; 'that's how I knew. I once blew a tent away in precisely the same fashion.'

'You might have told me!'

'Pardon me, if you reflect a moment, I think you will do me the justice to admit that I did.'

'You certainly said that the fowl-house would not be there.'

'Precisely,' said Geoffrey triumphantly; 'and the facts have borne me out.'

Mrs. Gird gazed at him with a severity which the twinkle in her eyes belied. 'Go,' she said, 'and put it back where it was.'

'I am afraid that is barely possible, but we might be able to make it pretty comfortable where it is.'

This proved to be so, and the fowl-house was re-erected not much the worse for the indignity to which it had been subjected by the draught of the falling tree.

'Here come the bairns,' said Mrs. Gird, looking with bright eyes across the clearing, as a couple of boys shot out of the shadow of the bush and darted towards her. 'Steady now, Mark, don't tear me to pieces; let Rowly have some too. Now shake hands with Mr. Hernshaw. That's right. Off you go to father. Take off your school clothes, and then you can get your tomahawks and amuse yourselves till tea-time. Aren't they just lovely?' This to Geoffrey.

'Vain woman!' said he.

'Yes,' she said seriously; 'it is true. I pride myself on my common-sense, but I'm a fool with my own.'

'They are the handsomest, the cleverest, the best-natured boys in the settlement,' Geoffrey said.

He was still smiling, but Mrs. Gird's bright eyes looked a long way into human nature, and she nodded.

'You're not a bad sort, Geoffrey,' she said, turning away.

'Well, of all the_____' Geoffrey began disgustedly.

'Where have you been this last month?' Mrs. Gird interrupted, leading the way to the house.

'At home, working.'

'I thought, perhaps, it was just possible you might be at Wairangi.'

'There is a good deal of the conditional mood about that sentence,' Geoffrey observed.

'And is there none of it about you?' Mrs. Gird asked shrewdly.

'I propose to occupy a portion of your valuable time in the discussion of my worthless self.'

'Very well—when we get inside. What's stirring in the settlement? Anything fresh?'

'Nothing much.' Then, after a moment's thoughtfulness, 'I saw Mrs. Andersen as I came by; things seem to be in a bad way with her.'

'Do you mean that you judged so from her appearance, or that she told you so?' Mrs. Gird asked sharply.

'The latter.'

'Then why not say so. She told you things were in a bad way with her—well?'

'That's all.'

'H'm. Well, it's a fact; they are in a bad way, and they are likely to be, unless_____' she pursed up her lips. 'Do you know a man called Beckwith?'

'Fairly well.'

'What kind of a creature is he?'

'I suspect him of honesty,' Geoffrey replied thoughtfully. 'He never stops working, and he's deadly silent. I think these be virtues.'

Mrs. Gird nodded, as though some previous account had received confirmation, then she laughed.

'Sven Andersen talks a great deal,' she said, 'and his English is as broken as his adopted country, *ergo* he is a fool.'

'No doubt you are right,' Geoffrey said.

'It is one of the data upon which our constitution is founded,' Mrs. Gird condescended to explain, 'that a foreigner whose English betrays him is necessarily an idiot.'

'Quite so; pardon my momentary forgetfulness. But what is your conclusion?'

'I was thinking that Andersen might be forgiven for being a drunkard and a brute, but it is impossible to pardon him for being a fool.'

'And so_____'

'And so, here we are at the house.'

Geoffrey took off his hat reverently as he entered the abode of the man who was dead and yet lived. Then he knew that his arrival was known long ago to the invalid, whose chair was drawn up in front of the window that looked out upon the clearing.

'Father is never lonely,' Mrs. Gird said cheerfully, as she wheeled the chair round towards the fire; 'there is always some one in sight from the window. Only the day before yesterday we had Finnerty chasing Robinson's pigs with a shot-gun, and that was enough to keep any one amused for a week.'

'It's marvellous how they carry on,' Geoffrey agreed. 'One half of the settlement appears to spend its existence in trenches waiting for the advance of the other half.'

'The mystery is how they manage to pay court expenses. Take the Finnertys and Robinsons, for instance; there is never a court day but what they are down on the order-sheet. If it's not Finnerty *versus* Robinson, it's Robinson *versus* Finnerty. Damages for assault, damages for trespass. Good Lord! they seem to be all mad together. Finnerty laid an action against Robinson for damages caused by Robinson's pigs. Defendant denied that any damage had been done, or that, if damage was proved, it had been caused by his pigs, and in any event he denied liability owing to the plaintiff not having a legal fence. Plaintiff alleged that he had a legal fence "acchordin' to th' act, yer reverence," and that in the alternative said fence had been removed by the Robinson family for fuel. Then they went at it hammer and tongs. Mrs. Finnerty, duly sworn, alleged that Mrs. Robinson was a liar. "You'll not be lis'nin' to that woman, your worship, for she's desavin' yez."—"Well, never mind that, get on with the evidence."—"It's like this, yer worship (wheedlingly); last Tuesday Mrs. Andersen come around to give me back some tay she'd borrowed a while back, and she sez to me, she sez—" —"Yes, yes, never mind that; come to the sow."—"Yes, your worship, and Mrs. Andersen was tellin' me she'd littered____" _"Who littered?" —"The sow, your worship." (Laughter in the court.) Magistrate, severely, "I won't have this noise. Well? (to witness), for goodness' sake, get along." And so on, *ad infinitum.* Don't look so shocked.'

'Me! I defy you!'

'Well, you ought to be. But what's wanted in this settlement is a good heavy top-dressing of horse sense, and that's a commodity which is pretty scarce anywhere. But I am stopping you from talking.'

Mrs. Gird seated herself with her arm across her husband's chair and looked expectantly at Geoffrey.

'I saw Sandy Milward to-day,' the latter said after a moment. 'He wants me to take over Raymond's job in the store.'

'What wages is he giving?' Mrs. Gird asked. Geoffrey shifted his position and looked foolish.'I ought to have asked that, of course,' he said, 'but as a matter of fact I didn't.'

Mrs. Gird shook her head. 'Not that it matters so much in this instance,' she admitted, 'because Major Milward is almost absurdly generous. Well, are you going?'

'I don't know. I could do the work very well; it would be less irksome to me than tilling the soil —supposing I could afford to consider my inclinations, which I can't. I am not a great deal of help to Robert, though I endeavour to do my share, and it has struck me that I might be able to assist him to better purpose if I were earning money independently.'

'Those are very good reasons why you should go; now let us hear one or two why you shouldn't.'

Geoffrey was silent awhile. 'There is only one,' he said at last slowly. 'You know that I was a good deal at Wairangi during the summer and autumn. It is a pretty place, and Major Milward has royal ideas of hospitality—you used to tell me jokingly what would happen.'

'Ah!' said Mrs. Gird, her eyes beaming. 'The one thing you haven't mentioned is that Eve Mil-ward is a lovely girl.'

'She is too lovely for my peace of mind.'

'Good boy. So that's the problem? Now let me think. I suppose you have never said anything to her? No. And you have no idea how she regards you. Well, as a friend, of course.'

'If I go,' said Geoffrey, 'it will be as her lover.'

'And as her father's storekeeper.'

'That is the crux of the whole matter. Are the two compatible?'

'Perfectly—in this country. You are not in England now.'

'Then do you advise me to go?'

'Not so fast, my young friend,' said Mrs. Gird, laughing; then she continued seriously: 'I believe in a man having the courage to avow himself and take his chance; but I should like you to have a good chance, both for your sake and for hers.'

'Thank you for that.'

'Well, I do not think it would be at all a bad thing for Eve; but I do not know if you accepted Sandy's offer that you would be in the best position to induce her to think so.'

'I thought you said_____'

'I said, or I meant, that there was nothing in the fact of your being employed on the station that need cause you to hesitate, but that's not saying that a position of dependence on a girl's father is a good one from which to woo her.'

'Then perhaps I had better not accept.'

Mrs. Gird sat looking absently at him, and it was some time before her reply came. Then she said: 'After all, the position is nothing; everything depends on whether you are the right man. Yes, that is the answer to the riddle. If I were you I should go. But, Geoffrey, let me tell you of two faults you possess: you are too unpractical in money matters, and you have no self-confidence. Why have you no self-confidence?'

'I don't know,' said Geoffrey, knitting his brows; 'I have and I haven't.'

'Well, at any rate try and be practical. Make a start with Sandy. Whatever wages he offers you, ask ten shillings a week more.'

'I couldn't do that,' Geoffrey said slowly. 'If I thought he would refuse me or argue the matter it would be all right, but he would say yes at once.'

'And that appeals to you as a practical reason for not asking him?' Mrs. Gird asked curiously.

'I don't know,' said Geoffrey; 'but it's why I couldn't.'

He looked so apologetic in his disability that Mrs. Gird conceded the point with a laugh. 'Young man,' she said, 'I doubt if you would be so scrupulous about your sweetheart's kisses.'

CHAPTER VI

THE SERVICE ON THE BEACH

MAJOR MILWARD left the store, locking the door behind him. It was Sunday afternoon. A native on horseback was scurrying along the beach with a tin of golden syrup under his arm, for which he had paid one shilling and fourpence in the belief that he was purchasing tinned meat. It is due to the Major to say that in this belief he fully shared. The store was closed against business on Sundays, but Major Milward, to whom serving at the counter was a pleasant relaxation, in which he was not supposed to indulge, occasionally managed on some pretext to obtain the key from the storekeeper when, if the opportunity offered, he would transact a little business *sub rosa,* frequently, as in this instance, with disastrous results.

The Major wore a sun helmet in compliment to the fine October weather, and a cigar, without which he was rarely seen, glowed between his teeth. In stature he was rather under middle size, but his figure despite his age was erect and active as a boy's. A pair of clear blue eyes looked steadily out on the world. He walked up the beach humming a hymn tune and looking well pleased with himself. The native, who had ten miles to ride, making twenty in all, was equally pleased as yet.

Presently the Major paused and pished irritably. He had recognised the tune he was humming and discontinued it on the spot. 'The air seems charged with the wretched things,' he thought. He stood a moment looking along the shining river in the direction of the bar, then turned in at a side gate and walked slowly up the path to the house. 'I wonder whether Hernshaw will get carried away like the rest. Mind too well balanced, I should say.' A shade of anxiety and annoyance crossed his countenance. 'I always thought her like that until—Bah! What makes religion such a cold, inhuman business when it's carried to excess? This Fletcher now, is there anything about him beyond what he *says?* If one wanted a fiver, would it be obtainable there sooner than elsewhere? If one needed sympathy, would it come more readily from him than from—Hernshaw, for instance?' His eye had caught sight of that gentleman on the verandah. 'No, by Gad! There is more quick humanity in that chap's little finger than in the whole of Fletcher's carcass.'

Geoffrey, his finger between the leaves of a book, looked pleasantly at the Major as he mounted the steps.

'Come for a stroll round,' the latter said.

Geoffrey rose obediently and dropped his book into the rocker. 'Miss Milward has offered to introduce me to Mr. Fletcher,' he said,'but I don't suppose it is urgent.'

'Not a bit,' the Major replied with alacrity. 'He is here then?' he asked in a lower voice.

'Yes, sir. But I will get my hat and come along.'

Geoffrey entered the wide hall and took his hat from the stand. He could hear talking in a side room and the door-handle turned as he passed. Reaching the verandah, he heard his name called, and turning he saw Eve Milward coming towards him, accompanied by a tall man of dark complexion. Geoffrey looked at him at first with indifference, then with more interest.

'Mr. Hernshaw—the Reverend Mr. Fletcher.'

The two men looked at one another and hesitated, then Mr. Fletcher, with a stiff inclination of his head, turned to Major Milward, who, having watched the meeting with curiosity, now came forward and shook hands with his visitor, making at the same time polite inquiries as to the success of what Mr. Fletcher was in the habit of referring to as the propaganda.

'Our efforts are bearing fruit,' said the latter, in his most clerical manner. 'Among the natives our ministrations have been more particularly blessed.'

'They would be,' the Major agreed.

'In the Waiomo valley more especially,' Mr. Fletcher went on; 'Heaven, in its goodness, has seen fit to bless our efforts in the conversion of every man, woman, and child.'

'What exactly do you imply by conversion?' Major Milward asked.

'Conversion,' replied Mr. Fletcher, 'is a turning from ways of darkness to those of light.'

Major Milward looked at Geoffrey. 'This will be good news for-you, Mr. Hernshaw,' he remarked. 'The Waiomo natives, I think you said, are owing the store some seven hundred pounds.'

'Seven hundred and forty-three fourteen nine,' said Geoffrey with stiff precision.

Major Milward got out a fresh cigar, and Mr. Fletcher, whose ardour appeared to have suffered a slight check, turned to Eve.

When Geoffrey and Major Milward set out on their stroll, they saw Mr. Fletcher and Eve walking slowly along the beach in front of them, their destination being the little village of Rivermouth about two miles distant.

The Major led his companion through the orchard where they decided that the fruit trees promised well, then round to the poultry pens, with their valuable and well-cared-for contents, and thence back to the beach. Geoffrey appeared thoughtful and preoccupied, and the Major glancing at him surprised a puzzled frown not due to anything in their recent conversation.

'I beg your pardon,' said Geoffrey with a start, becoming conscious of his companion's observation.

'I was suggesting that we should go as far as the village and see what is going on; or would it bore you?'

'Not at all. This sort of thing is generally interesting and sometimes amusing. I suppose Mr. Fletcher is a well-known revivalist?'

The Major shrugged his shoulders. 'I suppose so. The Church of England appointed him down here—to get rid of him, I expect.'

Geoffrey was silent awhile; then he said: 'Isn't it a little unusual for that denomination to go in for anything quite so—er—violent as I understand Mr. Fletcher's methods to be?'

'I thought so. In fact, I had an idea of dropping the bishop a friendly line on the subject. A parson is all very well to marry us and bury us and that kind of thing, but when he begins to distract our attention from the plain duty of sticking to our work he becomes a nuisance. I thought of suggesting that there might be room for a person of Mr. Fletcher's energies in the bishop's own immediate neighbourhood. By the way, that wasn't bad about the seven hundred and forty-three fourteen nine. I expect you got the odd money out of your head. But it is a fact that we shall not be sixpence the better for it. Fletcher doesn't know much about the natives and might expect permanent results.' The Major smiled grimly.

'Is he making many converts among Europeans?'

'A few of a sort among the men. Women, of course.'

The sound of a brass band had been audible in the distance for some time past, and as they now turned from the beach and surmounted a small hillock it burst on them in full blast.

A crowd was gathered on the sands at the foot of the hill, while another crowd of larger dimensions sat or lolled on the grassy slopes and looked on. Beyond lay the village, basking in the afternoon sunlight, apparently quite deserted. Major Milward descended the hill some distance and sat down. The crowd on the beach was arranged in a large circle. Geoffrey could see the tall figure of the clergyman at one side, with Eve and a few Europeans, male and female, close to him. The remainder of the worshippers were mostly Maoris, fully half of them being armed with brass instruments of one kind or another. A large native in a red jersey was walking majestically round the interior of the circle clapping a pair of bones and bawling out the refrain of the hymn: 'Wass me—and I s'all be wha-iter than snow! Wass me —and I s'all be wha-iter than snow!'

'Why, it's Pine,' said Geoffrey suddenly.

'So it is,' the Major agreed.

Geoffrey caught sight of Sandy lower down the hill, and the latter, observing him at the same moment, came up and sat down, clasping himself rapturously round the knees.

'Isn't he lovely?' he exclaimed with his solemn chuckle. 'I would not have missed this for anything.'

'Your enthusiasm does you credit,' Geoffrey said drily.

'Pine is the latest convert and the most enthusiastic. Observe the intensity of his conviction as expressed in his calves. How Fletcher can stand there and retain his mental equilibrium passes understanding.'

'No doubt the intensity of *his* convictions sustains him. After all, is this quite as ridiculous as it looks?'

'More so,' said Sandy.

'Sincerity is entitled to respect.'

'It is entitled to the respect it can command,' said Major Milward. 'We are not bound to respect a man because he has a sincere conviction that the earth is flat; neither are we under any obligation to respect him because he believes the Creator can be propitiated by more or less unmelodious howling.If it is a sense of humour that prevents me from joining the circle on the beach, then I am thankful I possess it.'

The hymn had come to an end, and Mr. Fletcher was now beginning to address his followers. His voice was powerful, and carried easily to those on the slope of the hill. He began by giving thanks for the success with which his labours had been blessed, and he went on to speak of the methods he had adopted for bringing the sheep into the fold. It was not those who came voluntarily to the House of God for whom the Church need feel its deepest concern. There was more joy in heaven over one sinner who repented than over a hundred of the righteous who needed no repentance. His predecessors had been content to guide and guard their flock, but for him that was not enough. There should be unceasing joy in heaven. The sinner should come daily into the fold, crying out for the salvation of belief. For it was one thing to know of God and another thing to know God. 'There are many,' he went on, raising his voice, 'who have put their reason in the place of their Creator and cried, "This is false, that cannot be; our reason denies the other." But later, when the spirit of God has possessed them with His knowledge, then reason falls back shamed before the over-reason of the soul.' He paused, and his voice dropped to a lower key: 'One such man I have known. With him, as with those of whom I have spoken, reason was the crown of his being. And reason told him that the Bible was false; that the story of Christ was half a lie; that there was no Creator. To what may such a man cling in the strong waves of earthly temptation? He was placed in a position of trust, and possessed the unbounded confidence of his friend. That confidence he betrayed.' The speaker hesitated a moment, and the audience, recognising something vital in the story, preserved a complete silence. Major Mil-ward, glancing at his companions, was arrested by the expression of Geoffrey's face and allowed his cigar to go out.

'Fortunately for him,' the speaker resumed impressively, 'his sin found him out. Then, as is the way with the sinner, he sought to fly from the judgment. Was it difficult? His sin was known only to two persons. Only to two!—two persons in all the world!' Again he paused; then suddenly his voice leapt out with startling clearness: 'To two! Nay, but to millions! He knew it himself —his conscience knew it—God knew it! The angels of heaven, whose number is as the stars of the firmament for multitude, knew it every one! The consequences of sin are eternal. Fly to the uttermost end of the earth, you shall not escape them.' His voice took a denunciatory ring: 'They will confront you in the hour of setting forth and in the hour of returning. They will cry to you, "Begone! Here also thou art known." Do you think to begin afresh as though your sin had never been? I tell you there is no spot on this earth or in the heavens above the earth where the consequences of sin shall cease and be no more. Is not that an awful thought?' He stopped and looked slowly round his circle of listeners; then in softer tones he began to point the moral of his story and to speak of the atonement of Calvary.

'He can talk all right,' Sandy said with unwilling admiration; 'but the moral didn't seem to hang to his little story too well. 'What do you think of him?' he asked, turning to Geoffrey.

'It seems impossible to doubt his sincerity,' was the reply.

Mr. Fletcher was now addressing the Maoris in their own language, and the crowd on the hillside, as though ashamed of the temporary seriousness into which they had been cajoled, resumed their original levity of manner.

'There are some fairly hard nuts for the parson to crack down there,' Sandy said. 'That's Hogg, the storekeeper, talking to the half-caste girl, and she's a Miss Wayte from up the river. There are seven girls in that family and they've all had to stick to their name. Some people think Hogg's going to marry her, but they've thought things like that about Hogg for the last twenty years. That's Howell, the shoemaker, pretty well in, they say, and tight as wax. His brother keeps the pub, the two-storey building beyond there. Most of the young men are from the coast settlement—you can see their horses in Howell's paddock. They work like furies all the week, real hard graft, mostly bush-falling, and on Sundays they get their horses and ride them backwards or sideways or any other way the fancy takes them, and tumble off here on to the sand and look at the girls.'

'And what about the girls?'

'The girls look at them and ask one another their names, and say, "Oh, *do* look!"and "Isn't he good-looking?"and "I *wish* I knew him."'

'And then____'

'That's all till next Sunday.'

'But in time, I suppose, they get to know him and marry him.'

Sandy shook his head. 'There are no marriages here,' he said; 'very few births and deaths only by accident. That's how it is that when the Government sends a man up here to collect statistics he always goes back a confirmed dipsomaniac'

'I have wondered why that was so,' Geoffrey said, and Major Milward laughed.

The band was now in full blast again, and the voices of the singers came at first with uncertainty through the hubbub. Then the voices mastered the air, and put the band back in its proper place.

The three waited until the service was over, and by that time the sun had set and the evening star glowed at the river mouth.

Major Milward rose and scanned the groups on the darkening beach below. 'Home,' he said succinctly. 'Go and fetch Eve.'

Sandy departed obediently, and in a few minutes returned with his sister. Eve took her father's arm, and the two young men following behind, the party made its way back to the house.

Lamps were glowing brightly in the big dining-room, as they went up through the sweet-scented garden on to the verandah. The Major went straight into the house, but Eve waited for the others. Her cheeks were glowing and her eyes sparkling as she looked from one to the other. 'I hope you both enjoyed the service,' she said.

'I did thoroughly,' Sandy replied; 'and during our walk home, Geoffrey has exhibited all the depression which could lawfully be expected of a man conscious of a misspent life.'

Eve smiled and looked wistfully at the person alluded to, but Geoffrey remained silent.

That night when he reached his room, he got out some writing materials and sat down to indite a letter. It was but brief, yet nearly an hour and two or three sheets of paper were expended, before it was finally sealed and addressed to the Rev. T. Fletcher, Rivermouth. Then he went out in his stocking feet and dropped it silently into the mail box.

CHAPTER VII

MR. FLETCHER READS HIS LETTERS

OWING to the delivery of all letters being deferred until the arrival of the weekly overland mail, it was three days before Geoffrey's letter reached its destination two miles away

The Reverend Mr. Fletcher boarded in the village, for though the Wesleyans and Roman Catholics possessed their mission stations, the Church of England had no local habitation within twenty miles of the county borders. The Mallows, at whose house he resided, belonged to the earlier pioneers, the family having been established in the days when the white man came alone into the native settlement and picked his wife from the bright-eyed kotiros of the hapu.[1] The founder of the family slept in the graveyard, beneath the manoa trees on the summit of the hill, and his grave vibrated eternally to the tread of the ocean rollers on the bar. His descendants were in every township and settlement throughout the county. Some had sailed away and were heard from occasionally; others had sailed away and never been heard from.

The Mallow who occupied the old homestead was a son of the founder of the family. He had married a half-caste woman, and had numerous olive branches with corresponding complexions. The sons had mostly disappeared—two were in South Africa, fighting the Boers. The daughters disappeared too, but more gradually. Now and then it became necessary to send one away to a distant relative, preferably in Auckland; and now and then one died of consumption. For many of the half-caste girls this was the dread alternative to marriage. As they left off their childhood the girls came to the window, where they could see the young men ride by, sitting loosely in their saddles, their hard bright eyes sweeping the beach. Sometimes at intervals of months, even years, the young men looked at the window. Then followed a season of danger and delight. The river was a sheet of silver in the moonbeams; the warm night wind breathed along the sands; the threatening of the bar was no more than a bee's drone. And there were dances occasionally here, and in the county township up the river, and at the settlers' houses; and though there might be a ride or a pull of twenty or thirty miles to the

---

[1] Maidens of the tribe.

place of entertainment, the attendance suffered little from that. But the young men went back to their work in the bush, felling and driving and forgetting, and sometimes the girls wished that they had never been born.

The coming of the Reverend Mr. Fletcher was a golden event in the lives of the two remaining Mallow girls, and they were naturally his earliest converts. Winnie was twenty-four and Mabel twenty-one. They were fine buxom creatures, with the glowing beauty of their mixed parentage in their dark skin and lustrous eyes. Though they had hitherto been among the gayest of the gay, nothing could now exceed the demureness of their conduct. It was tacitly understood that the clergyman was to marry Winnie, but the elder sister entertained the fear, and the younger the hope, that Mr. Fletcher would exhibit in his selection the usual perversity of his sex. As for the father of the family, he had never interfered in the love affairs of his daughters either for good or ill. He was an indolent, taciturn man, who appeared to live mainly on tobacco and reflection, supplemented by occasional financial assistance from his relations, but he left the management of affairs to his wife, who, for all her dark skin, was a European in her instincts. Mallow washed himself and brushed his hair only under pressure from his family. He preferred walking about the sands in his bare feet rather than in boots, and if the choice offered, he would hold companionship with a Maori sooner than a European, and with himself in preference to either. For all this he was an affectionate parent, and—which counted for a good deal—the best fisherman on the river.

Mabel had walked along the beach to Hogg's store for the letters, because Winnie was getting the parson's breakfast, and she now came back with the weekly paper, a bill for Mr. Mallow, and two letters addressed to the Rev. T. Fletcher. Mabel knew that one of the clergyman's correspondents was a local one by the postmark, and she judged that the writer was a man from the character of the handwriting. The other letter was plainly penned by a woman, but the postmark showed her place of residence to be at the other end of the world.

Mr. Fletcher was seated at his breakfast, a meal which for domestic reasons he generally took alone, and Winnie was waiting on him. He received the letters with a kindly smile, and allowed them to lie by his plate while he conversed with the girls.

'Mr. Raymond struck me as an estimable and well-informed young man. I am pleased to think he has found an employer so close at hand.'

'Mr. Hogg is going to open a branch store on the gumfield,' Winnie said; 'so probably he will send Mr. Raymond there by and by. Have you met the new storekeeper Mr. Hernshaw?'

Mr. Fletcher's brows contracted slightly. 'Yes,' he said; 'I saw him on Sunday last.'

'Isn't he nice-looking?' Mabel asked. Something of the old leaven still worked beneath the demure exterior of the younger sister, betraying itself now and again in chance remarks. Winnie made warning signals behind the parson's chair.

'He is not outwardly ill-favoured,' Mr. Fletcher admitted. 'Has he been long in the district?'

'Two or three years,' Winnie hastened to reply. 'He has a brother— such a nice boy—who used to be a shepherd on the station until this one came out. Of course Mr. Hernshaw's taking on the store is only a forerunner to something else.'

Mr. Fletcher looked interrogation.

'He and Eve are dreadfully gone on one another,' Mabel explained, with a roguish laugh. 'All last summer they were inseparable; so it is easy to see what his coming to live at the place means.'

Mr. Fletcher resumed his breakfast in silence, and the two girls exchanged glances.

'They will make a beautiful couple, don't you think?' Mabel asked, seating herself with her hands locked on her knee in an attitude that showed off the voluptuous curves of her figure to perfection.

Mr. Fletcher stirred slightly, and his eye fell on the letters. He laid his hand on them and turned to the last speaker. Her eyes were brown and bewitching, and he looked straight into them and read their meaning.

'Is it a fact?' he asked, with a half smile. 'Or is it just a conclusion drawn by lookers-on?'

'Do you mean are they engaged?' Winnie broke in sharply. 'Yes; or if they are not, then they ought to be.'

Mr. Fletcher regarded her fixedly with dark, cold eyes. Then, taking his letters, he rose abruptly and left the room.

'Bah, you flat!' said Mabel with disgust. 'You ought not to have said that, because it was silly, and I don't believe it was true.'

'He is in love with her, I suppose?' Winnie said, clattering the dishes together passionately. 'What do I care whether it is true? Every one is in love with her. Who are these Milwards, that they should have it all their own way?'

'They are the biggest people here,' Mabel replied good-humouredly; 'and they are ladies and gentlemen. Major Milward owns half the county, and what he doesn't own he's got a mortgage on, and I don't believe half these people who hold their heads so high ever pay him his interest. I'm sure we don't; and he's had a mortgage on dad since the year one.'

'Major Milward's a darling,' said Winnie, surrendering at once.

'So's Eve,' said Mabel; 'only she's so beastly beautiful.' The adjective belonged, properly speaking, to the days before Mabel was converted.

Mr. Fletcher, when he left the breakfast-room, went into his private sanctum and closed the door. His writing-table stood near the window, and he sat down before it and looked out across the tussocks to the shining wet sands. His face suggested that the alliteration now being uttered in the other room might, had he heard it, have roused a responsive chord in his bosom; for it was the beauty of Major Milward's daughter which occupied his thoughts at that moment. There was no truth in what he had just heard; it was the cruel spite in which even decent women sometimes indulge. Was it true about Hernshaw? His lips closed, and he crushed the letters he still carried unconsciously in his hand. His attention thus directed to what he held, he lifted first the English letter, opened it, and glanced at the signature. Then with a shock his wandering thoughts were arrested and he read it through. He read it several times, sitting motionless all the while. Then, as though seeking distraction, he turned to the letter still unopened, and here also there appeared to be matter of unusual interest, for a single perusal did not suffice him. By and by his eye sought the window again, and for many minutes he sat looking straight in front of him. A barefooted man was pushing a boat down into the tide: this was Mallow going fishing. A boy, leading a horse, went by close under the window. His mind disturbed by these movements, Mr. Fletcher turned his face from the window, and his eye fell on a text pinned to the wall: 'Be merciful, and thou shalt obtain mercy,' said the text in bold black letter.

Mr. Fletcher tore the local note across, and going to the fireplace, he put a match to it, and watched the pale flame curl up around it. A knock came to the door, instantly followed by the appearance of a lad of eighteen—the youngest hope of the Mallow family—who looked curiously at the burning paper in the grate.

'Your horse is ready, Mr. Fletcher,' he said.

The minister hesitated, thrust the other letter into his pocket, and taking his hat and riding whip from the wall, followed the boy out in silence.

Winnie had not anticipated Mr. Fletcher's stay in his study would be so brief, and she had gone up the bank to the well; but Mabel, who was on the watch, heard him and came out. 'What time shall you be back, Mr. Fletcher?' she asked.

'Probably not till this evening,' was the reply; 'but I do not wish the household arrangements disturbed on my account at any time.'

'Poor Winnie is sorry for what she said,' Mabel continued in a lower voice. 'She hopes you will forgive her, and not be angry.'

'It was a highly improper remark,' Mr. Fletcher returned, with a partial recrudescence of his colder manner; 'both because it was uncharitable and also because it was untrue.' He looked searchingly at her as he spoke.

'It was untrue,' Mabel admitted, 'if it suggested any more than that Eve Milward and Geoffrey Hernshaw are lovers.'

'That is a truth, I suppose?' Mr. Fletcher said, smiling.

Mabel nodded. 'I know,' she said. 'If not yet—then soon. But, now or soon, it is certain.'

Mr. Fletcher mounted his horse, with the girl's words tingling in his ears, and they kept time to the lumbering canter of his big horse as he moved along the beach towards Wairangi. Certain! Certain! But was there anything certain in this world?

At the moment the black-coated figure turned up the track to the stables Geoffrey was in the office behind the store, and Eve was with him.

The girl sat on a low seat near the door, and looked eagerly up into her companion's face. 'Could you not reconsider it?' she asked pleadingly. 'The case surely cannot be so one-sided as you think, else how may we account for the wise and learned men who accept it?'

'It would be no use,' Geoffrey replied. 'It is not that I *will* not believe, but simply that ray reason does not permit me.'

'Do you remember what Mr. Fletcher said about relying on our reason?'

'Yes. But it is all we have—or at least it is all I have.'

'What is it you cannot believe?'

Geoffrey smiled at the little eager question, but his eyes remained troubled. 'It used to be details,' he said; 'but I have reached a stage when I can regard them with indifference; it is the inadequacy of the sum total.'

'Do you think the story of Christ inadequate?'

'I think that the story of Christ would gain in beauty could it be purged of much that is inconsistent, and more that is incredible. But the moral teachings of Christ are one thing, and the Bible as an authentic account of the origin and history of the universe quite another.'

'Mr. Fletcher says that where the Bible is in conflict with our idea of what is probable, it is so as a trial of our faith.'

'That is a way of explaining it, of course. But you have mentioned Mr. Fletcher: if our own reason in these matters is to be distrusted, where is the justification for relying on the reasoning of another? Or is reason to be appealed to only when her answer is likely to be in the affirmative, and disregarded on all other occasions?'

Eve looked uneasy, then she laughed. 'Your arguments are more penetrative than mine,' she said; 'but for all that, I feel within me that the Bible is true. Would you not be glad to think so?'

Geoffrey hesitated a long while before he replied. 'Even to that,' he said unwillingly at last, 'I must say no. I have, like most men who have dipped into modern ideas, a picture of the universe such as is conformable with reason, and could I be convinced that the Hebraic account was the correct one, I should feel that I had suffered a loss, not reaped an advantage. The difference between the two shapes itself to me as though a house built for kings should have come by misadventure into the hands of a misshapen dwarf.'

Eve rose, looking troubled and disappointed. 'That seems to be final,' she said. 'If you have not even the desire to believe_____ What is it,' she interrupted herself to inquire, 'you find so attractive in science? For mankind it seems to offer little, and for the individual nothing.'

'That is so,' Geoffrey replied; 'but the road has gone only a little way into the darkness. It is paved with truths, and truths are hard to come by. This is one,' he added, laying his hand on a volume on the desk,— 'the book Mr. Fletcher advised you not to read.'

'Is the evolution of species so certain?'

'Either that, or the Creator has laid a trap for our reason.'

'Mr. Fletcher says that the *Origin of Species* does not disprove the Bible.'

'That is as well, because evolution nowadays is regarded as much a fact as gravitation. But the Church is wise, and I doubt if it would be possible to produce any argument which would disprove the Bible.'

Eve pondered awhile, then looked up more brightly. 'I do not despair of you yet,' she said. 'I feel that revelation is quite as certain as evolution, supposing that to be as certain as you think, and if you could feel the beauty of it as I do, you would be glad to think so also.'

This was the beginning of many similar conflicts between the pair.

CHAPTER VIII

THE PRIEST AND THE LOVER

WHEN the human mind suffers from a harassment of doubt it instinctively endeavours to relieve the pressure by thrusting its torment upon another. Geoffrey had no doubts as to the correctness of his position, and the argument in which he had just engaged seemed to him as elemental as might be the discussion of a flat earth. But with Eve it was otherwise, and consequently when she found Mr. Fletcher waiting for her on the verandah, she very shortly began to affect his serenity in a manner similar to that in which her own had been disturbed.

'Do you *never* have doubts?' she asked *apropos* of some dogmatic utterance of his.

'Doubts are of Satan,' replied Mr. Fletcher; 'put them behind you.'

Eve caught at something fresh. 'Is Satan a personage,' she asked, 'or merely an abstraction?'

'Can you ask that question with the Bible before you?'

'But does the Bible always mean what it says? Must we believe it all implicitly, no matter how incredible it may appear?'

'Why harass yourself with these doubts?'Mr. Fletcher asked. 'Put your faith in God, and He will make the path easy for you.'

'But—but—forgive me if I pain you—if there be one falsehood in the Bible, then the whole of it must be open to suspicion. If God had desired to reveal Himself to man, he could have made certain of achieving His object by appealing to his reason.'

'It is not for us to question the ways the Almighty in His wisdom has seen fit to adopt,' replied the clergyman severely. 'Nor must you forget that what we regard now as incontrovertible truths would have been rejected with ridicule on all hands at the time the Word of God was given to mankind.'

'That is no doubt true. But with what veneration would every one of us regard the Bible if we found that every fresh discovery in science only made its truth more apparent?'

'And are we certain that it will not be so? Science has reached no finality in its discoveries. The truth of yesterday is the doubt of to-day and the lie of to-morrow. In the pursuit of knowledge do we get any nearer the solution of that vital question, the fate of the human soul? And,' he continued, starting to his feet with something of his outdoor fervour upon him, 'the day of science is wellnigh spent. Everywhere its votaries are returning with the same story of the impenetrable barriers God has set against the expansion of human knowledge. Turn then, my sister, to the blessed figure of the Saviour, in whose strength lies your salvation and that of the world. What has science to offer us in comparison with that divine light? Put from you the consideration of the Old Testament, which is too hard for your understanding, and cling to the Saviour, in whose arms your doubts will pass like darkness before the sun.'

'Ah!'said Eve, her eyes shining, 'when you talk to me like that my faith soars upwards; but afterwards the strength goes from its wings and down I come to the ground.'

He stood still, arrested by her words, and the whole expression of his countenance underwent a slow change. 'Would you dwell for ever in that empyrean of belief?' he asked at last.

'How willingly!' Eve replied.

'Then link your life with mine, and it shall be my task and my delight to hold you there.'

The girl looked at him with puzzled eyes, then slowly the blood mantled in her cheeks and she drew involuntarily backwards.

'Yes,' he said, watching her; 'this is a declaration of love, no less. I have argued and wrestled with and half convinced you; but in the process I have become wholly convinced myself.'

If Eve had been rosy before, she was pale now. All the light of exaltation raised by his words had faded from her eyes, leaving her face cold and impassive. Her first emotions were those of reproach and disappointment.

'I do not know how to answer you, Mr. Fletcher,' she said at last. 'I suppose I ought to have seen what was in your mind, and perhaps you will hardly credit me when I say that I did not. I have never had the vaguest idea until a moment ago that you thought of me in that way.'

'If one of us is to blame for that,' said Mr.Fletcher, 'I am that one. But I do not press you for a decision now. In a matter of such moment it is only right that you should take time to reflect.'

'No, no,' said Eve, startled. 'My hesitation does not arise from any doubt as to my decision. I was wondering whether I had to excuse myself for any action which, however unconsciously performed, may have led you to believe that such a proposal would be acceptable to me.'

'I can think of none,' said Mr. Fletcher, smiling. 'But there has been no action of yours since I have known you which has not had the effect of more firmly convincing me that no other woman would be so acceptable to me.'

His manner was sincere and respectful, with, for the moment, but little of the assurance that ordinarily characterised it. Eve found herself thinking that if as a clergyman he was dictatorial and inclined to crush opposition by a display of brute force, it was not so as a lover. Yet the influence he had begun to exert over her faded with the disappearance of the cleric, and was not replenished by the advent of the admirer. Had Mr. Fletcher been fully conscious of his power, he might have preferred to elaborate his opening sentence instead of covering and obscuring it in the ordinary asseverations of affection.

In these few moments of reflection the girl had regained her self-command. The first feeling of something incongruous in this abrupt change of their relationship, the sense of loss and disappointment, almost amounting to a betrayal, she now, with a clearer mind, recognised as unreasonable, and, however evolved, she accepted the situation frankly.

'I am sorry,' she said gently, 'because it is impossible.'

'I have taken you very much by surprise, no doubt,' he said.

'I think that has no influence on my reply. I can only say that I do not regard you in the way that you would wish.'

'Perhaps at a later date,' Mr. Fletcher suggested, 'you will give me leave to address you on this subject again. It is probably unfortunate that my manner has not led you to anticipate such a disclosure. Forgive me if I press the point—I would not willingly abandon hope in a matter which so vitally affects my life's happiness.'

'I do not think it would be of any use,' Eve replied. 'If I were to yield to that you would have just grounds for believing that your wishes might ultimately be realised.'

'I am prepared to take the risk of a fresh disappointment.'

Eve shook her head. 'It would not be right for me to allow you,' she said; 'for I do not see any possibility of a change in my feelings.'

Mr. Fletcher moved a few steps from where he had been standing. 'Is there—may I ask—any objection which I should be forced to regard as insuperable?'

Eve looked at him steadily, her face showing a faint surprise. 'Do you not regard my disinclination as insuperable?' she asked.

'Not altogether,' Mr. Fletcher confessed.

The quietness of his manner had betrayed the girl into a serenity which now held her at a disadvantage, dimly felt, but not consciously realised. She met his reply with a smile, but also with a little catch of the breath. She was seated on the music-stool, her back to the piano, in the drawing-room to which she had led him on his arrival. Mr. Fletcher drew forward a chair and sat down in front of her. There was something in his strong face which held her gaze despite her desire to look elsewhere.

'Eve Milward,' he said, 'it is borne in upon me that I shall prevail against your disinclination, and that the day is not far distant when you will be glad that I had the resolution to try. Is there in your heart nothing to correspond with that prescient?'

Eve's blue eyes dilated in a sort of speechless fascination, and for a moment it seemed to her that she must yield not only the point he pressed for but the whole argument. Then with a little start she was back in the world of realities.

'I can only argue from my present feelings,' she said; 'and they are such that I must hope for your sake that you will at once forget this conversation and dismiss the idea from your thoughts.'

'The latter is an impossibility,' Mr. Fletcher declared. He was silent awhile, but his manner by no means showed a disposition to relinquish the struggle. Eve began again to feel that some concession he must exact from her, and filled with the desire for immediate escape, she debated inwardly what might be the consequences of allowing the renewal of his proposal at some—preferably distant —date.

'If,' said Mr. Fletcher, 'your only reason for denying me a continuance of hope is the desire to spare me the pain of an ultimate refusal, then I trust that you will reconsider it. I am not of such poor material that I cannot submit myself to the inevitable, but first let me be assured that it is the inevitable to which I am submitting.'

'If my replies do not now give you that assurance, Mr. Fletcher, it is possible they may be no more effectual later on.'

'At least you will be possessed of the knowledge of my feelings towards you,' Mr. Fletcher said, disregarding this suggestion; 'and your final resolve, if no more favourable, will at any rate be the result of mature consideration.'

Eve moved uneasily. It seemed that she was being asked so little that it was mere obstinacy to refuse. But also it seemed that she was being asked so much that there was very little more to be conceded. She had not reached her twenty-first year without receiving an offer of marriage, but she had never had a lover who pursued the matter with such pertinacity as Mr. Fletcher. That gentleman, indeed, seemed possessed of a fecundity of argument and a resolution to exploit it which must be allowed to be somewhat unusual in the circumstances.

'It is, of course, impossible for me to prevent you renewing the subject should you desire to do so,' she said at last.

'May I take that for a permission to address you again?' Mr. Fletcher asked at once.

It seemed that there was no escape on that road, and Eve became slightly exasperated. 'No,' she said, with more firmness than she had yet shown,

'I will not go as far as that. I could not in honesty take any responsibility for the infliction of a fresh disappointment, for I am convinced that nothing but disappointment for you could attend any renewal of the subject.'

'If you could bring yourself to dismiss that aspect of the matter from consideration,' Mr. Fletcher urged. 'No doubt I was inadvised to broach the question at this juncture, but do not let me suffer irretrievable harm as the result of an uncontrollable impulse of affection towards you.'

Eve felt that there was something extraordinary about this speech, but she was too agitated at the moment to inquire what. Surely it was impossible for her to refuse so gentle a plea, and yet_____

She heard a step that she recognised enter the dining-room, then return along the verandah. A shadow passed the window going and coming, then the wanderer entered the house and advanced along the hall. Eve's heart beat more rapidly in the hope of relief, but she did not move. Mr. Fletcher's attention was divided between the downcast face of the beautiful girl and the annoying movements without.

The step came along the hall and paused outside the partly closed door; there was a perfunctory tap and Geoffrey put his head into the room.

'Were you looking for me, Mr. Hernshaw?' Eve asked lightly as she rose.

Geoffrey glanced with an impassive countenance from one to the other.

'Good-morning, Mr. Fletcher,' he said. 'I am looking for Major Milward. There is a native outside thirsting for his blood. He charges him0020that he did on or about the 18th of October last feloniously and of malice aforethought supply him with one tin golden syrup in place of one ditto preserved meat, and he demands apologies and damages, or in the alternative—war.'

Eve laughed gaily, and Mr. Fletcher, as in duty bound, produced a dour smile, which did not by any means express his actual sentiments at that moment.

CHAPTER IX

THE RED LINE IN THE LEDGER

IT was Major Milward's custom to spend an hour or so of every morning in the office, when all matters of importance in connection with the estate were brought before him. Sandy had claimed that the real management of affairs was in his hands, and though there was a certain justification for this, it did not take Geoffrey many days to discover that the master mind belonged in fact to the head of the household. He was astonished at the clearness of judgment with which the Major dissected a commercial problem, and the far-reaching grasp of its possibilities which seemed to be present a few moments after the subject was first mooted. Nothing could exceed his keenness and shrewdness in entering into any speculation which seemed to promise profitable returns—unless it might be the laxity he displayed in pressing for his own after the venture had succeeded. Major Milward was above all things a companionable and good-tempered man so long as he did not meet with wilful or prolonged opposition. But there was something in his shaggy brows and bright blue-gray eyes which was calculated to impress strangers with the belief that here was a man with whom it might be dangerous to take liberties. Those who knew him well needed no such outward indication to be similarly convinced.

Geoffrey found himself liking his employer better every day, and whether or no this good feeling was reciprocated, it is certain that the Major appeared to take pleasure in the young man's society, dropping in at the store at other than his accustomed times, and allowing himself to be defeated at the chess table with perfect placidity. Sandy could have assured Geoffrey that there was no more certain sign of his father's goodwill than that.

One morning, a few weeks after the event recorded in the last chapter, Major Milward entered the office at the customary time. Usually the cigar between his teeth was the only thing he carried, but on this morning he had what appeared to be an old account book under his arm, which he placed beside him as he took his seat at the writing-table. It was mail day, and a little packet of correspondence lay waiting attention.

'Anything fresh?' the Major asked musingly, as he glanced through the first letter.

'There is one note from a man called Wadham, who has a kauri bush for sale.'

'Ah!' said the Major eagerly; 'what's he say?'

Geoffrey found the letter and laid it in front of his employer.

'"Sorry to have to let go . . . kauri getting scarcer . . . twice the money two or three years' time,"'read the Major in snatches. 'H'm! Hope so. "About three-quarters million feet . . . easily got out." Oh yes; write and tell him we'll take it if he halves the fire risk until we start cutting.'

'I suppose in that case we should fix a date when the cutting will begin,' Geoffrey suggested.

'He will probably think of that,' said the Major drily; 'and we'll let it stand over until he does. About the price—Sandy will tell you what it's worth.'

The Major returned to the letter he had been reading. Presently he said: 'I see Hogg writes that the lease will expire in fifteen months' time, and he asks with Howell's consent for a transfer to himself for ten years at the same rental.'

'Yes, sir, what reply shall I send to that?'

Major Milward referred to the index of the old account book and turned up a page. 'Just come here,' he said.

Geoffrey went round behind his employer's chair and looked over his shoulder.

'What do you make of it?' the Major asked after a moment.

'I take it to be a loan account for £480, on which there is £75 owing as interest.'

'That's the position,' the Major said, nodding approval. 'Write and tell him that when he has discharged arrears of interest on that loan and made a reduction in the capital amount, I shall be prepared to consider his application for this lease.'

'Is the rent account satisfactory?' Geoffrey asked.

'Yes, the rent is paid through another channel. That was the money you received from Howell a fortnight ago. Hogg is a sub-tenant.'

Geoffrey made a note of his instructions while the Major finished the remainder of the letters. Then the latter turned again to the old account book.

'I should like you to go through this,' he said, running the leaves through his fingers with a lingering touch,' and draw out a statement of what is owing in each case. You will find a number of accounts ruled off with a red line and those you can disregard. I have either been paid, or I am satisfied I shan't be, or I am content not to be. I should like a list of the others, but any time will do, and there is no hurry for a week or so.'

'Very good, sir.'

The Major rose, walked idly across the office and stood musing in the doorway.

'Everything satisfactory?' he asked finally.

'I think so,' said Geoffrey, a little puzzled.

'Don't feel bored out of existence? Satisfied with the money you are getting?'

'No to the first question, and yes to the last,' Geoffrey replied.

'There was a time,' the Major said, 'when I never saw a ship cast off for the old land but I wanted to be on board. Ever felt like that?'

'I have, often, but not now.'

'When you feel the craving return upon you and you are convinced that there is no place like England and no happiness away from it, tell me so, will you?'

'I will,' said Geoffrey, puzzled.

The Major nodded, seemed on the point of continuing the conversation, but finally departed without further speech.

Geoffrey sat at his desk with the pen arrested in his hand. That instinct of return, which man shares with all migratory creatures, and which years of restraint can deaden but never kill, lay for the time wholly hidden from feeling by the one passion powerful enough to subdue it. There had been a time when, had he yielded to the intense desire that possessed him, he would have taken the first boat available: when the very name of England filled his heart with a rapture such as the lover finds in the name of his sweetheart. All the while it had been in his power to gratify the longing had he so chosen. Of the many letters that reached him from his uncle and his cousins not one failed to speak of his return as otherwise than a more or less immediate event. Things had prospered greatly with his uncle. The Boer war, which had brought sorrow and suffering to thousands, had brought wealth to him, and in this increased prosperity he desired that his nephew should return to share. Mr. Hernshaw refused to entertain the idea that Geoffrey would settle permanently in the new land, but he offered to buy and stock a small farm for Robert, or to provide the capital necessary to carry on operations on a place already selected. This offer led to a species of compromise, by virtue of which and pending any ultimate decision the brothers drew on their uncle for £150 a year. This until his coming to the station had been the whole of their income, and it was easily absorbed in the expenses of living and the demands made on them by their section. It was not that Geoffrey was indifferent to money, or the ease and comfort it provides,—having been reared in comparative luxury it was next to impossible that he should be so,—but he had a *feeling* that before he could accept anything more from others he must first prove his ability to support himself by his own efforts. This—whether the incentive to it were pride or a desire to test his efficiency once for all by matching his strength against the world—was, he told himself, the venture which had drawn him from England.

Something of this passed through Geoffrey's mind as he sat listening to Major Milward's retreating footsteps. He wondered whether his employer's last words had been prompted by good-natured sympathy, or did they veil a knowledge of the facts of the case, and, if so, how was that knowledge acquired? 'When you are convinced that there is no place like England and no happiness away from it.' Had the word 'Wairangi' been substituted for 'England,' the answer must have been 'now'; for the place where love dwells is the only spot more desirable than that where we were born and bred.

Geoffrey's thoughts drifted easily from the father to the daughter. He reviewed the occurrences of the past two months, recalling every conversation, every chance word and expression of his beloved. At one moment it seemed impossible that the girl should be unconscious of his feelings; at the next—when he recalled the frank serenity of her manner—it seemed equally impossible that she should be aware. Could any girl be unconscious of the meaning of certain little speeches, hovering on the borderland of a declaration, such as love had drawn from him on occasions? He thought of her clear eyes, and admitted it might be so. He thought of her momentary silences, and hoped for the best. There had been something in her looks at times—he recalled the momentary heart-shock of finding her alone with Mr. Fletcher, almost instantly annihilated by the radiant smile which had welcomed his arrival. If ever there were welcome for a man in a girl's eyes, it was in Eve's at that moment. But perhaps it was not the man but the interruption that was welcome. Of course Fletcher was in love with her. Possibly he was on the eve of a proposal at that very instant, and if the proposal were unwelcome anything likely to avert it would have been as radiantly received,—a cow, for example. Geoffrey laughed and frowned at the same instant. He thought of Mr. Fletcher with misgivings. Not that he considered it likely that the clergyman would prove a dangerous rival, but on account of the power he possessed to create mischief if he chose. As it was, there was an element of difference in his relations with Eve which had not existed previous to Mr. Fletcher's arrival. For some occult reason, the fiercest heart-burnings grow out of and accumulate round a religious disagreement. It would seem that just at that point where reason becomes powerless she makes the most obdurate fight to retain her supremacy. The man who in one breath will tell you that religion is a matter of belief and not of reason, will in the next educe every argument reason can provide to convince you that belief itself is a matter of reason; and thus, with growing anger in its participants, a religious argument will whirl round in a circle like the fracas of a pair of bantams fighting in the dust. Fortunately the religious difference between Eve and Geoffrey had so far been of an impersonal character. Whatever feelings actuated the girl, the man's love kept all bitterness out of his side of the discussion, and probably Geoffrey was right in concluding that no taint of chagrin had clung to either party as a result of their mutual inability to convince. It was a great deal, however, to expect that this would continue to be so, and it was in the possibility of a coldness arising from this source, and in the growing influence of Mr. Fletcher, that Geoffrey recognised his most dangerous obstacles.

Geoffrey dipped his pen in the ink and automatically completed the task on which he had been engaged; then he sat down at the table and opened the old account book.

It began a long way back in point of time, and some of the earlier entries were veritable historical curiosities, the value of which was occasionally enhanced by a brief note written in red ink at the foot of the page.

'To Capt. John Shewn. Master mariner. On the hull of the schooner *Martha*, £250 at 8%.'

Interest appeared to have been forthcoming for two years. Then came a note in red ink, so faded as to be hardly decipherable:—

'*Martha* wrecked on the bar, June 12, 1852. Captain and all hands lost. Poor Jack Shewn!'

Lower down the page was a column of small amounts, debited to E. S., £5. Ditto £3, etc. etc. The account was closed with a red line.

Geoffrey turned the pages idly.

'To Joe Mallow, without interest, £100 to equip his boys for the West Coast goldfields.'

This appeared to have been repaid, but the Mallow account ran for two or three pages and concluded with a considerable debit. At the foot of the first page were the words:—

'Mallows said to have done very well at the diggings. Bought a schooner and loaded her with goods, chiefly agricultural implements— but also, it is said, large quantity of gold dust—and set sail for the north. Schooner sighted off Hokitika September '54. Never seen again.'

A little farther on was an account for £50 discharged by a contra of ten tons of gum. Gum was of very little value in those days. The loans on timber ran into very large amounts, and Geoffrey was pleased to see that they nearly always resulted profitably. The loans on real estate were more difficult to estimate, and it was the exception when any commensurate amount appeared on the credit side of the ledger. More frequently there was some such note as: 'Gave this bit for school-ground,' or less explicit, 'Church stands here,' or 'Allowed the family to continue at nominal rent on account of my friendship with the father.' But even in this last case there was nothing to show that the nominal rent had ever been paid. More often than not the red line went steadily across the page, and closed the matter up for good. It is not always in a man's ledger that he appears at his best, but Geoffrey found his heart warming as he read.

But he was fated to make a discovery that should bring the Major's business peculiarities home to him at his own door. In his idle turning of the leaves he came to a place where the pages adhered together, and absently lifting the paper-knife he divided them at the bottom and then at the top. Not until he had done so did it occur to him that the sheets had been intentionally sealed against him, and at the same moment his eye fell on his father's name. There was a sum of over £300 to the debit of the account, and not one penny to the credit. Beneath was the note:—

'I wish with all my heart that Mrs. Hernshaw had let me do more to help her. As good and noble a woman as ever lived.'

The red line crossed the page with more than its usual emphasis.

Stung as he was in his pride by the discovery of this unexpected obligation, Geoffrey yet felt the moisture gather in his eyes at the tribute to the mother he scarcely remembered.

The sound of an approaching footstep caused him to close the volume, and Sandy came in booted and spurred from his customary bi-weekly visit to the branch store on the coast.

'Did you ever look through this?' Geoffrey asked, indicating the account book.

Sandy opened his eyes and whistled. 'No,' he said; 'that's tapu.'[1]

'Some day,' Geoffrey said, 'and may it be far distant, you will read it, my boy; and take my word for it now, who have read many books, that you will never twice read anything quite so noble and so foolish as your father's private ledger. And if it be possible to pay a man's nature a higher compliment than that, then I confess I don't know how.'

---

[1] 'Tahpoo,' sacred.

CHAPTER X

THE GROWING OF THE CROP

THE potatoes on the ploughed land had done well, and now that the hoeing was finished they presented a picture of which Robert as its author was justly proud. A strip had been left for the cultivation of kumaras, and on this Robert was busily engaged. He had worked the soil up into long ridges during the past week, and was now employed in the pleasant operation of putting out the sets at regular intervals all down the ridges. The tubers had been started in a piece of rich soil near the house, and now and then, as his work demanded, Robert came down to the bed for a fresh supply of shoots.

He was returning from one of these visits when he caught sight of a large straw hat and a black stocking between the slip-rails. Lena Andersen, for it was she, came through the vegetable garden and greeted him with a little serious nod.

'Oh, Robert!' she exclaimed.

'How beautiful you look, Lena!' Robert said soberly.

It was a wonderful November morning, with just sufficient movement in the air to soften the intensity of the sun's vertical beams. The mingled odours of the standing forest came down the south wind, and the air was full of the liquid talk of the tuis as they sipped at the pendent blossoms of the honeysuckle trees. The crops were growing vigorously, the hardest of the work was done, and the reward of labour was in sight. Planting kumaras was a pleasant relaxation, calling for no physical exertion, and allowing the mind to wander at its will. So Robert, who would have scorned to pay a mere compliment, summed up his satisfaction with the moment by telling Lena that she was beautiful.

Lena seemed astonished. She had discarded the flour-bags from the day they had attracted the young man's attention, and was dressed in a gray print frock, with black shoes and stockings, all of which Robert had seen on other occasions. A wide rush hat rested on her sunny curls and shadowed her fair face and blue eyes. Altogether she was a sufficiently charming picture of a young maiden to justify Robert's remark; and if she were astonished, the astonishment probably had reference not so much to the words as to the quarter whence they emanated.

'Oh, Robert,' she said again, 'father has come back!'

Robert's face fell slightly, and he put the kumara sets back on the bed. 'Come and tell me,' he said.

They went together to a log behind the house and sat down side by side. A row of quince bushes formed a screen in front of them, giving the spot the privacy of a room. Their actions seemed to show that this was not the first time they had made use of the log.

'When did he come?' Robert asked.

'Last night; and he was awful. He chased mother with a knife round the house, and we put all the things against the door of our room; and at last I got the children out of the window, and we stopped together in the bush all night. He wanted to kill us all because he said mother_____'

'Mother what?'

'Oh, I don't know. . . . Something he said. I was glad when daylight came.'

'Why didn't you come up here?'

'Mother wanted to go somewhere else, and I said we would come here; and neither of us would give way, so we stopped where we were.'

'Where is he now?' Robert asked presently.

'He's at home asleep. Of course he will be sorry when he wakes; but what's the good of that? Oh, Robert!'

'Well, Lena?'

'I wish he was dead—I wish he was dead and buried.'

The wish found an echo in Robert's heart, but he moved uneasily.

'It's no good wishing I was dead myself,' Lena said, looking at him, 'because that would help nobody; and why should I wish we were all dead rather than him?'

'It's a shame, Lena; but I don't like to hear you say that. Let me do it for you, because there's no harm in my wishing him dead—and I do!'

There was a long silence.

'Do you think you will be able to come tonight?' Robert asked at length.

'I don't know— I might—I will try.'

'Does he stop long as a rule?'

'No. When he wakes up he begins to cry and carry on, but mother takes no notice of him. Then after a bit he says he will reform and never touch drink again, and then he goes away to look for a job; and that's the last of him—till next time.'

'Does he never give you anything at all?'

'Almost never.'

'Then how on earth do you live?'

'Mother gets money somewhere. Mrs. Gird gives her some, and other things. She gave me these clothes. Oh, I hate it!'

Robert looked contemplatively at the clothes and the desperate young face, then he turned away and gazed fixedly at the bushes.

'I was thinking, Lena, I might do a great deal for you—if you wouldn't mind.'

'What could you do?' asked Lena quickly, her eyes on his averted face.

'I could give you things, you know—clothes and such, anything you liked. I have plenty of money, and I could get a great deal more if I wanted.'

'Why don't you want?' Lena asked, her attention diverted by this surprising statement.

'I suppose it's pride,' Robert said, after a thoughtful pause.

'And don't you think I have any pride?' Lena asked. 'Besides, you do give me things, as it is.'

'Tea and sugar,' Robert observed contemptuously.

'More than that.'

'Soap,' said Robert, considering.

'Soap and—sympathy,' said Lena, with a little laugh. 'It sounds like that funny book, *Alice in Wonderland*.'

Robert looked round quickly. 'I meant practical things,' he said. 'Sympathy's cheap enough, Lena.'

'Sympathy is dear,' Lena averred.

'Would you let me give you some money?' Robert asked, sticking to the point as was his custom.

'No, I wouldn't.'

'Why not?'

'I don't know.'

'But if you liked me you would think nothing of that.'

'Then I suppose I don't like you.'

Robert tried a fresh tack. 'You take money from Mrs. Gird.'

'Yes, because if I didn't we might starve.'

'Would you take it from—Mr. Russell, or— Major Milward?'

'I daresay.'

'And yet you won't take it from me! Why?'

'Because.'

'Because what?'

'Because.'

'But that's no answer. You must have a reason.'

'Well, because I don't choose.'

'Very good,' said Robert, in a huff. 'I only meant to be friendly.'

Lena's eyes filled with tears, and presently they overflowed and a tear fell. Robert saw it, and his ill-humour vanished in an instant.

'There!' he said. 'Don't cry, dear; I won't trouble you about it any more.'

The term of endearment slipped out unawares, but it sounded natural, and Lena, happily, appeared not to hear.

'It's because you are my friend that I couldn't,' she sobbed. 'Don't you see?'

'No,' said the practical Robert after a tremendous strain. 'But never mind. No doubt you are right, and it's only my stupidity.'

'But you think me unfriendly.'

'No, I don't. I think you are the nicest, and the prettiest, and the cleverest girl I know.'

Lena laughed through her tears. 'Boo!' she said. 'What a baby I am. But I have been wanting to cry ever since last night. And to think it was you that made me after all.' She turned a pair of tear-bright, wondering eyes on the delinquent.

'You know, Lena,' Robert said seriously, 'that I would not willingly make you cry for the world. I would do anything to give you happiness.'

Lena rested her chin on her hand and regarded him steadfastly. 'Do you like me?' she asked. 'Do you—almost—love me?'

'I do love you,' said Robert.

Lena clapped her hands. 'Oh, you dear!' she said. 'How much do you love me?'

'A great deal,' replied Robert, labouring heavily in the strong seas of emotion. 'It—it covers everything, and goes right out beyond, beyond what I can see, or hear, or feel. But I'm a fool at words, and I couldn't make you understand.'

'But I do—I do!' Lena exclaimed in awed rapture. 'And what you said was beautiful and sweet. And why do you love me?'

'Because *you* are beautiful and sweet, and because I can't help it.'

'Would you like to help it?'

'No, indeed!'

Lena gazed rapturously at her captive. 'Tell me some more?' she cried.

'That is everything,' said Robert. 'I think of you always, and when I say your name to myself I see your eyes. I can always see you quite plainly when I think of you.'

'Then I must be always with you,' Lena said, putting two and two together.

'Yes, all day long.'

'And you never told me!'—reproachfully.

'I did not think it would be so easy to tell you.'

'Why not?'

'Because I was afraid of you.'

'Oh, you strange boy! Oh, you funny Robert! And you're not afraid of me any longer?'

'Yes, I am—a little. It seems too good to be true that you should be glad because I love you, and so I am afraid that it may not be true.'

Lena thought over this. 'Would you be very sorry if it were not true?' she asked with experimental curiosity.

'I should not care what happened to me after I knew that.'

'But it is true, Robert, it is. Because you love me, *I* don't care what happens. I don't wish any one any harm now, only happiness. I wish every one could be happy, I feel sorry for poor mother, and I never felt sorry for her like this before. And I'm sorry for father too—yes, I am. And I feel glad and *good.* And it's all because you love me; and you say, "If it were not true." Oh, Robert, if it were not true, and I knew it were not true, I should wish I was dead.'

'If I could express myself like that,' Robert said, 'how I would make you believe!'

'It was just beautiful as it was,' Lena declared; 'and I shall remember every word of it as long as I live. And now I must go back home.'

'You will come to-night?'

'Yes, if I can. Good-bye.'

They came out into the sunlight, and Robert glanced with diminished interest at the kumara sets wilting on the bed.

'I believe you are sorry I am going,' Lena said, watching him.

'Sorry!'

'Well, but you have my second always with you. Let her run along the rows, and help you plant the kumaras.'

'She is not like you.'

'Good-bye,' Lena said again.

At the fence she stopped, and they stood still for a space, looking across the garden at one another; then she waved her hand and went on. Robert watched the straw hat till at the bend of the road her face was again turned towards him. Again she waved her hand and stood to watch him. A whole minute passed. At last, step by step, she moved backwards till the bush concealed her.

Robert rubbed his eyes, picked up the kumara sets, and went slowly up the hill to his interrupted work.

The tuis had stopped singing in deference to his majesty the Mid-day Sun, but the little riro-riro who haunts the shadowy places in company with the fantail, popped out with a little silvery congratulation as Lena ran past.

'Thank you, you darling,' she said; 'but I can't stop to talk about it now.'

The fantail, perched on a supple-jack spanning the track, spread out his tail and made a dozen little grotesque bows and as many little rasping remarks, all with the kindest intentions.

'Oh, you funny little dear!' Lena said. 'I love you. I love every one and everything. And the world is just sweet.'

'Sweet—sweet—sweet—swe-e-t!' said the shining cuckoos in crescendo on the skirts of the bush.

Then Lena looked down on the house with the kerosene-tin roof which was her home, and saw her mother standing moodily at the door and her father gesticulating apologies at the slip-rail.

It was only a chapter from the past. She had seen it all before. The nightmare of his coming, the relief that followed his going; how well she remembered them. But now, somehow, she saw it all with different eyes. That was her mother in the doorway—that listless, untidy woman with the resentful eyes. Her mother! Oh, poor thing!

Her father turned at the sound of her approach, and looked at her curiously out of his bloodshot eyes. 'Vy, it's Lena,' he said at last in surprise.

'Yes, father,' said Lena gently; 'it's me.'

'Vy! she is bekom a womman,' the father muttered. 'She is grown great gel. Now I vill warrk and warrk and never touch him again. You vill see the goot faters I vill be and the goot hosbands. Vill your mother say I forgif you, Sven, dis las' time?'

Mrs. Andersen, who had been apathetically watching the pair, shrugged her shoulders.

'Mother has forgiven you many times, father; and always you need to be forgiven again.'

'Ah!' said the wretched man, thrusting his hands in his hair. 'It is true as my daughter says. It is true, and I am beast and brutes, but never more vill I touch him—dis time vill I svear.'

'I have heard you swear before, father,' Lena said sadly.

'But never as dis time. If your mother vill give von forgifness then I shall be strong.'

Lena looked imploringly at her mother.

'Well, then, listen to me, Sven,' said Mrs. Andersen. 'You have called yourself a beast and brute, but you may thank Lena there that you have not to stand up and call yourself a murderer as well. You came very near it last night. Do you see this mark on my cheek? Ay, you may well call yourself a brute, but when the drink's in you, you are worse than any beast. Husband or no husband, that's a true word. Now you listen to me, for as God lives I mean what I say. This is the last time. Do you hear that?'

'Yes, yes; I vill svear—I vill go on mine knees_____'

'And if you break your word and come again as you did last night, then—you may take the consequences, for drunk or sober I will have nothing more to do with you.'

For an instant the woman's eyes blazed with passion, then clutching her throat she went sobbing into the house.

'Oh, father, father!' said Lena, her eyes shining, 'do try, and we might all be so happy.'

'Yes, I vill try,' said her father, staring at the closed door. 'I vill try so as neffer before.'

'And you will succeed, father; and then how proud we will all be.'

'Yes, I vill socceed. I vill make you proud as neffer was. Dis time I haf no money. Ah, filty wretch dat I am!'

'Never mind that, dear; only try.'

'Yes. Soon I vill bring some money—every veek I vill bring money. And your mother vill forgif me more'n more, and you vill be proud.'

'Yes, I will be proud, for it will be very, very hard for you; but this time you will conquer, won't you?'

'Yes, dis time I am strong. It is nutting. I vill not touch him again; I have said it.' And the poor wretch snapped his fingers at his absent enemy.

Lena looked at him and sighed. 'When are you going, father?' she asked.

'Straight avay,' said Andersen, and lifted his swag from where it had been lying since the night before under the fence. Lena helped to adjust it on his broad shoulders and to secure the straps, swollen with the dews; then she looked at him long and wistfully and said, 'Remember.'

Her father nodded. 'Gif me the kiss for the kia ora.'[1]

Lena lifted her face to his. There was moisture on her cheek as she drew away, and she saw that there were tears in his eyes. 'Be strong, dear,' she said.

He nodded again and went blindly away down the track as full of good resolutions as ever a man in this world.

The nearest public-house was fourteen miles off, and besides he had no money.

---

[1] 'Well-wishes.'

CHAPTER XI

LENA CONSULTS THE ORACLE

LENA went soberly into the house. The youngest child, who had not yet passed the stage when an oatmeal bag would cover the greater portion of him, was howling himself into an apoplexy in one corner. Lena picked him up, and in his astonishment at her gentleness he stopped crying on the instant. Mrs. Andersen looked round suddenly at the abrupt cessation of the noise.

'Father's gone,' Lena said cheerfully.

'Good riddance to him,' said her mother.

'He was very sorry, mother, and he is going to be good; and there were tears in his eyes.'

'Yes, he's the sort that cries easily. Was there any money in his pocket?'

'He's going to work and bring us money. Oh, mother, I wish you could forgive him!'

'Let me forget him then.'

Lena looked wistfully round the wretched room, seeking for an inspiration that might thaw the frozen heart.

'It seems so hard,' she said, 'that all his trying should come to nothing; it seems so cruel. He means so well in his heart now, and he is so gentle and kind, and then the drink masters him and he becomes hateful. Why doesn't God help him? It would be so easy for God. Oh, I wish there were no more drink in all the world!'

Her mother laughed savagely. 'I've been wishing it for fifteen years,' she said, 'and there's been more and more all the time.'

'Poor mother!'

The woman caught her breath and sitting down on a stool with her face to the wall, began rocking herself to and fro.

Lena set the child on his feet and went and knelt down beside her. Her face was pale, but there was an absence of demonstration from her manner which seemed to speak of a sensibility unusual in one of her years. 'Poor mother! 'she said softly, possessing herself of one of her mother's hands.

'Don't,' said Mrs. Andersen peevishly; but the child persisted, and presently both hands were in her possession. 'Oh, Lena, Lena!' said her mother. 'I was not many months older than you when I married him, and I am only a young woman yet, and I have wished myself dead any day for more than a dozen years.'

'Yes, yes—I know.'

'How can you know, you child? If you had been a boy you could have helped me, but the boys came last.'

'I can help you, mother, and I will.'

'But it is too late. You must let me go my own way. If it had not been for you last night, everything would have been settled now. Why did I listen to you?'

'Oh, mother, could you ever be happy again?'

'There!' said Mrs. Andersen, pushing her away. 'You are only a child; you don't understand.'

'But I do, mother. I know what your going to Mr. Beckwith meant. I know *all* that it meant.'

Mrs. Andersen looked at her uneasily, a faint colour showing in her careworn cheek. 'What did it mean then?'she asked huskily.

'It meant that father would not be your husband any more.'

'It meant clothes for you and the children, and comfort and peace for us all,' Mrs. Andersen said slowly. 'It meant protection from what we had to endure last night and what we shall have to endure again.'

'Never again.'

'Yes, again. Well, we shall see.'

'But you have given father another chance?'

'One more.'

'And then? Oh, I wish—I wonder if we do right when we let him go away. Perhaps if we clung fast to him it would be easier for him to resist. We ought to let him go only by little and little till at last we could trust him altogether.'

'I've tried it all,' said Mrs. Andersen wearily, 'and I broke my heart over it; but now I don't care what happens. Bah! A man should not need a parcel of women to keep him straight. It's not natural.'

'Was he always like that, mother?' Lena asked musingly,—'even when you first knew him?'

'He drank a little, but I had never seen him more than merry. It was afterwards that I found he had no will of his own. Never you marry a man who can't say "No" and stick to it.'

Lena started and the colour deepened in her cheeks; then she caught her mother's hand and her eyes sparkled. 'Did you love father very dearly? 'she asked.

'I suppose I loved him or I should not have married him, but I hadn't the sense to see him as he was. But what do you know about love? Love is all very well, but it won't feed you or clothe you or keep the wind out of the house. How are we going to live now?'

'I suppose we can manage somehow. We have managed hitherto.'

'Yes—on Mr. Beckwith's money.'

'Oh, mother!'

'Yes—and oh, Lena! The world's none of my making. Would you have me sit by and see the kids starve while there is a way to prevent it? I suppose he has a right to be charitable if he likes, even though he does—love me, as you say. Come, are you thinking of any one but yourself? You wouldn't like it because people would talk, but what about the children? It's his idea, not mine. He says *all* and for good, and he never changes, and he is a just man and a good man, and your father isn't worthy to black his boots. There!'

'And is there no other way?' Lena asked restlessly. 'I do feel the truth of what you say, and I do want us all to be happy—us who have never known what it is—but is that the way to happiness, through—yes, I must say it — shame, and over father's misery?'

'I would take any road to happiness now,' Mrs.

Andersen said recklessly. 'The wonder is I have refrained so long. But I am a fool to argue with a child. Wait till you have been through what I have and then see how much morality is left in you.'

But even as she uttered the wicked words the miserable woman burst into tears and caught her daughter in her arms.

'No, no,' she sobbed. 'Don't listen to me; don't believe me. Oh, my little one, it's that or madness! Once you might have persuaded me; but it's too late. I love him.'

'Poor, poor mother!'

'And if he were to walk in now and say to me, "Come," then I must follow him to the end of the world, and that is the way with a woman.'

Lena looked out despairingly through her tears. Was it for her to deny the supremacy of love?

'Oh, mother!' she said, 'perhaps you are right and I am too young to understand; and maybe I only repeat like a parrot what I have heard, because I am incapable of forming a judgment myself. I will believe that you are right, if Mrs. Gird will say so too. May I go to her and tell her everything? She is not like other women; she will never repeat a word of it. Then, if she is against you doing as you wish, she may think of some way to help us. Say yes, mother.'

'Very well, then,' said her mother, worn out by the struggle, and glad to throw the onus of a decision on another. 'She knows nearly all about it as it is. Yes, anything to bring it to an end.'

So in the afternoon Lena set out to consult the oracle, whose shrine was in the dark bush, where the trees came down slowly one by one, and the tui's lustrous talk was always in the air so long as the daylight lasted. There was little to disturb him here, for the track ended at the Girds' doorstep, and beyond the forest stretched away to the south for forty miles without a break. And it needed little to disturb the tui, who for all his loquacity and gaiety has the reserve and pride of the aristocrat, shunning the places frequented by that sturdy foreigner the thrush, and turning his glossy back contemptuously on that vulgar little blackguard, the European sparrow.

Mrs. Gird was not visible in the clearing, and Lena, who had the distaste of the young for the sight of incurable sickness, went hesitatingly up to the open door of the house.

'The very lass,' said Mrs. Gird's voice from the dark interior. 'Come right in and take off your frock. Now, who says I haven't the power of summoning those I want? Yes, you may smile, father, but here's the maid in the flesh, and what's brought her here if it wasn't my summons? Well, Lena? You see father's been a bit poorly—oh, nothing to speak of—and so I'm stopping at home to cheer him up. And I've cut up my black velvet for you, because an old woman has no need of dresses in the bush; and it's been packed away ever since— well, never mind when, for it's good yet, and the very thing to show off the whitest skin and the bluest eyes in the settlement.'

'You are very good, Mrs. Gird,' Lena said awkwardly.

'Good! Good's-no word for me. I am simply a wonder of generosity when I like. Take off your frock; I'm dying to see what kind of a dress-maker I am. No, I didn't cut it out with the axe.'

'Oh, Mrs. Gird!'

'Well, then, that bit of thought-reading missed fire. Now, let me see. My! what lovely arms! Oh, if I only dared make it without sleeves! Mind the pins! Gracious! I believe it's going to fit. *Gently!* And the waist is like a dream—and the throat! Did you ever! Ain't I an artist? Ain't I just the most extraordinary clever woman in spite of my grammar?'

'You are very kind,' Lena said, her eyes beaming.

'I'm all kinds,' said Mrs. Gird. 'Now, let me see. We mustn't hide those pretty legs altogether. I should like it quite short; but you, of course—oh, you needn't tell me_____'

'I should like it longer than that other one,' Lena confessed.

'I knew it, and it's so stupid. Just when, for His own reasons, God has made a girl most attractive she begins to curl up her hair and her toes and get out of sight. It's just an invention of the poor miserables to whom clothes are necessary for survival. The wonder is that the hand-some people allow themselves to be imposed upon, and led by the nose or the clothes into all sorts of ridiculous disguises. It's indecent. Well, if you must; but not an inch longer. Now turn round. Ah, well, I suppose after all it's the girl and not the clothes! 'And Mrs. Gird sat down and re-garded her handiwork with thoughtful eyes, in which a gleam of anxiety played amid a deal of tenderness.

'So your father has come back?' she said presently, busying herself with the more perfect adjustment of the dress.

'Yes, last night; and he went away again this morning. He was terri-ble, but he was sorry afterwards.'

'The same old tale—and what next?'

'He has promised never to touch drink again, and he means to try—he means to try so hard.'

'Yes, a weak man's resolution and a rope of sand.'

'Oh, Mrs. Gird, is there no hope for him?'

'Hope, child,' said Mrs. Gird softly, her eye travelling to the still figure in the invalid's chair; 'we can no more help hoping than we can stop the beating of our hearts; but the order of things is not changed in deference to human desire. In the end we have to make up our minds to the inevitable. Hope? No, not a shadow.'

Lena stood silent and miserable while the frock was removed. The futility of hope is a tragic prospect to the young, to whom, indeed, it is little less essential than the air that fills their lungs.

'Come and sit down by me,' said Mrs. Gird kindly, 'and let us see if the world is really as black as it pretends to be. Does it seem so dark? Is there no gleam of sunshine anywhere?'

The colour rose in Lena's cheeks and she dropped her eyes. 'I was thinking of mother and the children,' she murmured.

'Yes,' said Mrs. Gird, watching the downcast face, 'and what of mother?'

'She has given father another chance — the last—after that____'

'The deluge'—as Lena hesitated. 'Well, I did not expect she would give him another chance; and that is something gained, I suppose, even if it's only time.'

'Oh, Mrs. Gird, mother seemed to say that you knew all about us, and she said I might come and talk with you—not on her account, you understand, but my own; because I want to know what is right and what is best for us all.'

'Ah, if there were any one who could really tell us that, Lena!'

'Mother has given him another chance, and if he fails she will leave him and go—to—Mr. Beckwith.'

Lena wrung her hands passionately.

'And that seems terrible to you?' Mrs. Gird asked gently. 'But of course and so it is—and yet, perhaps—probably—it will come to pass.'

'Oh, Mrs. Gird, could it ever be right?'

'No, it could never be right—that seems certain. But can we ever do what is perfectly right? Do we even know it? The best of human righteousness is only parti-coloured. Now and then, Lena, we all come to the place where the roads divide, and sometimes we know or think we know which is wrong and which is right, but we have to make our choice, and when we have made it there is no turning back.'

'But ought mother to do this?' Lena urged. 'I know that Mr. Beckwith is everything that is kind, and that the children would be well fed and clothed and taught, and when I think of them my heart says yes, but would that excuse it? Would anything excuse it? It seems that the price is more than we should be asked to pay.'

Mrs. Gird shook her head. 'It is for your mother to decide. I would help her if I could; but, child, this question is not for you or me. When a rat finds itself shut in a hole with just one gleam of daylight, it works and gnaws at that point until it gets through, and though there may be worse awaiting it on the other side, still it makes for the daylight, and that's just human nature. You, of course, look at the question from a moral point of view, and that is only right and natural in a young girl, but I'm not a moral person to the extent that I would drive a principle like a juggernaut, and so, frankly, I have no answer for you. There are some questions that fairly bristle with if's, and this is one of them. But the hour for deciding is not quite yet, and it may never come. Meanwhile, let us eat and drink and be merry.'

And that was all Lena learned from the oracle that day.

Mrs. Andersen asked her daughter a few leading questions, which elicited the unfruitfulness of the errand, and then there was silence between them. It seemed to Lena that there was only one subject for discussion with her mother, and that for the present was exhausted. A meal had to be patched up for the children, and this, thanks to the generosity of Mrs. Gird, proved less difficult than on some other occasions. By the time it was over the sun's beams gilded only the trees on the higher ground. Lena tidied herself and put on her hat, her heart beginning to resume the elation of the morning. Usually her mother watched her departure in silence, as though her trust or her indifference were too deep rooted to provoke a care, but this evening she opened her lips to ask—

'What do you two do with yourselves every evening?'

'We read,' said Lena.

'What?'

'History and myth-ology and things.'

Mrs. Andersen said no more. It was about this time of the day that Mr. Beckwith frequently dropped in for an hour. Geoffrey had described him as a silent man; but though he did not say a great deal, there was frequently a great deal in what he did say.

It was probably better for Lena to read history with Robert Hernshaw.

CHAPTER XII

AN EXCURSION IN LITERATURE

It had all come about through the unpacking of the box of books and Robert's offer to Lena to lend her any volume she cared to read. But one day Robert discovered that history became more intelligible when it was read aloud, because the movement of words was then sufficiently rapid to create pictures, an effect which was not produced in the course of the slow finger-following perusal which his want of practice necessitated. So Lena became the reader. She had a musical voice, full of delicate shades of feeling, and it flowed trippingly over proper nouns in a way that took Robert's breath away until he became used to it. Then in that alien country the Old World scenes, as depicted by the genius of the historian, took fresh being, and they saw the wild English and Saxon hordes, the men who were not to be denied, swoop down on the sacred land, where was yet the dying clasp of the Roman. Other parts of the book they merely skimmed, picking out the battles for special attention, as children pick plums from a cake. But the history of the English till the Conquest, the stirring story of the dominant race through the stormy five hundred years of its childhood, that was a thing of which Robert never grew tired. 'What beggars they were!' he would say, rapt in admiration. 'No wonder their children conquered the world.'

'But,' Lena suggested with misgivings, 'they were always being subdued and ruled over by foreign kings—Norsemen and Danes.'

Robert puzzled over this, and at their next meeting he had an answer ready. 'It was because they were so headstrong that none of their own race could rule them,' he said. 'They were always quarrelling, and their jealousy of one another was so fierce that they could put up with any king so long as he was not one of themselves. I can understand that quite easily. But the people themselves never paid much attention to the kings, and they went straight on as they liked. And if foreigners landed anywhere the English just swallowed them, and remained as much English as they were before. Even after William the Conqueror it only took a few generations to chew the foreigners out of existence, and England was more English than ever. But now just look, and here's the difference—when the English came they found the country full of people, like it might be the Maoris, and they went clean over them and wiped them out, every man Jack, barring a few that got among the mountains and managed to hang on till the English forgot all about them. But did any race ever do that with the English? No; peace or war, they were the better men. And they kept right on, and here they are still; and it's only just exactly what you would expect from the way they began.'

The reading of the pair was somewhat erratic. The library contained a considerable number of books of reference, and they treated these as seriously as anything else, having but a dim idea of their proper use. The Classical Dictionary had an alphabetical arrangement, which made it somewhat disconnected reading, but it opened glimpses of a remote and surprising world, and they followed its devious path eclectically as far as E. Robert learned and remembered a great deal from this work. Among other things he acquired the knowledge that there was once a poet called Ury Pides (a monosyllable) who wrote plays, and had the misfortune to be devoured by dogs; and he heard also of a gentleman of the name of Archie Medes. Mr. Medes, it appeared, was a mathematician of some eminence in his day who was still supposed to be remembered on account of his invention of the water-screw. But Lena vetoed the Classical Dictionary after awhile, because its contents were occasionally such that she had to stop reading and refer hurriedly to Z, or even, which was safer, to the back cover. There was no system in their examination of the shelves. Robert would select a book, chiefly by its external appearance, and say, 'Try this fellow,' as though it were a special variety of potato. And Lena would take it and begin respectfully at the first word on the first page — unless, indeed, it happened to be in a foreign language, when they would both stare at the mysterious characters, so clear to the eye, so opaque to the understanding. Lena had the devouring curiosity of a high intelligence, and she made an attempt to embark on these strange seas with the aid of a dictionary; but there was considerable contempt mingled with Robert's awe of the unfamiliar characters, and in the end, that they might not lose sight of one another, Lena had to put back to the shore. Their preference, they told one another, was for works of an educational character, but occasionally they were seduced into the enthralling arms of fiction, and stayed there night after night, forgetful of the world. It may be that their understanding grew more rapidly in those hours than when their fare was of a plainer description, for there they found, as nowhere else, life spread before them in its completeness. Danger lurked here, perhaps, but it remained unobserved. Their feet passed lightly and unconsciously over the delicate ground, and the trail of the serpent, if existent, was unmarked of the young readers.

Occasionally the volume proved to be poetry, and at first the unfortunate poets were returned incontinently to the shelves, as being on a par with the foreign books from the point of clearness, and but little in advance of the Classical Dictionary as regards rational sequence of ideas. But there proved to be a great many of them, and Lena at last decided that it was impossible to disregard the poets entirely.

'If there were nothing in them,' she said,' would your brother have them?' — an *argtimentum ad hominem* which appealed forcibly to Robert, and led to a plunge into the *Idylls of the King.* Lena was enraptured, a fair proportion of her delight being due to the discovery of her ability to understand; and even Robert was pleased with the fighting and colour of that legendary world.

'How grand it would be if it were all written out plain like Green's *Short,* he observed; and Lena laughed till the tears stood in her eyes. Green's *Short* was Robert's first love, and it became in time the literary standard against which he measured all works, prose and poetry indifferently.

One evening Lena came to a word in her reading which arrested her attention like the sound of a bell. 'Oh, Robert,' she exclaimed,' Shakespeare! Fancy, we have never thought of him once till now. It's like the name of a great country that every one hears of, and to think that we can go there any moment we please!'

'I did look at him,' said Robert. 'He's very close print and a bit long-winded; but there's grit in him in places. He's the man that invented, "Very like a whale."'

'He never did,' Lena replied indignantly. 'He wouldn't be so vulgar.'

'Well, I'll bet you twopence. I saw it with my own eyes. It's in a piece called *Hamlet,* and it made me think that he might be worth looking into.'

'You thought that because he wrote, " Very like a whale "?'

'Yes,' Robert alleged stoutly.

'Why?'

'Well, it seemed to me that a man who could invent a bit of slang that would keep fresh for three hundred years might have something in him.'

It was just this ability of Robert's to find at all times a reason—whether founded on a misapprehension or not—for the belief that was in him that held Lena's respect, even when she found him totally unable to share her literary enthusiasms. Robert's critical judgment appeared to be an instrument of two strings—awed admiration and cheerful contempt—and where the author failed to arouse one he got the other with distressing certainty. Nor was Lena able to console herself with the idea that this lack of appreciation was due to a want of understanding. Robert could crack nuts on occasion, and frequently there was shown to be nothing but dust in the interior. What Robert, in fact, asked of his authors was that they should create pictures of greater or less. distinctness, and where he found, after due trial, that no such effect was produced, he would have nothing of them. Thus, much of their first distaste for poetry arose from the failure of an attempt to read a poem called *Fifine at the Fair.* Robert thought the title sounded promising, and he got ready for more or less vivid experiences.

After a page or two Lena looked up slily, but Robert was all attention. 'Any sign of Fifine yet?' he asked.

Lena hesitated, and scanned the immensity ahead.

'Or of the fair? 'Robert asked further.

Lena shook her head.

'Well, try him a bit farther on. Maybe he's one of the sort that doesn't get going till he's warm.'

So Lena turned a page, and resumed—

'And consequent upon the learning how from strife grew peace from evil good came knowledge that to get acquaintance with the way o' the world we must not fret nor fume on altitudes of self-sufficiency but bid a frank farewell to what we think should be and with as good a grace welcome what is we find.'

'Ah, well,' said Robert, 'he don't seem to be able to get down to it, even when he takes it on in prose! '

'It isn't prose; it's just the same as the other,' said Lena, exasperated. 'But I suppose we are not clever enough to understand!'

'Let's look,' said Robert. Then, after a careful perusal, 'He's talking about some chap who's been bumping his head against a stone wall, and found out the wall's the harder of the two, and he's made up his mind that it's a first-class wall, and just where it should be, and he's going away to look for a gate. That's what it means. But the chap's mumbling in a fog. *Fifine at the Fair!* What is Fifine? I took it for a girl; but maybe it's only a kind of hardbake." And Robert closed the volume.

They missed a good many pearls from the difficulty they encountered in opening the oysters.

But Shakespeare draws with a great net, and the most unlikely fish yield to that universality of cast. Lena submitted unreservedly at the first tear, and thereafter she was but a slave to the caprices of the giant. Robert held out doubtfully for awhile. The great wind that blew across the ocean deafened and blinded him. But one night Uncle Toby remarked, 'A plague o' these pickle herrings,' in such a surprisingly natural manner that Robert became entangled and was drawn kicking to the shore.

As time went on Lena developed a surprising power of dramatic utterance, only a degree less wonderful than the insight that inspired it. The untutored girl, by sheer sensitiveness of nature, caught the pulsations of that mighty heart till her own blood vibrated in unison. She was the two wicked sisters; she was Cordelia; she was Lear.

'O, reason not the need:

('Oh, Robert, doesn't it make your heart stand still?')

'Our basest beggars

Are in the poorest thing superfluous:
Allow not nature more than nature needs,
Man's life is cheap as beast's: thou art a lady;
If only to go warm were gorgeous,
Why, nature needs not what thou gorgeous wear'st,
Which scarcely keeps thee warm. But, for true need,—

('How right that is now and always! And to think that this was written three hundred years ago!')

'Do not laugh at me;

For, as I am a man, I think this lady
To be my child Cordelia.

And so I am, I am.

Be your tears wet? yes, 'faith_____'

('And so are yours,' Robert interjected softly.)

'I pray, weep not:

> If you have poison for me, I will drink it.
> I know you do not love me; for your sisters
> Have, as I do remember, done me wrong:
> You have some cause, they have not.

No cause, no cause.'

And so to the conclusion:—

> 'Vex not his ghost: O, let him pass! he hates him much
> That would upon the rack of this tough world
> Stretch him out longer.'

Lena looked up, the tears trembling on her lashes, her eyes shining with a strange passion. 'Isn't it lovely, lovely? Isn't it the most beautiful thing in the world?'

Robert looked at her and was silent. In those moments it seemed that his practical common-sense could not call her back to the earth of their lives.

CHAPTER XIII

THE VOICES

AT last the sun was going down. Never before in Robert's experience had there been a day of such duration. More usually the daylight was inadequate to the duties of a settler whose heart was in the performance of his work. But to-day the sun had displayed an unheard-of reluctance to complete his portion of the universal contract.

The last of the kumaras had been duly set out in the row. There had been time to do some more or less necessary weeding in the vegetable garden, to earth up the melons afresh, even to strew rushes on the strawberry patch, and to nip off the sly runners whose ambition it is to establish themselves before they are discovered; but still the sun delayed high up, as though he also would commemorate this day of days. But the instinct of the lover turns with longing eyes to the night, and when love's promises point also in the same direction, then the day becomes a stumbling-block and time itself a rack.

But the sun was going at last. In a languorous glory of reluctant adieus he dipped the horizon and whirled his last beams across the bush-clad hills. The tuis were making a light supper amid a wild mockery of cat-calls and resplendent jests, and flocks of kakas[1] rose high into the sky, and flew screaming away towards the advancing shadows.

'Good evening, Mr. Hernshaw,' said a demure voice among the quince bushes, and the blood rose duskily in Robert's tanned cheeks.

Lena looked at him steadily, with shy, sparkling eyes, her face catching the tell-tale reflection.

'Oh, what gooses!' she said, laughing softly. 'What has come over us?'

'I suppose it's because we love one another,' Robert explained soberly.

Lena sat down on the log a little distance away and continued her scrutiny of his face. 'I feel afraid of you,' she said presently.

'Afraid!'

'And—I think—I like it. But why should I begin to be afraid *now?*'

'Do you think it is because you love me?' Robert asked.

---

[1] Parrots.

'I don't know,' said Lena; then she added, 'I am all a mystery to myself now.'

'Has the day seemed long?' Robert asked presently. 'I have done millions of things, and some of them hardly wanted doing yet, just to kill time; and it seems as though there were no more work left for to-morrow.'

'Let us go and see,' Lena said, jumping up; and together they went and inspected the kumara plants and the strawberry patch and the vegetable garden—even extending their examination to the potatoes on the other side of the hill, until it became almost too dark to see.

'How nice everything is, Robert, and how hard you do work! Should you be glad if there were no more work after to-day?'

'I should not be glad—no.'

Lena's eyes flashed suddenly in the darkness. 'You would not be?'

'No,' said Robert decidedly.

'I like to hear you say no—say it again.'

'I will if you will say yes.'

Lena's lips parted in tribute to this little bit of artfulness. 'Now,' she said, shrinking a little, 'do you I-like me? '

'No, I will not say no to that.'

'You have, twice. What was that?'

'Only a morepork. Lena, do you love me?'

'Yes, I suppose it was, but it startled me.'

'Come closer to me. And—did you answer my question?'

'Yes. There are two yesses for your noes.'

'But we were talking about a morepork, and I want to be sure. I will put the question again.'

'No, not yet. How sweet the bush smells! There's the jasmine scent I never could trace.'

'It grows close to the ground and has a red berry.'

'Robert, I think I will go home.'

'Home? So soon? Very well.'

'Now you are angry. Perhaps I should not have come, either to-day or yesterday.'

Robert said nothing.

'Now you are going to be cruel.'

'I am saying nothing at all.'

'Ah! that is how.'

Robert paused at the door of the house. 'So there is to be no reading to-night?' he said.

'Do you want it very much,' she asked—'tonight?'

There was a subtle undercurrent of meaning in the girl's words which appeased Robert's disappointment. Here was the sweetest romance in action, and he stopped to prate about books!

'Come, then,' he said, and led the way to the slip-rail.

The sky was crowded with stars in whose light they were visible to one another so long as the road lasted, but the bush track was like the jaws of darkness itself. There were bright jewels winking among the branches, now obscured, now suddenly reappearing, but the blackness below remained unsolved. Only the sense of touch formed a key to the enigma; the sole of the foot, the tips of the fingers. Robert felt a warm flutter against the back of his hand and caught at it. Then they went on, their fingers interlocked in a thrilling speech. Now and then one stumbled and caught at the other with a low laugh. When their feet brushed against vegetation they turned aside; to lose the track might be serious. The distance to the next clearing was not great, but touch is the slowest and most cautious of the senses, and he provides an immensity of detail. They spoke little and that in whispers, but their hands interchanged messages, warning, restraining, guiding, passionate.

Thoughts they had none, the senses dominated the situation; each was engrossed in the other; each was as much the other as if their spirits had changed dwelling.

When Lena came out into the starlight on the hilltop she drew a deep breath and turned to look back. The bush stood black and insoluble; it seemed impossible that the entrance to it could ever be found again.

'I wish you had not to go back,' she said.

'I might wish it as much.'

'Shall you be able to find the track?'

'Quite easily. I have found it before.'

They went across the chalky summit till the light of the hut below was visible. There was a sound of talking—a woman's voice in mono-syllables; a man's low, urgent. The words were not audible. Lena's hand tightened sharply on that of her companion; Robert placed his other hand over it and held it till the pressure relaxed. He had heard the voic-es on other occasions. A warm, languorous breath rose out of the hol-low where the sun had slept all day, but the night air breathed sweet and pure across the hill summit.

'Do you love me, Lena? "

Lena drew impulsively half a step nearer. 'Listen,' she said, 'and you shall judge. There have been things to make me miserable to-day. I should have been wretched, ashamed, in tears; but all day long my heart has been stumbling and bounding, and I have been happy, happy, happy I This is the most glorious and beautiful day that God ever made. If I lived for a hundred years I should remember it when I died—every instant of it. That is because you love me. That is because I love you. No. Don't say anything, because I am going to make you sad. Oh, Robert! It began at twelve o'clock; it ends now—it ends now.'

'Why are you crying, Lena?'

'Because of the voices. For me there is poverty and the shadow of shame. Oh, I understand it all! There was that in the darkness that told me its strength; and I would bring you everything that is dear and pre-cious, and have only my rags and the shadow of a disgrace that is cer-tain.'

'Bring me your dear self,' said Robert, 'and I shall have the most pre-cious thing in the world.'

'Would you not some time reproach me when people should point and say, "Her father was a drunkard; her_____"'

Robert put his hand quickly to her lips. 'Lena,' he said, grieved, 'do you think no better of me than that?'

'Never with your lips—no, no; but with your heart. Would it be enough that I loved you?'

'Enough!'

'Oh, how you say that! But it is because you cannot now think for yourself that I think for you.'

'Very well; but you must not prevent me doing the same by you. And if we think for each other, the result is the same as if we each thought for ourselves. That is love. We do not want anything but one another. That is the whole world. At least it is so with me. You have told me you love me; you cannot be so cruel as to let anything prevent me making you my wife.'

'Your wife! Oh, Robert, what would Geoffrey say?'

'When he knows you, he will certainly be as amazed at my good luck as I am, and he will probably say so.'

'That is just sweet of you to say that, but____'

'How old are you?' Robert interrupted.

'I shall be seventeen in two weeks.'

'We are both rather young, I suppose,' Robert considered in his practical way.

'Seventeen is not very young,' Lena said.

'Not *very* young. What I said was, it's *rather* young. But after all Juliet was a good deal younger; she was not fourteen, and Romeo—how old was Romeo?'

'It doesn't say; but he loved another girl before he loved Juliet, and so____'

'Probably forty,' was Robert's rapid diagnosis.

'Will you love another girl when you are forty?'

'I always go on as I begin,' Robert replied confidently; and Lena, beneath her amusement, was conscious of some justification for the egoism.

'I wish we were just a little older,' she said presently.

'Let us both wish,' said Robert.

Beckwith, as he climbed the track on the other side of the hill, heard a subdued laugh like a peal of fairy bells; the sound was not repeated, and he went on his solitary way.

'Geoffrey will be here in a day or two, and I will tell him all about it. Then I will see your mother—and your father, if I can, and after that____' The rest was conveyed through the twining fingers. 'Will you be ready for me when I say come?'

The twining fingers made their own reply.

'And you will not try to think for me any more— as if I could not tell quite well for myself what is good for me?'

'You shall do as you please.'

'But will you do as I please?'

'Hark!' said Lena.

From the hollow beneath came the sound of a closing door, followed by a profound silence.

'I must go,' she said. 'Yes, I will do as you please. Only I will not come any more in the evenings. That would not be right—would it?'

'Right?' Robert echoed doubtfully.

'Well, not wise. It mattered little what the waif Lena Andersen did, but Mrs. Robert Hernshaw is different.' Her voice lingered shyly and tenderly on the words.

'Say it again,' said Robert, delighted. 'Well, where then shall I meet you?'

'Here, so that if I am wanted I can hear mother's voice. Now go, and I will wait until you find the track.'

'Let me watch here until you are safely home.'

'I should be more Content to know that you were on the track.'

'Well then, good-night, dear'

'Good-night, Robert.'

It was easy to bid good-night, but their hands clung together and were not so easily parted. The eternity of the past meets the eternity of the future in that passionate clasp of lovers. In their interlocking fingers is the bond that holds creation. And these two were dumb.

Suddenly an owl screamed harshly on the edge of the bush; there was the pad, pad of some agitated creature—animal or human?—going by a few yards down the hill.

Lena drew back sharply. It seemed that spirits had been whispering at her heart, but she could not catch the words. Robert had moved away, and unconsciously she whispered his name. He was at her side in a moment. Had she called him, she wondered, and why? Then a memory came to her, and she laughed softly.

'I do forget why I did call you back.'

'Was it because you had forgotten to kiss me?' Robert asked at once.

'That is not right. You should say, "Let me stay here until you do remember it."'

'Yes, of course, but if he had been as near to you as I am, he would have said as I did.'

'She was up on the balcony,' Lena said wistfully after awhile.

'And he was down in the garden.'

'I will give you one—kiss—if you like.'

They leaned together in the dim starlight, and for an instant their lips touched; then tremblingly and with burning cheeks they parted.

Mrs. Andersen was sitting idly at the table. She looked up as the girl entered, and so searching was her glance, or so dazzling was the lamplight after the darkness, that Lena shut her eyes.

'Do you love him, Lena?' her mother asked suddenly.

'Yes, and he loves me; and he is coming to see you and father. And, mother, mother, I am the happiest and the luckiest girl in the world!'

CHAPTER XIV

THE INCIDENT ON THE BUSH ROAD

GEOFFREY'S discovery in the private ledger caused him considerable perplexity. Without evil intention, in a fit of absent-mindedness indeed, he had come into possession of a fact which had been deliberately concealed from him. How was he to act? To seal up the pages again was to preclude the possibility of discharging the obligation under which his family laboured. While he retained the consciousness of the debt he must lose the power to allude to it. To leave the pages open, on the other hand, meant that the Major must be taxed with his generosity and the money returned. This, to Geoffrey, seemed a hard and ungrateful act, and one which, however delicately performed, would be certain to hurt Major Milward's feelings. That the Major would prefer the memory of his good action to the return of the cash disbursed was a foregone conclusion — the note that closed the account meant that or nothing; and though, doubtless, the good deed remained even after its pecuniary aspect was discharged, yet Geoffrey could feel no enthusiasm in this view. Where was the money to come from? It meant that the obligation was transferred, not discharged. Why his uncle rather than Major Milward? And yet, he dared not be so beholden to the man whose daughter he sought to marry. At all costs the credit and good name of his family must be rehabilitated, and since the sons of the dead man were incapable of the task, the obligation devolved on the brother.

This decision was not arrived at immediately, because in the interim Geoffrey was in constant intercourse with the unconscious Major, and it seemed then so much pleasanter to let things be, to preserve a complete unconsciousness of what he had learned, or to accept the obligation frankly and generously and there an end. Indeed, it was only after consultation with Robert that the course to be pursued became fixed and irrevocable.

Geoffrey had not lived for three years in his brother's society without discovering that there was good holding ground for vessels inclined to drift, and on one or two occasions he had let down an anchor with good effect. The recollection of this occurred to him one morning as he was returning up the beach with Sandy from their customary swim, and he at once expressed the necessity for making a trip up the river.

'You will take the sailing boat, I suppose?' Sandy said.

'Not if you want it. Anything will do—or I could ride.'

'Eve has been wanting to pay a few calls inland for some time past, and I don't know when I can make it convenient to go with her. I was wondering whether you would mind acting escort.'

'I shall be delighted if Miss Milward will condescend to accept my services,' Geoffrey replied, with his will on the curb.

It was not often that the storekeeper showed such care in his choice of language, and Sandy glanced at him out of the corner of his eye as he said: 'Let us go round to the kitchen, then, and make inquiries.'

Eve was not in the kitchen, where a couple of bright-eyed Maori girls were busy in the preparation of breakfast, but they found her gathering the scarlet hibiscus blooms in the garden, her long fair hair, alive with sunlight, falling below her waist.

'This is one of the seven wonders of the world,' said Sandy, possessing himself of a handful of the golden tresses; 'but it is not often that our weak eyes are suffered to behold it.'

And indeed Geoffrey stood by like a man dazzled with excess of sunlight.

Eve drew herself laughing away, the colour deepening in her cheeks. 'Tell me at once,' she said, 'that you have come for me because breakfast is late.'

'I shall never marry,' said Sandy gloomily, 'to be thus continually misjudged.'

'Look, Mr. Hernshaw,' said Eve, suddenly extending a double handful of the gorgeous blossoms; 'can you match these in the gardens of England?'

Geoffrey shook his head. 'Neither the flowers nor the gatherer.'

'Aha!' said Sandy. 'An extra plate of fish.'

Eve let the flowers fall to her side and looked with twinkling eyes from one to the other. 'What is it, then?' she asked.

Sandy explained. 'The only condition Mr. Hernshaw makes is that you won't talk religion. Farming, sheep-shearing, anything like that, but religion he bars.'

'Rubbish!' said Geoffrey, half annoyed.

'I shall take Prince,' said Eve, her eyes sparkling. 'May I take Prince, Sandy?'

'Ye-es. You won't be able to talk religion on Prince. He won't stand it. He believes in the other thing. I rode him to the gum-store one day last week, and I don't believe we exchanged a single heavenly word going or returning. Better take the mare, Evie.'

'That is because you don't understand him,' Eve said gaily. 'Tell the boys to get Prince in, Sandy. And now you do really deserve to have breakfast.'

They galloped together along the hard sandy beach, thence at a tangent through thick groves of tea-tree on to the steeper grades of the bush road. Prince's solitary misdemeanour so far had been to shy at a bullock, emerging heavily from the growths by the roadside; but he plainly watched every inch of the way with the profoundest suspicion, and—at any other pace than a gallop—when he was not sidling away in one direction, he was edging across the road diagonally in the other.

'What is it he is always expecting?' Eve asked laughing. 'Do you think horses believe in ghosts?'

'Horse ghosts or human?'

'Suppose intelligence takes us farther away from the perception of such things. What if a spiritual universe stands revealed at the bottom of the scale, and perhaps again at the top, and we, being out of sight of either, have only a vague legacy of dread coming to us out of the past!'

'Is this the thin edge of a religious argument? '

'I will give you a race to the big pine tree.'

'Done.'

'You see when he gallops he forgets or becomes indifferent. That would seem to show that it is not anything he expects which absorbs him, but the things he actually sees. I wonder that spiritualists have never thought of using animals for their mediums.'

'Asses,' Geoffrey suggested.

'You are the most sceptical person of my acquaintance, Mr. Hernshaw. What *do* you believe in?'

'I believe that the sun is shining, the woods are green; that a bell-bird is singing somewhere in the ranges; that we are together.'

'You have good ears. Listen.'

Faint, yet clear, came the silvery peal like the ringing of a bell in fairyland. They reined in their horses and remained motionless till the sound ceased.

'They are very rare,' Eve said. 'I have not heard one for years. Yet father remembers when the bushes were thronging with them. Then the tuis are not so plentiful as they were. Soon the forests will be as silent as a graveyard.'

'Soon they themselves will be gone.'

'I hope I shall not live to see it,' she said passionately.

'Yes, civilisation is a ruthless thing. One is sometimes tempted to ask if it is worth the cost, but we are bound to think so. That is a thing we dare not disbelieve.'

'What wonder if it be true, as the bushmen believe, that the forest demands its toll of the destroyers. It needs no stretching of the imagination to believe that in this great silent outburst of life there is a soul that can offer resistance. Stephen, our bushman, is a firm believer in—in—what should one call it?'

'Vegetable vengeance,' Geoffrey suggested.

Eve laughed and pouted together. 'Uto[1] is the word,' she said,—' payment in expiation—and he supports his belief by many gruesome instances. (Do believe in something!) Have you heard him tell of the night he spent in the bush with Jim Biglow?'

'No; I have not heard that one. Only about Mark Gird.'

'Do you believe that?'

'About Gird? I may believe it and attach no importance to it. The really miraculous thing would be if a coincidence of the kind never occurred. What did it amount to? A certain man dreamed that a tree had fallen and struck Gird. He says he dreamed it twice. That may be so, though the pathology of dreams allows of a vision appearing to the waking mind in duplicate. Any way, it was a natural enough dream for a bushman, even in its association with Gird, who had worked with him frequently. Thousands of bushmen must have dreamed similar dreams,—possibly the bushman's nightmare usually takes the form of a falling tree. But in

---

[1] The word 'utu,' meaning price, is also frequently used in the same sense.

113

this case it happened that the coincidence established itself. There is no more in it than that.'

'I do not envy you your religion of science which reduces everything to the same dead level of the commonplace.'

'Let me try to give you a more pleasing idea of science. It is not a religion. It may be more aptly likened to the making of a road into the unknown. This road is being built stone by stone, backward into the past and onward into the future, and both ends have the same destination. Now and then the road crosses the old, worn track of a belief or a religion, and the crowds using that track are annoyed and endeavour to break it to pieces, to turn its course, to undermine it; but all the while the labourers come on, bringing their stones and setting them and pushing yet farther forward. Every stone in that road fits into the stones next to it, and locks and binds them together; when it fails to do so it is rejected and another takes its place, and so the work goes on. The formed road men call Knowledge, and on it rests the foundation of the civilised world to-day. The extremities of the road are where the labourers in science are for ever probing the abyss and securing fresh foothold for the great journey; but its destination is that to which all religions alike turn their gaze—the origin of things, the fountain of Truth, the Absolute.'

'That is very striking,' Eve said, after a pause. 'But does not science itself deny the possibility of man ever reaching finality by its means?'

'Science recognises that at some remote date she may reach a point where her tests will no longer meet with response, where the abyss will not yield to the plummet, and all the accumulated knowledge of the ages cannot carry her forward one single step.'

'Yes—and then?'

'Then,' replied Geoffrey, smiling, 'it may be justifiable for man to give a guess as to his Maker. He will at least have exhausted every avenue accessible to reason.'

Eve looked around her with musing eyes. The yellow road, blotted here and there with shadow, wound gradually downwards through the unbroken forest. On its margin, fern-tree and palm and springing sapling formed a continuous curtain of greenery at the feet of the lofty trees. A sweet earthy odour mingled with the honeyed breath of a myriad flowers. High in the flaming rata trees the wild bees hummed. Now and again a pigeon flew with a silky whisper of wings from one bough to another. The tui's note sounded briefly, a scatter of pearls. No jarring sound broke the serene peace of this temple of life.

'Is there nothing,' she said dreamily, 'that comes to you through the leaves out of the great Unknown?'

'Yes,' he said steadily. 'Law, unchanging, adequate, unconfused.'

'And to me—Love.'

They rode on for awhile in silence. 'I do not deny your love,' he said at last. 'That may well be the reverse of the coin. But love that is bound by law, and law that is inspired by love. Is it possible we are on mutual ground at last?'

She looked at him eagerly.

'Teach me your love,' he said, 'and learn my law in exchange.'

Not until the words were spoken did the light of another meaning leap into his gaze and cause her eyes to swerve aside from his.

'That, I suppose, is Sven Andersen,' she said quietly. 'Who is the other man? '

Geoffrey, following the direction of her gaze, looked down the road, which had here taken a sudden turn. Three or four acres in the angle had been cleared and burnt, save for a few kahikateas and ratas, rising scorched and leafless from the black soil.

In front of the clearing was a low weatherboard building with a narrow verandah, and beneath its shelter, seated on a rough form, were two men. Sven Andersen had a pannikin on the seat beside him, and in this he was engaged in stirring up a decoction of vinegar and sugar. The other man sat with his hands in his pockets, his legs stretched out, and his eyes gazing straight before him.

As the riders approached Andersen appeared to make some remark to his companion, who turned his face in their direction. For awhile the two groups looked indifferently at one another. Then a singular thing happened.

Eve, becoming conscious of some change in her companion, turned quickly towards him. He was regarding the man on the verandah intently, with eyes full of expectation. The man for his part had risen to his feet and was looking with equal intent-ness at the passing horseman. There was a strange glittering in his eyes and a mocking smile on his lips.

It seemed to Eve that the recognition of the two men was mutual, that that exchange of electric glances must result in speech—speech of a startling nature. But no—the horseman rode steadily by, the man on the verandah stood smiling in silence. In a moment the curve of the road brought the scene to an end.

Eve was unconscious of the tension to which she had been subjected till she surprised herself by a long breath of relief.

'Who is that dreadful man?' she asked.

Geoffrey was gazing thoughtfully, moodily, straight in front of him, and for a moment made no reply.

'He was a friend of mine in the old country,' he said carefully at last. 'His name is Wickener. I believe he is mad; but pardon me if, for the present, I say no more.'

The girl felt a strange stirring at her heart. 'Forgive me,' she said; 'I had no right to ask you. I had no idea that it mattered.'

Then Geoffrey turned and looked at her. There was compassion and a shadow of fear in her eyes. There was anger and revolt and love in his.

'If that man were to represent my past,' he said on the impulse, watching her.

'Then I should be sorry for you.'

'Sorry?'

'Yes, because of the man.'

Suddenly he reined his horse close to hers. 'Eve,' he cried passionately, 'could you ever give me more than the compassion you might extend to any hunted creature? Is that the best you have for me now and always? '

'Why do you ask me now?' she inquired, regarding him thoughtfully.

'I suppose because it is the most inopportune moment I could select,' he replied with bitter reflection.

'I have not noticed that anything of the kind was characteristic of you,' Eve said after a pause.

'You have never before seen me stake my life on the hazard.'

Eve was silent, but her eyes still continued to scan his face with the same frank seriousness, not unmingled with something like reproach.

'I wish I could feel that I understood what was in your mind,' she said at length.

'There is nothing there but love and devotion. There has been nothing else there from the moment I first beheld you.'

'Why do you feel ashamed to tell me so? Is it against your will that you—love me?'

'No, no. How can you even imagine such a thing? The whole of me consents. Consents! The whole of me is one impulse towards you.'

'Then why are you ashamed?' Eve repeated steadily.

'It is true,' Geoffrey admitted. 'Even now I cannot forget that I am your father's servant.'

A light glowed in the girl's eyes and a smile flickered for a moment about the corners of her lips. 'You are not ashamed because—because the moment is inopportune?' she asked.

Geoffrey looked puzzled awhile. Then he understood, and shrank from the understanding. 'It is impossible,' he said, 'that I should tell you the story now.'

The girl's face trembled as she turned away and set her horse in motion.

'Then ask me nothing,' she said huskily.

CHAPTER XV

THE MAN FROM ENGLAND

IT was two days since Sven Andersen had set off full of good intentions for the future, and he was still within a dozen miles of his home. Where he had been in the meantime was best known to himself; but for all improvement that had been wrought in his appearance he had better have remained elsewhere. As he moved along the dusty road, talking and gesticulating to himself, occasionally pausing to glare savagely at some object by the roadside, or, still worse, to express amusement at his thoughts in a harsh laugh, he had the look of a man well advanced in intoxication; but he was not drunk, unless drunkenness be given a wider interpretation than is usually allowed to the word.

'Either drunk or mad,' was the reflection of a person watching him approach from a verandah a hundred yards or so down the road. 'Not drunk in his gait,' he added awhile later; 'mad then.' And the man rose to his feet and went into the house.

A counter ran across the room in front of the door, and behind this stood a young man busy with an account book. Piles of cheap prints, stacks of tobacco, candles, soap, and other universal necessaries on shelves round the walls showed the nature of the business sought to be conducted.

The man from the verandah seated himself on a cabin-bread case near the doorway and announced the approach of the supposed madman. 'Who is he?' he asked with a faint interest.

The storekeeper craned his neck eagerly to look along the road. 'Why, it's Andersen,' he said, relapsing into indifference. 'He's not mad; he's a foreigner. He's probably drunk; any way, Mr. Wickener,' he added, 'he generally is.'

But Andersen seemed neither drunk nor mad as he entered the store and nodded composedly to its occupants. Then he approached the storekeeper and whispered something in his ear.

'Not a taste,' said the latter aloud. 'Dry as a sack of gum dust, I give you my word.'

Andersen looked over his shoulder at the other man and continued his solicitations aloud. 'Von leedle tree finger, M'Gregor, like a goot fellow?'

'I haven't got it, Andersen. I tell you there isn't such a thing in the place, so that's enough about it.'

Andersen sat down and ran his eye over the shelves. 'You haf de Pain-killer?' he asked presently.

'Not a drop,' said M'Gregor, lying cheerfully; 'the men at the camp on the new road took the last bottle yesterday.'

'Vot dat red bottles, like a goot fellow?'

'Sauce—Worcester. And this is castor oil, and that's sheep dip, and yonder's embrocation, and the spirits of salts is under the counter.'

'Ach, Mac's the poy for the jhoke,' said Andersen, laughing boisterously and turning a pair of mirthless, bloodshot eyes on the other person present. 'Dat Vooster's horse, I vill take him,' he concluded suddenly.

'The price is two shillings a bottle,' said the storekeeper, without moving.

There was a short pause.

'I have not the pleasure of this gentleman's acquaintance,' said Mr. Wickener, coming forward with a smile; 'but sooner than the matter should terminate here, I would request permission to act as host to this excellent company. I should esteem it an honour if Mr. Andersen would drink my health in Worcester sauce or embrocation, or any other beverage he might prefer.'

M'Gregor handed over the bottle without more ado, and leaping on the counter, unhooked a tin pannikin from a string in the rafters. Andersen withdrew the stopper, and giving the bottle a shake poured the contents into the tin.

'Here's your very goot healts,' he said, nodding to Wickener, and drained the pannikin to the bottom.

'An inside like that must cost a shilling or two,' M'Gregor opined.

Mr. Wickener seemed much interested. 'Have another,' he suggested; 'or perhaps you would prefer a little embrocation? Fill' em up again, M'Gregor.'

Andersen, however, professed himself satisfied, and picking up his pikau, betook himself to a seat on the verandah. Wickener lifted the empty bottle, smelt it curiously, and followed the other outside.

'A nice morning, Mr. Andersen,' he said; 'warm, but just the weather to make one relish a cooling drink. Are there any after-effects from Worcester sauce, by the way?'

'It is the hollow,' Andersen explained; 'the crave to fill him. When man has warrked mooch in bush and wet and rheumatism, then Vooster's horse very goot.' He got out a briar pipe and felt tentatively in the bowl with one finger.

'Tobacco?' suggested Wickener with alacrity. 'M'Gregor, tobacco and matches. You live somewhere about here?'

Andersen's face darkened suddenly, and he clenched the pipe in his hand till the knuckles whitened; then he pointed vaguely along the road. 'I got vife in the bush,' he said.

'Good place to keep one,' Wickener observed, surveying the landscape; 'room, in fact, for more than one.'

'My Gott, there is not room for one,' was the rapid response. 'Should man have more than one vife? Gott prevent him!' Andersen twisted himself on his seat and laughed harshly.

'So that's the way the wind blows?' Wickener said, his eyes glittering. 'Domestic unhappiness, eh? Woman! What follows? Alcohol, Worcester sauce, embrocation. Curse them, and I'll give you curse for curse. Begin!'

'Ach, the wretches!' said Andersen.

'_____!' said Wickener.

Andersen clenched his hands. 'All day you leave them and warrk, warrk, then you kom back. Vot you find? Nuther man's drunk all the visky.'

'True bill,' said Wickener. '_____! Set' em up again.'

'They got no decent like a man; they got no feeling like a man. She all flower and pretty things on top, and underneath the devil.'

'_____!' said Wickener.

Andersen drew back and regarded his companion. 'You haf a vife too?' he asked.

Wickener dropped back into listlessness. 'What about the man? 'he asked.

Andersen hugged himself and looked cunning, but he did not reply.

'Don't be in a hurry,' said Wickener. 'The best pleasure is in anticipation.

Combine poetry with justice. Don't hit a man when he's down— because you can't hurt him enough. Hit him on the top of a precipice if possible. Andersen, I like you. Have another Worcester. No? Then name your drink.'

Mr. Wickener's liking was evidenced in the fact that a week later the Swede was still domiciled in the store as the guest of his singular companion.

M'Gregor, the storekeeper, who had been ready enough to accommodate the English stranger with board and lodging, raised no objection to this addition to the family when he understood that all charges were to be borne by Wickener. The Englishman's tastes were peculiar, no doubt, but his payments were made in advance, and he showed a lordly indifference to details which appealed favourably to a man whose predilections were all in the opposite direction. If M'Gregor troubled himself at all to find a reason for the Englishman's patronage of the other, such reason was probably associated with Andersen's morbid craving for liquid excitement, Wickener seeming to take a pleasure in indulging his *protégé*, in season and out of season, to the top of his grotesque bent. He had, however, privately admonished the storekeeper to beware of the admission that there were any spirituous drinks on the premises.

It was not until Wickener had been a fortnight in the house that he discovered that the Maori woman who did the cooking, and whose shrill voice was occasionally heard from the kitchen, was the storekeeper's wife. The lady, in fact, was the first to supply the information, and though M'Gregor seemed disposed to minimise the fact, he did not actually commit himself to a denial of its accuracy. Her features were plain, even for a Maori, but she was young and her eyes were brilliant, and once the ice was broken, she was not indisposed to be communicative. Mr. Wickener had many questions to ask, and made full use of his opportunities. He appeared, so far as could be gathered from casual remarks, to have come straight to his present habitation immediately on his arrival in the country. He was absurdly ignorant on the most ordinary colonial matters, and, it may be added, indifferent; but trivial things occasionally interested him to the point of enthusiasm. He had a stock question with regard to every Maori name—what did it mean? It seemed to astonish him that every hill, vale, creek, clump of trees, rock had its own individual designation. 'Well, what is the name of this place? Eh? What's that? "Why-kick-her-why-whack-her "? Really, I have no notion.'

Tapaia considered his humour of the most exquisite character, and was always ready to provide him with a name or a meaning, for the pleasure of hearing him mispronounce the former, and of noting his frequent astonishment at the latter. It is characteristic of Maori names that they are descriptive often to an embarrassing degree.

'So "wai" is pronounced "wy," and means "water,"—I see. Then "Wairangi "will mean "watery-sky"?'

Tapaia laughed heartily. 'You got the cart before the horse,' she said. '"Wairangi "will mean "skyey-water." That Major Milward, his place "Wairangi."'

'Ah!—Major Milward—a settler, I suppose?'

'Major Milward the big rangatira,' Tapaia explained with respect. 'He the first of all the European to come here. This time he got the sheep station, the kauri bush, the gum-field, plenty big stores. You know my husband?—-he the storekeeper before.'

'Oh, indeed! and who is the storekeeper now?' Wickener inquired with polite interest.

'Mr. Raymond come after my husband, then Mr. Hernshaw.'

'Hernshaw? Surely you have mentioned the name previously?'

'He and his brother have a section in the bush near to Mr. Andersen.'

'Yes, yes, of course, so you told me. And one of them is storekeeping for this Major—er—Milward? That will be the one who was born here, I suppose? By the way, I think you told me one of them was born here, while the other emigrated only a year or so back? Or am I confusing the families?'

'No, that is right; but Geoffrey Hernshaw is the storekeeper, and he is the one from England.'

'Oh, indeed! that will be a nice change for him,' and Mr. Wickener smothered a yawn.

'Major Milward any family?' he asked presently.

'He two children here—Eve and Sandy. Eve the pretty girl.'

'Aha! Any chance for a young man of my complexion? '

'That Hernshaw's girl, I suppose? 'Tapaia replied, laughing. 'Kapai[1] you make a try, perhaps.'

Mr. Wickener looked with smiling reflection at a fly-blown almanac on the wall. 'Hernshaw again,' he said quietly. 'No, no, dear lady; though

---

[1] Good.

the contemplation of Mr. M'Gregor's happiness must ever provide a powerful incentive, there is no guarantee that I shall be equally fortunate. Once bitten, twice shy.'

The friendship between the Swede and the English stranger developed rapidly as the days wore by. Neither seemed to find his lack of occupation galling, or to be in a hurry to move on elsewhere. The spot was a lonely one, but little disturbed either by travellers or customers, and but that Wickener had learned from Tapaia that the land for thousands of acres around was her private property, he might have wondered at the singularity of M'Gregor's choice in establishing himself so far from civilisation. The pair spent most of their day in the shadow of the tree ferns on the edge of the sweltering bush road, retiring into the denser growth when the heat became unbearable to the unaccustomed Englishman.

Mr. Wickener was soon in possession of the family history of the Andersens, and it formed a constant subject for discussion between the two men.

'Yours is not exactly a strong case, Andersen,' Wickener remarked thoughtfully once, 'because there is a certain amount of culpability on your side. Still that does not excuse the other man. Nothing excuses the other man. Make a note of that.'

'Nuttings,' Andersen agreed.

'By the way, you have never been the other man yourself, I suppose? Ah, well, don't protest! How far have you got? Have you reached the boiling-oil stage yet?'

Andersen nodded morosely.

'Yes,' Wickener mused, 'it's interesting, no doubt, and picturesque, but it passes. The law of evolution holds even here; by and by you will come to higher things.'

'What things?' Andersen asked.

'The higher hatred, my boy; perhaps even to the perfect hate that passeth understanding. For observe the analogy between love and hate. The first distaste that precedes dislike and develops loathing. So, by obverse stages, the full-blown passion of love. Treasure these words, Andersen, my boy, for I shall not always be by to instruct and guide you. Then comes the brooding on the beloved or hated image; the hundred situations, fervently conceived and as intensely desired. The passive mood becoming the active, the drawing of the loved or hated one's attention, the threat, the promise, and so on up the scale, through all the heightening tones, to consummation—devoutly to be wished.' He stopped, his glittering gaze fixed on a point opposite to him, and was silent.

'Is yours the hate porfect?' Andersen asked after awhile.

'Sometimes I am inclined to think so, my friend; at others I seem to descry an unattainable greatness just out of reach. Contrast my stage and yours. You would kill Beckwith by slow torture of—shall we say?—a few days' duration, then an end. Afterwards what will you do? You cannot expect two such passions in a lifetime; the gods are more chary of their gifts. Keep it, keep it, my boy, to warm your bones when you grow old. As for me, I can wait. I have become an artist in the matter. Nothing but the best will satisfy me. I want the supreme moment. If I could enthrone my man above the world, if I could load him with all that the earth, or better still, with all that he himself holds desirable, I would do it that in the next instant I might tear him down and leave him naked and accursed.'

The man's voice was light and bantering, and a mocking smile played across his features; yet Andersen, only partly comprehending him, shuddered as he listened.

'Vot you do with your man ven you got him?' the Swede asked with a shrinking curiosity.

Wickener stretched himself and laughed. 'We are discussing your affair, my boy,' he said placidly, 'and it is a peculiar one, because, as I have already told you, there are two sides to it. Take my advice and don't hurry. The killing stage passes, the lust for violence goes by. Live up to the great idea, and some day you may reach that sublimity of hatred that would dictate the words, "Beckwith, take her!"'

CHAPTER XVI

MR. WICKENER GOES AFIELD

ALTHOUGH, as has been said, Mr. Wickener spent most of his time in Andersen's company in the vicinity of the store, yet he did make a few excursions farther afield, and on one occasion he was absent a whole night. Of these journeyings he said nothing to Andersen, neither did he invite that gentleman's society, even though the Swede might happen to be a witness of his departure. Affable and companionable as the Englishman had proved himself, there was yet a certain aloofness in his manner which forbade question.

One of these rambles, for it seemed to be nothing more, brought him out above the river in the neighbourhood of the Hernshaws' section. It was a blazing summer afternoon, when to the idle man the mere thought of labour is a horror, yet there was a young man busily hoeing at the crops on the hilltop, and whistling as he worked. The whistling was good, and Wickener, when his astonishment at its mere possibility had been overcome, found himself listening with enjoyment. All the birds of the bush and the settlement appeared to have combined to produce that melodious theme. There was the solemn chuckle of the tui, as at some joke really too exquisite for ordinary laughter; there was the plaintive trill of the riro-riro, in whose nest squats the cuckoo's offspring; the jarred bleat of the fantail; then the rollicking music of the European thrush, the scream of the parrot, the squeal of the morepork; finally, the ventriloquial crescendos of the shining cuckoo. Now and then a bird answered sleepily from the bush. 'Tonk, tonk!' said the tui. 'Wait till it gets cooler and I'll talk to you.'

Mr. Wickener had found a tree easy of ascent and climbed into the fork. After awhile he was in danger of going to sleep himself.

The whistling began again presently, half a dozen birds together apparently, then there was a little gurgle of amused laughter much closer at hand. Fully awakened, Mr. Wickener peered down. Something white was passing underneath his hiding-place. A hat with a girl beneath it—a girl with the sunniest curls in the world. Mr. Wickener obscured himself still further and watched.

The girl came out of the bush, crossed the road, and slipping through the rails, walked soberly towards the young man on the higher ground.

Presently the latter looked up and espied her; next moment they were together, walking hand-in-hand to the house, the girl's face turned upwards, the man's down.

'Young love,' said the watcher to himself, with a cynical twist of the lips.

The pair passed out of sight behind the house, and there was a long ten minutes of waiting; then the girl reappeared, walking backwards, laughing and talking, every motion of her body a poem, the man after her, slowly, like a worshipper. A few moments of delay and the girl turned and ran towards the slip-rails.

Wickener examined her as she came, with a curious feeling of likeness about her to some one he knew. To whom? She was too lovely to be forgotten had he ever really seen her before. The girl passed with light step under the tree and away down the track out of sight. The watcher sat quiet for a moment, then let himself down and followed.

It was only a short distance through the bush to the bare hill above Andersen's house, and Wickener was hard on the girl's heels as she reached the slip-rail.

'Pardon me,' he said, raising his hat as she turned. 'Have I the pleasure of addressing Miss Andersen?'

A new face in the settlement was a thing as startling as rare, and this one appeared to have sprung suddenly out of the earth.

'I am Lena Andersen,' the girl said after a moment.

'I am fortunate in discovering you so easily, Miss Andersen. I trust I am guilty of no discourtesy in addressing you here rather than in the house.'

Lena looked at her interlocutor. He was a man probably thirty-five years of age, with a fair skin, a trim brown beard, and singularly bright eyes. There was nothing insolent or repulsive in his manner, which, on the contrary, was full of a polite respect.

'Will you walk into the house and see mother?' Lena suggested.

'I will not disturb Mrs. Andersen on this occasion,' said the stranger, after a moment's hesitation, which included a glance at the building; 'more especially as my business is with yourself. I am the bearer of a message from your father. He is some distance away, but I happened to have—an appointment in the neighbourhood, and so_____' Mr. Wicken-

126

er concluded the sentence with a friendly smile.

'I hope father is well?' Lena said with more animation; 'and I'm sure it is very kind of you to trouble. Where is he now?'

'So far as my information permits me, he is at a place called "Why-kick-her-why-whack-her," but you are probably more conversant with the peculiarities of Maori topography than I am.'

Lena looked puzzled. 'And what is the message, Mr____'

'Wickener is my name. The message I am afraid is rather a prosaic one. It consists in fact of five effigies in gold of her gracious majesty the queen. I will ask you to relieve me of their responsibility.' And Mr. Wickener handed her the coins with the humorous suggestion that his fingers were being scorched.

'And is this really from father?' Lena asked, looking at the little pile of sovereigns in her palm. 'Oh, sir, I am glad, not altogether for the money's sake, but on account of something that passed between us when he went away! Will you tell him that from me, with my love?' The girl's face was dazzling in its animation, and there was a suggestion of tears in her eyes.

'I fear I can hardly promise to deliver any message, Miss Andersen,' Wickener said slowly, and for the first time avoiding her direct gaze. 'It is not absolutely certain that your father will remain at the place with the mysterious name, or, indeed, that I shall return there. I would not, if I were you, take any steps in the matter.'

'What—not even thank him?' asked Lena in surprise.

Mr. Wickener appeared to reflect a moment. 'Forgive me,' he said, 'if what I am about to say should betray a closer knowledge of your family affairs than you would naturally care to be in the possession of a mere stranger; but from a knowledge of your father's character I am bound to think that it will be best to accept his offering without comment or even thanks.'

'Oh, sir,' said Lena, 'how can we do that?'

'I make the suggestion, Miss Andersen, with the best intentions. After all, the matter is in your own hands, and I have no kind of right to interfere.'

'I should be glad to follow advice given with the kindest intentions,' Lena said gently; 'if it were not that I must appear ungrateful to father.'

Mr. Wickener smiled pleasantly. 'Believe a man of the world of probably twice your years, Miss Andersen,' he said, 'that the expression of gratitude in so many words is not the safest way to ensure a continuation of gratuities. I do not presume to think that that argument will influence you, but I perceive a number of children in the background, as it were,'—he waved his hand towards the rear of the paddock, where a portion of the flour-bag brigade were noisily disporting themselves—'on whose behalf a certain amount of sordid calculation would be, to say the least, excusable. Forgive me, if my candour appears offensive.'

'You are very good,' Lena said. 'I can only thank you for the trouble you have taken and for your thoughtfulness.'

'No thanks,' said Mr. Wickener. 'Delighted to be of service.' And with a generous exposure of his hair he took his departure.

'A good action is its own reward,' mused Mr. Wickener, as he descended into the bush. 'Also two and two make four and p-s-h-a-w spells pshaw!' He repeated the word with varied inflections of disgust once or twice aloud as he went his way. 'Pshaw!' Engrossed in his thoughts, he followed his feet without attention and presently they struck against a root and brought him to a standstill. He found himself on a narrow, worn track in place of the wide road he remembered to have traversed in his coming. Retracing his steps, he came on two tracks and, following one at random, arrived in the course of a few minutes at three more.

'Ah, would you! 'said Mr. Wickener ad-monishingly to the silent forest. 'You don't catch old birds with snuff,' he reminded the landscape. With careful steps he returned to the original track and went doggedly down it. 'A path like this leads somewhere,' he soliloquised; 'and somewhere is where I desire to go.' Presently he found himself in a clearing with a house at the farther end. In front of the house was a group of three people—a woman and two boys, the latter busily engaged in chopping firewood.

Mr. Wickerter made his way through the stumps, becoming the cynosure of all eyes before he had traversed half the distance to the house. They were keen eyes, all of them, and the keenest belonged to the lady.

'Pardon this intrusion, madam,' he began; 'I am a stranger in this neighbourhood, and I have had the misfortune to miss the road.'

'Then you are the first man that has ever done it,' said Mrs. Gird.

'There is only one road in the whole of the north country, and if you miss that you are completely done.'

'This is consoling,' said Wickener, taking another look at the lady. 'What should you advise in the circumstances?'

'I can think of nothing more appropriate than tea,' said Mrs. Gird cheerfully. 'Mark, run and see if the kettle is boiling. Stay a moment; this is my eldest son, Mark—Mark Gird.'

'Wickener is my name,' said the Englishman for the second time that day, as he shook hands with the boy.

'And this is Rowland,' said the lady, bringing forward her second son.

Mr. Wickener repeated the hand-shake and remarked that they were fine children.

'My husband is an invalid,' Mrs. Gird said, leading the way to the house. 'He was injured some years ago by an accident in the bush. I mention the fact that you should not be shocked, as he is very sensitive of the effect of his appearance on others.'

'I am grateful for the information, madam.'

'It is plain that you are from England,' Mrs. Gird said bluntly; 'a colonial might have felt as you do, but he would not have expressed himself so happily.'

Mr. Wickener bowed, 'Your diagnosis is correct,' he said. 'I have been less than a month in the country.'

Mr. Gird sat erect in his chair, the light still burning in his sunken eyes. No motion of the pupils, no flutter of the eyelids greeted the stranger, only in the depths of the eyes was a light that seemed to betray consciousness and showed that the motionless figure lived. What passed behind that sealed countenance—what thoughts, what memories, what sufferings, who shall say? Day after day, week by week, year in, year out, he sat there, forgotten of Death, like a shattered idol. Did love penetrate through that mask of death to the vital spark within? The woman thought so: in that faith she framed her life and that of her children. May be it was all a delusion; may be the thoughts she uttered as his were her own; may be there was room there for neither love nor reason, for neither regret nor hope. Ah, but the woman knew better! What though the gates of the senses were closed never to be undone, yet love spoke direct from spirit to spirit, and there was no message too trivial, none too strenuous for that ethereal messenger.

The table was already set for the evening meal, and Mrs. Gird invited her visitor to a seat without more ado.

'My stay in the country has not yet been long enough to diminish my sense of the hospitality of its inhabitants,' Mr. Wickener observed as he seated himself.

'Hospitality is rather a large word with which to describe acts of common humanity.'

'Happy is the country where common humanity is so broadly interpreted.'

'That is very nice, but don't run away with an exaggerated idea of our virtues,' said the lady. 'We are an extremely mixed community; for instance, there is probably as much hatred per square yard in this settlement as would suffice to keep two nations embroiled in constant warfare.'

'Do you tell me so? But the Lord loveth a cheerful hater.'

'Then we are certainly His chosen people,' said Mrs. Gird dubiously. 'But aren't you confusing your text? I remember that the Lord loveth a cheerful giver.'

'Probably you are right,' Mr. Wickener reflected. A moment later his lips had framed the word 'Pshaw!' 'There should be enough scope here for people to live independently of their neighbours,' he said presently. 'You, for instance, must find a difficulty in living up to the traditions of the settlement.'

'Beyond our boundary there are a hundred miles of native bush land, sacred to the kiwi and the wild pig, so that we are preserved on that side. On the other we have the Andersens, with whom we simply refuse to quarrel.'

'An excellent *casus belli*,' said Mr. Wickener. 'These Andersens appear to make but little use of their section,' he added.

'You passed the place? But of course you did; that was where you missed your road. No, the father is a great deal from home. He is a bushman by trade; a splendid worker when he likes, but not so much given to liking as might be wished.'

'Poverty and neglect seem to be written large on the place, and from what I saw of the family, they deserve a better fate than to be sequestered there.'

'Whom did you see?' Mrs. Gird asked with interest.

'A young woman of prepossessing appearance, whose speech and manners seemed to be above her station.'

'That would be Lena, the eldest girl—yes. But you must not be surprised at poor people speaking good English; we are a very long way ahead of your countrymen in that respect, you know. Your people are handicapped by the fact that they have lived for hundreds of years in small communities, hence the language has been broken up into innumerable dialects. Our facilities for communication, on the other hand, enable us to speak one language, and our educational system ensures that that language shall be the best.'

Mr. Wickener bowed but did not discuss the subject. Instead, he fell back on his stock amusement of Maori names.

'Pray enlighten me,' he said, after a few remarks on this head; 'how is it that the native nomenclature is framed in the likeness of excellent, but apparently unanswerable conundrums? "Why-carry-me," for instance, and "Why-make-a-row," the two names you have just mentioned, and "How-marry-her,"-and "Whaty-whaty-why-how,"—an excellent and typical specimen, by the way—do they, by any chance, mean what they say?'

The Gird boys were too well bred to make any audible comment, but they watched Mr. Wickener with the intensest delight and appreciation from that moment; nor was it many days before the fame of him had run through the settlement even to its farthest outposts.

'Are you proposing to settle in this country, Mr. Wickener?' Mrs. Gird asked by and by.

'No, madam; suspicious as my actions may appear, my intentions are, I assure you, innocent. I am a mere bird of passage—here to-day, gone tomorrow. A bird possessing the loquacity of—shall we say the jay?— and the curiosity of the magpie.'

'From what part of England are you, Mr. Wickener?'

'From many parts of late, madam; but York is the county of my birth.'

'My husband is a Yorkshireman; so also by birth are our neighbours the Hernshaws.'

Mr. Wickener showed polite interest. 'The latter, I presume, are settlers?' he asked.

'Yes, their section adjoins the Andersens. The elder brother is away for the present, but the younger is at home.'

'I wonder if I have seen him this afternoon. Is he by any chance given to amuse himself by whistling?'

'That is certainly Robert,' Mrs. Gird said, smiling. 'He is a nice boy—hard-working, sensible, straightforward, a good sample of the colonial-born youth at his best.'

Mr. Wickener had it in his mind to ask if colonial-born youths were also adepts at love-making, but he held his tongue, and the meal shortly came to an end.

Mark was deputed to guide the stranger on to his road, a task which he undertook with considerable eagerness.

'The rippling of the waters,' said Mr. Wickener as he stepped outside and caught the music of a neighbouring creek. 'Who would have guessed that poetic answer to the conundrum—" Why-carry-me"?'

Mrs. Gird nodded. 'By the way,' she said, 'what is the meaning of York?'

Mr. Wickener acknowledged the shaft with a smile and a bow, then he followed his guide across the paddock.

Mrs. Gird, as she stood in the doorway, remembering how little information had been vouchsafed to her in comparison with that which had been supplied by herself, was inclined to add to the loquacity of the jay and the curiosity of the magpie the secretiveness of the raven.

But she was destined to see a good deal more of Mr. Wickener, who, from whatever motives, developed a habit of calling at the house whenever, as happened not infrequently, he had occasion to visit the settlement.

CHAPTER XVII

THE CLOUD IN THE SKY

'It's a pity you ever found it out,' said Robert, 'if you are going to let it worry you. I had an idea that there was something of the kind, but it was mostly while father was alive, and if mother could bring herself to take it surely we can.'

'You knew her better than I ever did, Robert.'

'That's the pity of it.'

'You mean if I had known her I should have had no doubt as to how I ought to act now?'

'Something of that.'

'I can't bring myself to seal up the pages again; there would seem to be something underhand about an act of that sort.'

'Then don't seal them.'

'But what am I to do?'

'Nothing.'

Geoffrey looked thoughtfully at his brother, his face slowly clearing. 'I am not sure but what you are right, and if it were not for one thing I should be certain of it. But the one thing seems to make all the difference. I am going to ask Eve Milward to marry me, and I don't want to owe her father £300 at the same time.'

'I am glad you are going to do that,' said Robert heartily; 'and if I were you I wouldn't waste a moment before it was done. As for the money, it's none of your doing, and you are far more likely to do harm by harping on it than by letting it slide. Eve's not likely to trouble nor is the Major. Pride's a proper thing in its way, no doubt, but you can easily have too much of it, seems to me.'

Geoffrey was silent, but his countenance looked much more hopeful than when the matter was first broached.

'And there is another thing,' continued Robert, 'since we are at it, and that's Uncle Geoff. It has seemed to me for quite a long time now that you're treating him pretty hard. Seems to me there ought to be no question of pride between you and a man who has done for you as he has.

It's little short of a sin to keep him at arm's length in the way you do, and how he manages to put up with it beats me. Pie's the sort that if you wired to him for a few thousands, he'd want to get up in the middle of the night to cable it to you.'

'It's true. I'm an ungrateful sort; but it's the confounded stiff-necked way in which I am made, Robert.'

'Well, it may be. But if you want to marry Eve Milward, you will have to come down from that. I know you are a great deal cleverer than I am, Geoff, and better educated and that, but it's struck me of late that I've got most of the common sense.'

'I am convinced of it. Go on.'

'Well, I was just about to say that if you are not going to accept anything from Uncle Geoffrey, you won't have much of a prospect to lay before Major Milward. Have you thought of that?'

'Not very deeply, I am afraid.'

'Well, I would; or — which is better than thinking — I would act. Write home to uncle, tell him the whole story, and throw yourself on his generosity. There's no doubt what the result will be.'

'Then you think I am not capable of earning a living for myself?'

'Why shouldn't you be? But it's much simpler to have a good round sum in the bank, and it gives you a great deal more confidence, especially when it comes to interviewing a wealthy man like Major Milward. Besides, a bird in the hand doesn't prevent you going after the bird in the bush; it's the very thing to make you.'

'As to the round sum in the bank, you can hardly be speaking from experience, Robert,' said Geoffrey, smiling.

Robert looked slightly uneasy. 'It's a good thing for every one,' he said, 'but it's more necessary to some than to others. You've been brought up as a gentleman, and are more fitted to make money by your brains than your hands, therefore it's almost a necessity for you. As for me, I can get along all right, and my wife won't expect a great deal just at the first.'

'You speak of that problematical lady with some assurance.'

'Not more than I feel, however,' Robert said.

Geoffrey looked up a little surprised, and something in his brother's countenance caught his wandering attention. 'Is it possible the lady is not entirely problematical?' he asked.

'It's Lena Andersen.'

'Lena! Good heavens! Why, you are only children!'

'We don't mind that,' Robert said; 'and we shall get over it in time.'

'Of course. I beg your pardon. But you astonished me a good deal. Lena? Yes, I remember her,' and Geoffrey's face, despite his endeavours, clouded slightly.

'She is a very clever girl,' Robert alleged anxiously. 'You should hear her read Shakespeare and—and Green's *Short.*'

'That's something, Robert, isn't it?' Geoffrey said kindly. 'And she promised to be a very pretty girl too.'

'More than that,' said Robert. 'And good—good as gold. Too good for a rough chap like me.'

'She doesn't think so, however, nor her parents probably.' Geoffrey remembered with misgiving the untidy woman at the slip-rail and the stories current in the settlement of the drunken father. 'I suppose you are not contemplating doing anything just immediately?' he asked.

'Well, I am,' Robert confessed. 'You see the family is in rather a bad way owing to Andersen's habits, and then there is a good deal of talk in the settlement about Mrs. Andersen, and I should like to take Lena clean out of it all before worse happens. There is not a brighter little girl living, Geoff; but she's very tender-hearted, and that sort get hurt easily and badly.' Robert's honest, eager eyes clouded suddenly.

'And how would you get her out?' Geoffrey asked sympathetically,

'There is only one way, Geoff.'

'But aren't you afraid of taking a responsibility like that?'

'No,' said Robert, squaring his broad shoulders, 'I'm not afraid. At the worst she would be better off than she is now. I have tried to think for her as well as myself, but I can't find any better way. If you see any road out but that I should be glad to know of it.'

'I should like to see her first,' Geoffrey said. 'Is it possible we can do so this afternoon?'

Robert found his coat in silence, and together the brothers set off on their errand.

Now Lena had descried Geoffrey as he rode past on his way to the section, and anticipating this conclusion to the interview, she had tidied the house and arrayed herself in the black velvet frock which was Mrs. Gird's gift. Robert had heard nothing of this garment, and he was consequently as much surprised as Geoffrey at the smart and lovely appearance presented by the young girl as she came out of the house, blushing divinely, yet with a certain charming self-possession, to meet her prospective brother-in-law and her lover.

Lena stood a little in awe of Geoffrey. He lacked, she thought, the serene disposition of the younger brother, and his manner, except when roused, was silent and sunless. Her awe, however, was tinged with admiration for his good looks and his learning, which she and Robert supposed to be without a parallel in New Zealand, if not in the world.

The beauty and naturalness of the young maiden, however, had instant effect on Geoffrey, dismissing completely the cloud of doubt which had gathered round the idea of the Andersen family, and enabling him to tender his congratulations sincerely and hopefully. For a moment the mother with a possible future and the father with a certain past dropped out of sight

'If you only knew how nice it is of you to say that,' Lena said. 'My heart has been sinking lower and lower in anticipation of this interview, and now it is quite easy after all.'

'That is the mistake one continually makes,' Geoffrey said. 'Opposition, if there is to be any, will come, as it always does, from an undreamed-of quarter.'

'I wonder where—there is only father left now.' Lena looked seriously from one to the other.

'Don't inquire too strenuously of the Fates, and happily they may forget us and pass by on the other side of the way.'

Lena led her visitors into the house, where Mrs. Andersen was waiting to receive them. The children had been smuggled out of the way, and except for a suppressed giggling in an inner room, an unusual peace reigned throughout the establishment.

Mrs. Andersen, with a closer acquaintance with the facts than her daughter, had also had her doubts of Geoffrey, and his attitude in the matter consequently brought her great relief. The whole responsibility for the affair rested, as she knew, on her own shoulders. But for the almost criminal neglect she had shown as to the girl's actions, the engagement of Robert and Lena would probably not have come about so speedily, if at all.

'Of course, you think it quite wrong of me to let things come to this pass,' she said when Robert and Lena had disappeared to discuss their new happiness.

'Probably it was not preventible,' Geoffrey replied.

'But they are such children.'

'In years, no doubt; but Robert has a very wise head on his young shoulders, and Lena, unless her looks belie her, is a young lady of some intelligence.'

'She is no fool,' the mother conceded. 'So you are not put out about it? I was fearing you would be. Robert, of course, might have done better, but she is a good girl—a real good girl.'

'Robert might very easily have done much worse.'

'But the trouble is they are in such a hurry. They want to get married at once—to-morrow if they could; and how they are going to live I don't know. I know what it is when there is no money in the house.'

'As far as that goes, Robert is quite able to keep a wife,' Geoffrey said thoughtfully.

The door of the room whence the giggling proceeded had been opening and closing narrowly at rapid intervals, and on each occasion there had been a row of round blue eyes, one above the other, fixed with varied expressions, ranging from horror at the bottom to mere curiosity at the top, on the visitor who had come in connection with that mysterious affair, Lena's marriage. Now, as Geoffrey ceased speaking, the door suddenly opened wide; there was a whisper, a giggle, a rush, and with a wild whoop the Andersens scattered across the sunlit paddock. Geoffrey looked after them and his original misgivings returned. Was it possible that, in taking Lena, Robert was burdening himself with the support of the whole family, not omitting the mother? And if it were not so, what, in the alternative, was to become of them?

Whether or no Mrs. Andersen guessed what was passing through her visitor's mind, her next remark fell appositely on Geoffrey's thoughts.

'One thing,' she said, not without a taint of bitterness, 'Lena has never been accustomed to extravagant living, and after what she has had to put up with for years, it won't take a deal to make her happy as the day is long. And Robert needn't be afraid that the rest of us will trouble him—not that he's likely to worry, for he's a dear, good-hearted boy, but we're not coming on him to keep us. And so, when you think it over, you can just reckon on their two selves and nobody else.'

'I suppose her father is not likely to raise any objection?' Geoffrey asked, his mind considerably relieved.

'Andersen will do as he is told. It's not for the like of him to come raising objections if the rest of us are satisfied.'

'I think it possible Robert may be able to do a little to help you all by and by,' Geoffrey said cautiously. 'But I quite agree with you as to giving them a fair start without encumbrances. In fact, that does seem to me very important, so much so that should anything occur to—to render you in need of assistance, I hope you will let me hear of it instead of Robert.'

'Nothing will occur,' said Mrs. Andersen evasively. 'We're past all that. Then you are going to let them get married right off?'

'So far as I can be thought to have a voice in the matter,' Geoffrey said, 'I surrender it freely. They shall please themselves. Robert is at least as capable of weighing the pro's and con's as I am.'

Meanwhile Robert and Lena had ascended to a ledge on Bald Hill and were sitting overlooking the hollow.

'To think that I have been misjudging Geoffrey all this while,' Lena said. 'Nothing could be kinder than the way he spoke to me. It made me feel as though I were a princess in disguise and he had found me out.'

'Geoff is the best fellow in the world,' Robert agreed enthusiastically; 'and he behaved just exactly as I told you all along he would behave.'

'Did I look nice—a little? I know I blushed and felt like a gawk, but did it show through?'

'Not through the velvet. My, what a beauty! Where did you get it?'

'Mrs. Gird made it for me quite a long time ago. It's real velvet, not common velveteen, and it must have cost a heap of money.'

'It's nothing to the dresses I am going to get for you directly, Lena. I've mapped it all out—satins and valencias and that. You'll see.'

The valencias puzzled Lena a little, but she was none the less appreciative, and she nestled closer to her lover and slipped her hand into his.

'We are getting closer to it,' Robert said solemnly. 'This is a big step to-day, and there is only your father to think about now. Are you glad?'

'Are *you*, Robert?'

'Sometimes I think I've no right to be as glad as this. I ought to wait and give you a chance of some one much better than I am.'

'I don't want him,' said Lena. 'I wouldn't have him if it were ever so— the disagreeable, stuck-up thing! We are such dear friends, Robert— such kind companions—and you can talk calmly of some one coming in between to part us. I wonder at you!'

'It's only my great happiness, Lena. It makes me suspicious some-how. It's like that chap we read of who found a big diamond and dared not even pick it up to look at it for fear some one would grab it or it would melt away.'

'How strange! I have felt like that ever since—that first day. And I thought you were so practical and unimaginative.'

'You see I could be hit here,' Robert said wisely. 'I could be hit hard, and I know I should take it badly; so it makes a man disguise his true feelings a little and keep his eyes open more than ordinary.'

Lena laughed softly. 'But it's all true,' she said. 'We take pain to our hearts as a matter of course, but we walk round happiness with suspicion.'

'So, Lena, we will not tempt Fate longer than we need, and—is there any reason why we should not get married almost at once?'

'And yet there are people who say that this young man is not as clever as his brother,' Lena said, patting his hand.

'And what do you say?'

'I say as you say,' said Lena, springing to her feet. 'There goes Geoffrey. Let us run down and say good-bye to our brother.'

Geoffrey, seeing their approach, reined in his horse at the slip-rail.

'Good-bye, Geoff, and good luck,' said the younger brother.

'Mrs. Andersen and I have been discussing your prospects, young people,' Geoffrey said, looking from one to the other; 'and we are agreed that there are no clouds of any importance in the_____'

Geoffrey was interrupted by a horseman who came suddenly up out of the bush, raised his hat to the group at the slip-rail, and set his horse at the hill.

A complete silence attended his advent and succeeded his departure. Geoffrey's sentence remained uncompleted. It was as though a
cold blight had fallen on the happy group.

The man was Beckwith.

CHAPTER XVIII

MRS. GIRD ADVISES

MRS. GIRD, who was every one's friend, yet had partialities of her own. She held human nature to be a dear and comfortable as well as amusing thing, but even she preferred to observe it through the veilings of civilisation rather than to contemplate its proportions in the rough. Such is the exaction of sex. The brutal did not dismay her, but it affected her animal spirits, and keen as was her sense of humour, it frequently proved inadequate to the naked problems of life. Of what kind was the soul of her—a tragic, a mocking, a tender thing—none could say, though many conjectured. Only one man had been permitted to gaze into that depth, and it closed and sealed itself for ever on the day that his shattered body was carried into the narrow house. To the sensitive the tragedy of the thing lay in that the woman made no sign. Neither at the time nor afterwards did she show a wound. Her face was turned to the future, and if the past ever rose like a ghost in her path, at least no one knew of it but herself. She made no confidences. That sin and suffering were; that it was necessary to fight and subdue them, her whole life attested; but that they existed for her she never admitted either by word or deed. Yet her power in the settlement was a thing remarkable and apart. No ordinary interchange of mutual sentiments and amenities explained it, for the amenities were merely sources of amusement to Mrs. Gird, and her sentiments were her own. It was not that she supplied a spring of compassion that might soothe if it did not materially alleviate suffering, for the waters she administered were tonic and not seldom bitter with the bitterness of death. But a largeness of nature covered all. No vagaries of the human machine astonished her. There was no pettiness in her reproofs, no narrowness in her awards. Wrong, no doubt, she often was, but it was with the large wrongfulness of humanity. Yet Mrs. Gird had her partialities. To the young and the beautiful her heart turned instinctively, and with none was she on more intimate terms than Eve Milward. And Eve, recognising that it was so, gave her in return a wealth of love and sympathy defiant of obstacles.

Mrs. Gird was not free with her kisses, but she embraced Eve Milward and looked at her keenly, 'Sad and *twenty,*' she said. 'How's this?'

'How is Mr. Gird?' Eve asked.

Her hostess paused before replying, and her face stilled to calmness. She undid the buckle of the girl's saddle, pulled it off and, releasing the horse from its bridle, looked with significant eyes at the questioner.

'It has been a long road,' she said, 'but the end is not far away now.'

'Oh, Mrs. Gird!'

'Ah, my dear, I understand that you do not know what to say! Why say anything? There is nothing to be said. His was a fierce vitality—the vitality of a man struck down in the heyday of his youth and strength. It has taken ten years of torment to quench his spirit, but the work is nearly done. Ten years of smouldering agony, and even now I do not know whether to thank God or curse Him.'

Eve had paid her visits and, until the return of Geoffrey from the section, had come to spend her time with Mrs. Gird. The sun still found its way into the clearing, though the shadow of the high bush on the margin was gaining rapidly on the sun-dried paddock. They went together to a log in the cool shadows. Before them the land rose in a bank of tree ferns, vivid with the new season's growth. Higher up stood a huge rata in full flower, its top, where it caught the sunlight, appearing as though freshly dipped in blood, its lower branches clotted in deepening shades of crimson and crimson-purple till they were lost in the undergrowth. Over the emerald sheen of the tree ferns spread a faint blood-coloured stain from the scattered stamens of the rata flowers.

Eve looked around her, her face still and pale, at a loss for words. At the evidences of toil everywhere, the blackened trees, the fallen logs, some with deep axe marks in them, the wilting grass among the stumps. Then, the untouched virgin forest, the tree ferns, the rata, weltering in his vivid summer garment. It seemed that the task set was too great, that God had forgotten—nay, that 'the beautiful blue heaven was flecked with blood.' With a little shiver she turned to her companion and put her arms round her.

'I am sorry for you, Mrs. Gird,' she said gravely.

But the elder woman made no sign,

'Who can tell,' Eve continued in the same voice, 'why God has afflicted you like this—you and him of all people? Who can tell why God permits such things to be? But I believe that He will recompense you in the end—if not in this world, then in some other. He must; it is incumbent on Him, or there is no justice anywhere.'

Mrs. Gird smiled gently as she took the girl's hands. 'Let us talk of something else, dearie,' she said. 'Of life and its fulness, of the paradise that is in the gift of these soft fingers. Tell me about yourself.'

The desire for self-revelation that follows the tender emotions stirred in the girl's breast, yet she was silent.

'Is there nothing to tell?' Mrs. Gird asked.! No fresh scalps? No new lovers?'

'Old loves are the best,' Eve replied, smiling, but averting her face from the other's keen scrutiny. 'Every day I find myself looking back with greater tenderness on poor Mr. Linkworthy. He was so nice, so considerate, so heart-broken, and now so married.'

'What about our friend the new minister?' Mrs. Gird asked, keeping to the point. 'He always speaks of you in terms of the highest admiration.'

'Is it a breach of confidence to speak of these things?' Eve wondered.

'I cannot see why, so long as it is not done from the housetop.'

'Well, Mr. Fletcher proposed to me. He was very urgent, and put his case, as it appears to me, extremely well, but_____'

'The case did not appeal to you?'

'Not at the time, but afterwards it has seemed to me better than I thought, and I don't know really what might be the upshot of a second display of its good features.'

There was a chill levity in the girl's tone which rang unpleasantly in her listener's ears. 'Is there any chance of such a second display?' she asked.

'Exceedingly good, I fancy. In fact, that was where the urgency revealed itself. Mr. Fletcher was by no means pressing for an immediate reply; on the contrary, he refused, I think, to take one, and he spoke of the results of a second, or perhaps even a later proposal, with a confidence in which I by no means shared. Still his judgment was possibly better than mine.'

'Why do you speak like this, Eve? Do you love the man?'

'Well, since you ask me—no; though I like him well enough, and as a minister I have the very highest opinion of him.'

'My dear child,' Mrs. Gird said bluntly, 'when a woman marries she marries a man and not a profession.'

'Yes, of course. Still it is Mr. Fletcher's profession which forms the inducement in this case. It is the case of the reed seeking support from the bank, the vine and the oak, the—the rata and the rimu.'

'Your similes are plentiful but dissimilar,' Mrs. Gird said. 'Do you know the story of the rata, for instance? How he lodges no larger than a speck of dust in the fork of the rimu, how he germinates and sends down roots and puts forth branches until finally_____' Mrs. Gird ceased speaking, and Eve, following the direction of her gaze, saw in the heart of the tortuous rata branches the dead trunk of the throttled rimu which had nursed it into being.

'What is the meaning of your parable?' she asked more soberly.

'It is capable of various interpretations, but let us take the one you yourself suggested. There is the profession dominating all, and there is poor human nature squeezed out of existence.'

'What of that, if the thing supplanting is more beautiful than the thing supplanted.'

Mrs. Gird turned impatiently aside. 'Don't let us confuse our minds with this rubbish,' she said. 'There is nothing so misleading as a simile, because in contemplating its justice we are apt to lose sight of the fact that it merely illustrates in place of supporting an argument. And this is serious. There is nothing more serious in life than this. We must grapple it with both hands and discover its nature. Eve, be sincere, be your own self and help me. Why should you desire support of that kind? Religious support, I suppose you mean. What has happened to you?'

But Eve, despite her real desire to become confidential, found a difficulty in overcoming her present mood of indifferent levity. 'Theologically,' she said, 'I am unsound; my faith is weak, and my credulity is gone in the wind. Surely it is in accordance with the order of things that we should seek to bolster up the weaker side of our natures.' Then she added with compunction, as her gaze met the other's, 'Forgive me; I can't help myself.'

There was sincerity there at all events, and Mrs. Gird determined on other tactics. 'Well, we shall not get that straight, apparently,' she said. 'But what about Geoffrey Hernshaw? Has he also met refusal?'

'Mr. Hernshaw is among the few who have not honoured me with a proposal,' the girl replied lightly, but there was a trace of uneasiness in her manner.

'Have you ever given him the opportunity to do so? Well, not exactly that. But have you never checked him when it seemed he might be likely to consider the occasion suitable?'

Eve picked up her gloves and stretched them between her fingers. 'I believe,' she said, truthfully at last, 'that Mr. Hernshaw would have proposed to me to-day if I had permitted him.'

Mrs. Gird could not conceal her disappointment. 'Is there no chance for the poor fellow?' she asked, her eyes on the girl's downcast face.

'There might be,' said Eve; 'I can't say. I do not know my own mind.'

There was that in the hesitating speech which drew forth to the full the maternal instincts of the elder woman. 'Dearie,' she said, 'it's a pity you have no mother, for just now and here she would have put her arms round you and all would have been right. I might have had daughters of my own if—well—I am an old woman, not so old as years go, but very old in experience, and wise in the knowledge of the pitfalls and snares that are set all over the valley of life. It may be that, if you could confide in me as you would in your mother, I could give you that in return which is worth having, if it be only a rough woman's sympathy and it may be that, in telling what you know of your mind, you will come to the knowledge of that which is at present concealed from you.'

'Dear Mrs. Gird, it is not that I do not wish to tell you, for I do, but I have a strange difficulty in speaking. Perhaps it is the intuition that things are bad, and that no amount of considering can put them straight. But you shall judge. You have asked me about Mr. Hernshaw.' The girl hesitated, and her manner took on a charming diffidence, while the colour mantled slowly in her cheeks. 'I like him extremely well; I suppose I may say I—love him. At least there is no man for whom I feel anything comparable with what I feel for him, but'—and the colour receded from her cheek—'there is a serious difference of opinion between us, so serious that, were it the only obstacle, it would still, I am afraid, be a barrier we could not pass. He is an agnostic'

Mrs. Gird's countenance had changed momentarily during this speech, but she now sat up with a great deal of cheerfulness. 'So'm I,' she said; 'so's every one, or something akin to it. What does it matter?'

Eve shook her head. 'Don't you see,' she said, 'that a difference of that kind is vital; that nothing can overcome it; that it must ultimately drive us apart as completely as the poles, as well in this world as the next? One may agree to differ on a thousand subjects, but not on this one; one may change one's opinions on a thousand points, but not on this. For this goes to the root. Other differences depend on the point of view, on the soundness of the reasoning, but this is beyond reason; it involves the fate of our souls, and may not be disregarded.'

'Stay a moment, young lady,' said Mrs. Gird shrewdly. 'I believe a few minutes back you confessed that theologically you were unsound, that your faith was weak and your credulity gone in the wind; that, I think, was the flippant manner in which you described your religious short-comings. Am I to understand that, in the face of this difference—which, mind you, is vital—between yourself and Mr. Fletcher, you are debating whether or no you should immolate that gentleman on the altar of mar-riage?'

But Eve was not to be bantered from her train of reasoning. 'If I have confessed that I am not so firm in my beliefs as I would desire to be,' she said, 'I know at least that a marriage with Mr. Fletcher, whatever disadvantages it might otherwise possess, would place me beyond the possibility of any further retrogression.'

'And Mr. Fletcher is willing to take the risk of himself falling from his high estate? But of course he is. And you? Might it not by the same rea-soning be counted as righteousness on your part to lend a helping hand to poor Geoffrey?'

Eve smiled reflectively and a soft light grew up in her eyes.

'However,' Mrs. Gird went on quickly, 'we can deal with the obstacles better when they are all before us. Now for the second.'

'The second?'

'I understood you to say there was more than one. Let us have the whole case against Geoffrey Hernshaw, and then we will take the items *seriatim.*'

Eve moved uneasily, her mind busy with the scene of the morning. Again she saw the figure of the strange man, erect on the verandah, his eyes glittering, his face full of a triumphant mockery. Again she heard the fatal passionate words that seemed to breathe in one breath love and despair. 'The compassion you might extend to any hunted crea-ture.' Hunted! Her cheeks grew hot. What story that was not shameful could account for that word? If there were not guilt in Geoffrey's countenance, there was mastery in the face of the other. Then the evident shrinking from her questions; the complete silence he had maintained as to the incident, and its singular effect upon him. Was it fear? Afraid, and of a man! In a country where, through the primitiveness of their lives, all men are of necessity compelled to face danger in one shape or another, it is only to be expected that the natural aversion of women to pusillanimity in the opposite sex should be accentuated *beyond* the ordinary, and the mere thought that the man she loved allowed himself to be held in subjection by another brought a curl of contempt to the girl's lips, while it brought also a pang of distress to her heart. Yet surely the thought did him an injustice. Afraid he may have been, but not with any mere physical fear.

Mrs. Gird awaited in silence the result of the girl's reverie, her eyes scanning her face with wondering curiosity.

'I know of no other obstacle,' Eve said at last; 'but I have reason to think there is something I might consider one if I knew it. That sounds ungenerous, I know, but I cannot help it; the suspicion has been forced upon me.'

'What reason?' Mrs. Gird asked, surprised.

'I doubt if I ought to mention it even to you, Mrs. Gird,' Eve replied hesitatingly. 'My discovery of its existence was an accident, and the discovery was not pleasing to Mr. Hernshaw. If,' she added slowly, 'it concerns something he desires to conceal, I have certainly no right to speak of it even to my nearest and dearest.'

'Pooh,' said Mrs. Gird, 'there is nothing wrong with Geoffrey. I will wager the thing is a mare's nest; that it can be explained in a few words. But I'm all in the dark. It seems you trust neither of us, and at least we have this in common, that we are your lovers.'

'I will trust you, Mrs. Gird,' the girl said, with more resolution; 'and the mere fact that I do so should be an indication that I trust him. It was this morning, while we were passing M'Gregor's store, that the thing happened. There was a man there, a stranger—but I cannot explain it. He knew Mr. Hernshaw; he seemed to denounce and challenge him, and Mr. Hernshaw knew him, recognised him. There was nothing said, but there was an effect of something said which, had it been spoken, would have been dreadful to hear. Do I give you an idea of the scene? Mr. Hernshaw seemed to shrink away as though from a blow—that was at first. Afterwards he looked straight at the man and passed him without a word. But it is hopeless to try and make you understand the effect it all had on me. I was so startled that I spoke without thinking, and it was then Mr. Hernshaw alluded to himself as hunted. I believe I made an effort to discover what he meant. I gave him an opportunity to explain the scene, but he did not do so. That is all—except that the stranger was not alone. Andersen was with him.'

'Andersen,' Mrs. Gird exclaimed sharply. 'And this happened at M'Gregor's store. What was the appearance of the man?'

'He was a dreadful creature — cruel and vindictive-looking; but I seem only to remember his eyes.'

'Fair or dark?'

'Fair. Yes, I recollect, he had a brown beard.'

Mrs. Gird's eyes wore an introspective look. 'It is curious at least,' she said musingly; 'but don't let us jump to conclusions. After all, there are a thousand things which a man might find a difficulty in explaining to a girl. Even the best of men—even your paragon of virtue, Mr. Fletcher, might not be disposed to have his past laid bare in every particular. And Geoffrey is a good fellow, isn't he? — a warm-hearted, sensitive, intelligent, sweet-tempered man. They're not common, my dear, and sometimes that sort gets into scrapes quite easily. Supposing—it is only a supposition—there had been something in his life which we, no less than his present self, would prefer not to have been, shall we ignore the present and remember only the past?'

'That depends,' said Eve slowly. 'There are some things it would be impossible to forget,'

'No doubt, and do not regard me as a special pleader on behalf of what is criminal and vicious; but the sins impossible of forgiveness are not for Geoffrey Hernshaw.'

There was a note of reproof in the elder woman's voice, and the girl recognised it with a heightening of colour.

'After all, Mr. Hernshaw's affairs are no concern of mine,' she said; then with a sudden surrender she cried: 'Oh, why am I so hard, so cruel, so suspicious!'

Mrs. Gird knew and smiled tenderly upon her, but she offered no explanation.

'Come into the house,' she said; 'I have something to show you.'

Eve rose and followed her hostess. In the bedroom she came to a standstill and pointed to a picture on the wall. It was a small engraving, such as might cover the page of an illustrated paper. To the right and at the back, infantry and horsemen were moving forward in extended order, men falling and shells breaking overhead as they moved. To the left the trenches of the enemy, the point of attack, belched forth a torrent of lead. In the foreground was a peasant, an aged man, ploughing with a team of horses. His hands, holding the reins, knotted themselves strongly round the haft; his calm eyes looked straight ahead.

'How singular!' said Eve. 'What does it mean?'

'Common-sense, my dear,' said Mrs. Gird.

CHAPTER XIX

'I HAVE NO MOTHER'

IF the innumerable prayers offered up by a suffering and desiring humanity were of a sudden to receive fulfilment, it is probable that the recipients would be less full of thanksgiving than of surprise at the unforeseen consequences of their action, while, were the favour belated, it is inconceivable but that the surprise should be largely flavoured with annoyance.

Mrs. Andersen was past the stage when any reform in her husband's conduct was prayed for or even desired. So when Lena conveyed to her the subject of Mr. Wickener's message, and it seemed that her old prayers had at last received attention, there was far from being any corresponding feeling of gratification in her breast.

'Let him keep his money,' she said roughly. 'We can do all right as we are.'

But the money was not returned, nor were the sums that dropped in subsequently, all at the hands of the same courteous and agreeable messenger. And in consequence the appearance of the family improved greatly. In course of time the whole of them became clothed, and it was thus possible to distinguish the males from the females, a matter which had for years presented an insoluble enigma to the settlement. Out of the enigma emerged, it may be said, a girl a few years younger than Lena, four sturdy boys, and another child, as yet nondescript, all dowered with their mother's clear skin and fine features, and their father's blue eyes. Mrs. Andersen herself had shared in the improvement. She no longer hung listlessly at the door, indifferent as to appearances both in her person and her surroundings. Her good looks returned, and a young woman in fact, she began shortly to suggest that fact by her appearance. The male settlers, who had been in the habit of nodding hurriedly and passing by on the other side, now drew closer and lifted their hats. The women showed a tendency to place her name on their Sunday afternoon visiting lists, and only Mrs. Gird shook her head and waited with misgiving for the denouement. It was not long in coming. The heart expands rapidly in the sunshine, and whereas in the shade of poverty growth is slow and subject to relapses, in the light of prosperity it comes rapidly to a head. So, while poor Lena, in the hope of her father's complete reformation, filled the house with singing, her mother was rapidly making up her mind to a course of action which must make his success or failure a matter immaterial to her.

'Mr. Andersen,' said Wickener one day in his lightest tones, 'I have been guilty of a little subterfuge with regard to yourself and your family, as to which it is due to you that I should offer an explanation and an apology.' He paused, glanced at the other, reflected a moment, and went on, 'I have already pointed out to you that your case has a weak spot, and I will now tell you wherein that weak spot consists. You have left your family for some considerable time past without means of support. Pardon me, I beg of you; you shall have your say by and by. Now a woman, a good-looking woman—and Mrs. Andersen is certainly that—without means of support is, owing to the inherent vileness of human nature, subject to special temptations over and above those which are provided by her own disposition. For that excess of temptation you and you only are responsible. Understand me,'—Mr. Wickener's voice stiffened slightly—' you only. Now, to put the matter on a correct footing, I have ventured—impertinently perhaps you will consider—to present your family from time to time with sums of money; not very great amounts, but sufficient at any rate to keep the wolf from the door.' He paused, looked at Andersen, who was scowling darkly, smiled a little, and continued with increased gaiety of manner. 'These sums, Mr. Andersen, I have—very repre-hensibly no doubt in the interests of truth—-represented as coming from you, as emanating, in fact, from a fond husband and devoted father as the result of stern manual toil. As such and such only the offerings I speak of have been received.'

Andersen's frown turned slowly to a look of bewilderment. 'You haf done dis,' he said; 'for why?'

'My object I have already explained. I desired to put your little affair on a proper footing. I desired that your wife should have no temptations other than those which are inseparable from her nature. She is now, through your good conduct, in that happy position; and henceforth, if she falls, her blood will be on her own head.'

Andersen stared at his companion, the muscles of his face twitching.

'I am a rich man, Andersen,' Wickener went on reflectively,—' rich beyond the dreams of avarice.' He stopped, plucked a fern frond from the ground, and crushed it with a sudden fierce ruthlessness between his fingers. 'And I can afford to gratify my little whims and make my little experiments. But in this case I have thought twice, and I have resolved to stay my hand. I will be frank with you, completely frank. You have a daughter; she is young, she is beautiful, she is charming; if it were possible for me to think so, I should say that she is also good.' He rose to his feet. 'But,' he continued quickly, 'however that may be, for her sake I abandon the experiment. Now, listen to me. Go back. Get up now from where you are sitting, don't stay to bid me good-bye, turn neither to the right nor the left, but go back—back into the house where your wife sits, and it may be—who knows?—that you will not be too late.'

But Andersen looked up at him shamefaced and sat still.

'Stay,' said Wickener, 'you shall not go back empty-handed, but as a man and a conqueror. Here. Now, lose no time.'

With the 'here' was extended a little roll of bank notes, and then at last Andersen rose trembling to his feet. He seemed moved to the utmost of his nature, and with the simple action of a child dashed the tears from his eyes.

'Gott for effer bless you, Mr. Wickener,' he said hoarsely; 'but no, dat I cannot do. I am a villains, a beast, a dronk, but also I am a man. I vill not take your money, Gott forbid! I vill not go back to mine vife with the false in mine hand, dat is lies. But I vill go from here now as you say, and I vill waark; waark is plenty for me, and soon then I vill go back as you told me, but dis ting I cannot.'

'Fool!' said Wickener savagely. 'Take it—what is the trash to me? It will buy nothing, it will keep nothing. Do you think Fate will wait your convenience? Pay me back if you will, but take it now and go.'

'I cannot,' said Andersen. 'Shall I buy her faith with anudder man's money? No, by Gott!'

Slowly Wickener, his eyes fixed on the other's face, drew back his hand and restored the notes to his pocket.

'Have your way, then,' he said. 'You are a fool, and you lose the game. Perhaps it was not worth winning. Console yourself with that reflection when your time comes if you can. Shake hands, Andersen. God knows the human race is a set of damned fools, especially the men; but it can't be helped, and it is of no great consequence anyhow. Nothing matters—after all, it is a happy thought that nothing does matter. Make a note of that. We may shake up the box of tricks till the details rattle like the devil, but the game plays itself out to the predestined end and Death cries "Domino!"every time. Rattle it as you will, the game is in the box. That's fatalism. You have chosen to go against the pieces. It has been tried, millions have tried it; but go on. Good luck to you, and goodbye.'

Within twenty-four hours Mrs. Andersen had taken the irrevocable step, and Wickener's wisdom was justified.

Lena had been sent on some trivial pretext to a distant part of the settlement, and she returned home to find the house cleaned and swept, but empty of its inhabitants. At first the girl glanced round with no suspicion of the truth. The absence of the children was unusual but not inexplicable. Going into the room which she shared with her younger sister, she was struck by a sense of difference, of a bareness in her surroundings. She returned quickly to the living room, then to her mother's bedroom. Her heart sank like lead in her bosom. A blindness came to her eyes; she felt sick and faint, and groped through the gathering darkness to a seat, sitting huddled and trembling, sick with shame and horror. Even the presence of death might not so have wrought on her susceptibilities. All the wearing apparel in the house save her own had disappeared. The nails in the walls and doors were empty. That no word or act of hers should interfere with her mother's intention she had been sent out of the road, cozened with a lying message. Her mother's last word had been a lie.

'God forgive her, God forgive her; I never can.'

She got unsteadily to her feet and went blindly, her hands before her, to her own room. There she threw herself on her bed, face downwards, recklessly, but in a moment she was up again.

No, no; she was mad; she was dreaming; it could not be; God was not so cruel. The bare walls stared at her in mockery. Every empty nail struck sharply to her heart. Suddenly something white on the dressing-table attracted her—a letter, a sheet of paper, hurriedly folded and bearing her name. Clutching it, the girl returned to the bed, and endeavoured to steady her trembling nerves. For awhile the black characters writhed like centipedes across the sheet, then slowly they settled themselves and began to convey a meaning.

'I have done my best (wrote her mother), and I can bear it no longer. Forgive me if you can. It was for your sake and the children's I listened to him first, but afterwards—well, I have told you that. He has a room for you, Lena, if you will come, and you shall have everything you want.

He is a good man. But if you are going to desert us there is money in the cracked teapot in the cupboard. You need not be afraid to take it, 'tis your father's. What will you do? Oh, dear, do not be hard on me!'

The end was blotted and smudged, and the whole composition showed evidences of hurry and agitation. But to Lena these facts made no appeal. To her the note was bald, brutal in the overwhelming confirmation it offered of the shameful and terrible fact. The 'Do not be hard on me' might as well have been addressed to a stone for all effect it had on the girl's outraged feelings. Gentler thoughts might come with time, but there was no room for them now. Again she threw herself on the bed, her face on the pillow, her hands clutched in the counterpane. Everything was over; the worst had happened; welcome death, death the healer, the consoler. Darkness settled rapidly on the house. One by one the stars came out and shot their slender rays through the uncurtained window. Hour after hour she lay almost motionless, her eyes wide open. When she moved at all it was to bury her face in the pillow in an agony of shame.

'God forgive her, God forgive her; I never can.'

Her feet and hands grew cold, the blood raced in her temples. Every aspect of the dreadful business whirled and struck through her brain. Her father, Robert, her friends, her acquaintances—the effect of the news on each of them. Robert was lost. She had lost him. That was all over—all done with. But if love were lost, what was left? The question shot away unanswered into the blackness.

'Why did I let him love me? I knew, I knew. But it was so sweet, and now I have hurt him. Oh, poor Robert! God forgive her for that; I *never* can. And it can't be undone. Nothing can undo it. God Himself could not undo it even if He would. If I live I shall have to face it.' Suddenly she sat up in the darkness, dashing the hair from her eyes. Her breath came and went in hurried, fearful gasps. 'Soon—to-morrow—in a few hours. Oh, I can't, I can't! It is too much!'

She slipped her feet silently to the floor and stood listening guiltily in the darkness. Presently she began a cautious move forward towards the living-room. A few steps brought her to the door. She could see dimly now, but the floor was heavily shadowed, and her foot striking some obstacle it moved noisily. As the sound died away, another arose outside the house: a quick footstep, followed by a rap on the wall.

The girl stood rigid, listening.

'Lena!' said a man's voice eagerly.

No answer.

'Lena, is that you? Speak to me; it's Robert.' Silence.

'Dear! Are you there? I know everything. Beckwith has been to me.'

Still no movement within.

'Lena, Lena! Listen to me. Let me see you. Let me speak to you. Oh, my darling, what are you doing in there alone? I heard you move. Answer me.'

A faint rustle; a sound as of small objects being shifted hurriedly but with an attempt at noiseless-ness from place to place.

'Lena (with increased anxiety), let me hear your voice. Just one word. Are you angry with me? I have come at once, as soon as I knew. I have not deserted you—like the rest. I love you, Lena. You are mine now—only mine. Nothing could make any difference in that. Only say one word.'

Silence.

'Then if you will not come to me, I must come to you. Answer me, dear. I am determined. Will you force me to break in the door?'

'Robert.'

'Yes, Lena.'

'Go away. I do not love you.'

'That is the first lie you have ever told me, Lena. Come out and say it with my arms round you if you dare.'

'Leave me alone. I want to be left alone. I do not want ever to see you again.'

'I shall never leave you alone. What are you doing there without a light?'

'I do not want a light. I want nothing but to be left alone.'

'You shall never be alone again. Come out to me or I shall come and take you.'

'You shall never take me. I will kill myself first.'

Then in a flash there came on Robert the meaning of the silent house, the darkness, the faint noises as of searching hands. On all strong natures the imminence of danger acts like a tonic. The nerves steady themselves for resistance, the muscles brace themselves for action, the intelligence becomes acute. So, in less time than it takes to state, Robert's plan was made. He ran his hands lightly over the door and drew back.

'Lena,' he said from the increased distance, 'if I go away now, will you promise to go straight to bed?'

What her answer was he never knew, for in the next instant he had thrown himself with all his weight on the door. The wooden latch snapped like a carrot; there was a crash as the door swinging back struck the window frame, splintering the glass in the sashes. A chair, galvanised into activity, hurled itself against the opposite wall, and the girl was in his arms.

'Lena, you are mine. I have a right to take my own.'

'I never will be yours. I do not love you. I have another lover.'

He kissed the rebellious lips fiercely into silence. 'So much the worse for the other then,' he said; 'for when I lay hold I never let go.'

'No, no; it's a lie. I love you. You are splendid. You are my hero, my master. But I will never marry you.'

'We shall see,' said Robert, and bore her from the dark house into the dim starlight.

'I will take you to Mrs. Gird's now. If you will not walk I shall carry you.' Suddenly he began trembling, and the girl slipped through his arms to her feet. Still he held her, his hands shaking as with palsy.

'Robert, Robert, what is it?'

'Nothing, Lena,' he said in a shaken whisper; 'I was thinking. It's the slip-rail—I forgot to put it up. I was thinking of going back to do it, but I didn't go; I came straight on.'

There was a silence.

Gradually Robert's strength returned and with it the fixity of his purpose.

'Lena, will you do as I tell you?'

'Yes, Robert; in everything but the one thing.'

He took her hand and led her out of the paddock down the road on to the bush track. Three times during the journey he stopped, put his arms round her and kissed her passionately. She offered no resistance.

'You are mine. I will go to the Registrar's Office to-morrow.'

'I will never marry you, Robert.'

Again—

'Do you love me, Lena?'

'Yes, with my whole soul.'

'You cannot live without me.'

'I will try.'

And for the last time—

'You are mine, doubly mine. I won you tonight. You cannot go back to that other lover.'

'No. Robert, were there any bullocks near the slip-rail?'

'Never mind that. You are going to be a good girl. You will do as I tell you.'

'In everything except the one thing.'

He set her down on a log and went away to acquaint Mrs. Gird. It was some minutes before he returned. He lifted her and kissed her again. 'Are you a good girl now?'

'I will never be good.'

'Kiss me.'

She obeyed.

He led her to the house, passed her to Mrs. Gird and went silently away. Lena tried to speak but words refused to come. She wanted to apologise, but how to do it she could not remember. Mrs. Gird led her without speaking to her own room, put her in a chair and began to un-lace her boots.

Lena complained querulously. She did not want to go to bed. She wanted to lie down anywhere.

Her hostess continued disrobing her in silence and soon the task was complete. Frozen, motionless, she lay in the elder woman's arms.

'Sleep, darling, and you will be better.'

'I can't sleep. I do not want to sleep; I want to think.'

'Then let it be of the sweet days that are coming. Let it be of forgive-ness and compassion. Child, do you guess what your mother suffered all these years?'

'Mrs. Gird, I have no mother.'

'Little one, can you pray?'

'No, no; let me be.'

'That will I not. Come closer to me. Do I not know what suffering is?'

CHAPTER XX

ON THE BEACH

THE bloom of enthusiasm had worn off the religious revival at Rivermouth; there had even been a considerable backsliding. As a fire cannot be kept going without fuel, so an enthusiasm of this nature fails when the supply of converts is exhausted. The Maoris were the first to drop off; singly and in twos and threes they retired yawning and in search of fresh excitement. The band seceded in a body. It was in this way.

One of its prominent members having occasion to visit the Kaipara chanced on the farewelling of a contingent on its way to South Africa. The little town of Helensville was lavishly decorated in honour of the event. The heroes of the hour (six in number) were being triumphantly conducted to the railway station amid the cheers of the crowd and the braying of the local brass band.

What was that martial, that divine air? The dusky bandsman's heart bounded in his breast. He also was a patriot. He also was prepared to meet the hereditary foe Kruger in single combat. Great feelings entail action. The bandsman stepped forward into line, placed his instrument to his lips, struck the right note and launched impromptu on 'The Soldiers of the Queen, my lads.' It was the triumph of music over matter. For two days he remained in the township, studying the new airs, then he returned home.

The band met that night; the new music was played and received with delirious enthusiasm.

'Boys,' said the Prominent Bandsman, amid the wildest excitement, 'religion no good. That the ol' fashion'd. Patriotisnt!—that the ferra!'

And patriotism, as exemplified in martial airs, was the vogue from that hour.

Pine, who, through his conversion taking place somewhat late in the day, had never joined the band, was left out in the cold by these manoeuvres of his tribesmen. He had had the foresight to repress any religious cravings on the part of his family, and thus while the less thoughtful of the converts were growing daily leaner and sadder, he remained cheerful and well fed. Clothes, however, were another matter, not forthcoming without money. Pine's boots had reached that stage of decrepitude when repairs become no longer possible. Something had to be done and soon. He stood for some time outside the local boot shop, gazing longingly on the numerous specimens of the shoemaker's handicraft exposed for sale. The prices were marked in plain figures, but how to obtain the sums mentioned was not so clear. Pine, however, was never lacking in courage, and after one or two glances through the open shop door, he walked cheerfully in and seated himself in the workshop.

Howell was quite accustomed to being watched at his work, so he merely glanced over his spectacles at his visitor and went on with what he was doing.

Pine watched the deft fingers with little clicks of admiration. 'By gorry!' he exclaimed at last. 'Te pest ferra you makit te poot.'

'Good boots, eh?' said Howell.

'Te pest! You makit all dese poots?'

'Every man Jack of them,' said the shoemaker, not uninfluenced by the other's admiration.

'I tink you te pest pootmaker. Dese other ferra makit te poot no good. You te pest, I tink so.'

He got softly to his feet, and with many ejaculations of astonishment and admiration perambulated the shop, feeling the leather and expatiating on the ingenuity of the pakeha[1] at every step. At length he came to a standstill before a pair of watertights.

'Num'er ten, I s'pose so,' he remarked.

'Tens, yes.'

'I tink dese poots fit me,' Pine said tentatively.

'Just about your size, I should say,' replied Howell, sharpening his knife to cut a fresh strip of leather.

Pine kicked off his uppers and squeezed himself slowly down into the watertights. 'Te pest! 'he remarked when the feat was accomplished. 'How you look?'

'First-rate! Couldn't fit you better if they were made for you.'

'I tink I take dese poots,' said Pine. 'How much the utu[2]?'

---

[1] white man

[2] 'potoo'; price.

'Thirteen and six.'

'Py crikey, te sheap poot! Dirteen and hiki-pene! I s'pose one poun'.'

'No,' said Howell, with a virtuous shake of the head. 'Thirteen and sixpence is the price.'

'Py gorry, te gooroo poot for te little money! I tink I take dese poots. I pay to-morrow.'

'No, you don't,' said Howell. 'You pay now.'

'No money dis time,' said Pine; 'but s'pose to-morrow—ah, prenty money!' He waved his hand to indicate the magnitude of the revenues that were falling due to him at the time mentioned.

Howell picked up a thumbful of sprigs. 'No money, no boots,' he said inflexibly.

Pine sat down on the bench, and extending his legs, regarded the watertights critically.

'I tink too small,' he said presently.

'I can stretch them for you,' suggested the bootmaker.

'If stretch, I tink soon bust. No gooroo te leather, p'r'aps so. You makit all dese poots?' he inquired coldly, casting an indifferent glance round the shop.

Howell admitted the charge.

Pine shook his head. 'No good your poot,' he said. 'If wet, soon bust; if dry, too hard. I tink no one puy dese poots. Why you make more?'

The shoemaker's little eyes shone fiercely over his spectacles.

'S'pose half-crown,' said Pine finally; 'ah, I take!'

'Go away,' said Howell, incensed.

Pine removed the watertights, clicked disparagingly over them, and resumed the tenancy of his own property; then, with a final glance of disfavour at the shoemaker's wares, he lounged into the street.

It was mid-day, without a cloud to intercept the intensity of the sun's beams, nor a breath of wind to temper them. The river lay like a sheet of glass, returning tint for tint the colours of the sky. Some distance off the shore a yacht lay becalmed, her white sails spread in invitation to the reluctant breeze. The beach was all but deserted. No sound issued from the houses, or through the wide doorways of the stores, or even from the hotel. Only from the schoolhouse among the trees there came a continuous hum, which on long listening developed into singing. On the far end of the beach Mallow was rolling up his fishing-net, which had been spread out to dry in the sun. All the activity of the township seemed vested in his sole person, and as though ashamed of this divergence from his neighbours, he sat down in the middle of his labours and got out a pipe.

Pine meditated joining him, but the beach was long, and he was low-spirited at his recent failure, and so he sat down where he was. The yacht afforded a pleasant resting-place for the gaze of an idle man, and despite the fact of its being becalmed there were more evidences of activity about it than were discoverable elsewhere. Figures were moving about, busying themselves with the ropes, and presently the white sail slid down and disappeared from view. Then a dinghey at the stern was pulled alongside, and two figures stepping into it, it began to make for the shore. The hollow sound of the oars in the rowlocks, and the voices of persons conversing, travelled clearly across the still water. Pine soon identified one of the occupants of the boat. He belonged to the county township, and did the lion's share of carrying on the river. The other man was a stranger. Pine had all the curiosity of his race as to strangers, and rising to his feet, he sauntered down the beach in the direction of the approaching boat, arriving in time to put his hand on it as it reached the shore.

'Hallo, Pine! Good-bye, Mr. Wickener. Start back first streak of daylight in the morning. I'll knock you up at the hotel, unless you care to sleep on board.'

'I should prefer it,' said Mr. Wickener, 'if it would not inconvenience you too much.'

'My troubles. Well, ta-ta. See you again.'

Mr. Wickener turned to find the Maori regarding him with great intentness.

'Your name Wickerer?'

'That is my name,' Mr. Wickener replied, smiling.

'Where you come from dis time?'

Mr. Wickener indicated the upper river.

'You belong-a New Tealan'?'

'No, sir, I am from England.'

Pine regarded him with exhaustive earnestness. 'Where your wife?' he asked.

The Englishman moved restively, but continued smiling.

'You leave your wife up to your place in Inglan'?'

'Really,' said Mr. Wickener, 'your interest in my family affairs is flattering to the verge of embarrassment.'

Pine regarded him with intense thoughtfulness, taking in every peculiarity of his person and every detail of his attire. A sparkle of gold in the Englishman's teeth attracted him, and he craned his neck to obtain a second view. 'You got te false tooth?' he asked, frowning.

Mr. Wickener looked musingly at his inquisitor. 'Now,' he said *sotto voce,* 'I understand the genesis of "Why, why," "How, how."'

Pine stepped sideways to observe a ring on his victim's finger. Then he subjected him generally to a searching stare that sought to tear the mystery out of him. The very apotheosis of curiosity was in that keen, rolling scrutiny. In its earnestness was summed up all the imperative necessity for knowing on which the existence of his savage ancestry had depended. 'Where you buy that hat?' he asked.

But Mr. Wickener thought it was time to bring the inquisition to a close. 'Where did you buy those boots?' he retorted.

Pine acknowledged the shaft with a backward step and a dusky blush. He had been hit in a vulnerable place, and he regarded the stranger for the first time with respect.

'Your name is Pine, I think?' said Wickener in his turn.

'Dat my name. All same Inglis' pin.'

'Ah! Hence the pointedness of your attack. Now, let me see. So this is Rivermouth.' The Englishman looked smilingly along the sultry beach,

'That the hotel,' said Pine. 'Dat the good hotel, my word.'

'By all means,' said Wickener amiably. 'Let us go there.'

'You got te money?' Pine inquired cautiously, with the idea of avoiding misunderstandings.

'I probably have an odd shilling. At any rate, the responsibility of the visit shall be mine.'

Pine led the way for a few steps with alacrity, then came to an abrupt halt, struck by a disconcerting recollection. He had taken the pledge!

'Come along,' said the Tempter, pausing and jingling a pocketful of coins.

Pine saw the necessity for rapid thinking. The pledge had been taken on the impulse of the moment without due forethought. It had never included the possibility that an Englishman with a pocketful of money should offer to shout for him. Plainly the matter had been misrepresented. This was not in the bill. So far as paying for drinks out of his own pocket was concerned, certainly and by all means nothing should exceed the rigour of his teetotalism in that respect, but in this case the responsibility was clearly with the other party.

'All ri', said Pine cheerfully, 'I come.'

They entered the silent hotel, where, after repeated knocking, some one was found obliging enough to serve them; then they returned to the beach.

'What you do now?' Pine asked.

'Now,' replied the Englishman, 'I have a visit to pay. I want to see Mr. Fletcher.'

'Mita Fretchah!' exclaimed Pine, drawing back. 'My gorry! I tink p'r'aps you tell him I not 'total dis time.'

'I am a pattern of discretion,' Mr. Wickener replied. 'It is possible your name may not be mentioned.'

'Dat te best,' said Pine innocently. 'Why for you go see Mr. Fretchah?'

Mr. Wickener returned smilingly to the landscape. 'A charming spot,' he said; 'so restful, so Rip-van-Winkleyan. Where does Mr. Fletcher reside?'

'I show you. He live Mr. Mallow's place. That ol' man Mallow along te beach. He te small rangatira but te good fisherman. Some times ago his wife was say: "You go get tree, four schnapper for te brekfas."'Pine cleared his throat and his eyes began to roll. 'When he get out he look an' see he leave all his bait ashore. He only got one small pipi, all same's dis,'—Pine indicated a cockleshell on the beach with his dilapidated boot toe. 'But ol' man Mallow he te pest fisherman. He tink a big tink, den he say: "Good 'nuf!" First he catch te pakerikeri, dat te small ferra fish, all same's sprat; den te pakerikeri catch te kahuwai an' te kahuwai te good bait mo te schnapper. By'm-by te boat so full, he sit on te side and put out big hook for te shark. Plenty big ferra shark come along dat times an' ol' man Mallow he catch 'em seven an' tie 'em all round te boat. By'm-by Missus Mallow come along down-a beach an' she see ol' man Mallow pull for th' shore like te debil after him an' dirteen big ferra whales comin' in over'm bar. Ol' Mallow he pull an' pull an' soon he tumble out on-a beach like he dang'ously dead. "My glacious!" he say; "dat pipi te strongest bait ever I seen it." He te good fisherman, my word!'

Mr. Wickener nodded his appreciation of the story. 'I have done a little fishing myself,' he said, glancing at the stolid back of Mr. Mallow, who sat over the half-rolled net, his eyes fixed in contemplation on the river. 'So this is the place?'

'I go talk to ol' man Mallow,' Pine said. 'By'm-by I see you again.'

Mr. Wickener was received by Mabel Mallow, who spoke of Mr. Fletcher as absent, but likely to return at any moment. Meantime she invited him into the parlour, gave him a comfortable chair, and adjusted the sun-blind.

'Mr. Fletcher is somewhere in the township,' she said, smiling at the visitor, 'so that he is sure to be back to lunch. It is not often one can speak so certainly about him.'

'Then I am fortunate,' said Mr. Wickener. 'I should be sorry indeed to miss him, having travelled a considerable distance with the express object of seeing him.'

Mabel could think of nothing to say, so she smiled again with additional sweetness and straightened an antimacassar on the sofa.

'I am an old acquaintance of Mr. Fletcher's,' said the gentleman, his eye on the girl's well-proportioned figure; 'though, as I have not seen him for some considerable time, my visit is likely to take him by surprise. I presume he is quite established—one may say domesticated here?'

'It depends on what you mean by domesticated,' Mabel returned roguishly.

'At least,' said Mr. Wickener, smiling, 'a powerful incentive to become so is not lacking.'

No girl had a keener ear for a compliment than Mabel, but she was not anxious just at that moment to allow herself and the parson to be connected in the stranger's mind. She rewarded the speaker with a dazzling glance as she said: 'Mr. Fletcher perhaps finds his incentive a little farther away than Rivermouth.'

'Indeed?' said Mr. Wickener, pricking up his ears.

'At Wairangi, for instance,' Mabel continued in the same tone.

Mr. Wickener started slightly, and a look of intense reflection gathered in his eyes. 'Just so,' he said musingly,—'just so.'

'There is Mr. Fletcher now,' Mabel cried suddenly, as a shadow passed the window. 'I will tell him you are here.'

Left alone, Mr. Wickener rose, crossed the room once or twice rapidly, his mouth twitching, his eyes glittering. There was something daemonic and deadly in his tread, and it is probable that Mabel, had she come upon him now, would have had a difficulty in recognising the smiling visitor of a few moments before.

A strong step in the passage brought the restless movements to a standstill, and Mr. Fletcher, hat in hand, appeared in the doorway of the partially darkened room.

'Good day,' said the clergyman. 'I hear you wish to see me.'

Then he looked at his visitor; his sombre, handsome countenance stilled suddenly, and he stood like a man turned to stone.

CHAPTER XXI

THE DIVIDING OF THE WAYS

IT is doubtful whether at this time Mr. Fletcher still entertained the conviction as to the result of his love-making which he had expressed to Eve on the occasion of his first proposal. There had been much in the interval to create doubt even in a mind of unusual determination, and it is not conceivable that a man of Mr. Fletcher's character should allow himself to dwell for any length of time in a fool's paradise.

To begin with, the frankness and pleasure with which the young girl had been wont to meet and welcome his visits were things of the past, and it was rather as a guest than a master that he was now received by the fair mistress of Wairangi. Religion had always formed the staple of conversation between them, but there had been little diversions into mundane subjects full of charm for the man. Eve had a twin capacity for radiance. She had the radiance of an angel when some chord of her spiritual nature was touched and a radiance of sheer wickedness, responding to motives less exalted. Both were alike fascinating, and the clergyman and the man basked delighted in their respective beams. But now when they were alone religion took entire command. However the conversation might begin, a few steps carried it into the midst of a theological discussion. Religion stormed and carried by assault the most unlikely situations. It diffused itself through the atmosphere; the very landscape became saturated; finally, even Mr. Fletcher rebelled.

'Religion is not everything,' he said once in uncontrollable impatience, the man in him aware of something more immediately desirable.

'Oh yes, it is,' said Eve quickly; 'everything. There is nothing of any importance but that.'

It was a common remark of hers; and Mr. Fletcher was silent, for in a different sense he recognised that there was nothing else. Why, by his precipitancy, had he lost command of that one weapon? For the command was gone. It was no longer master and pupil, authoritative and respectfully recipient; it was no longer high discourse based on sacred and not-to-be-disputed texts. It was war—war without prospect of truce. Eve brought up her big guns and planted them fair in the open, where the masked batteries of the enemy put them quickly out of action.

'But you refuse to examine your side of the case. Don't you see how unfair that is? You tear science to pieces, but you refuse to stand or fall by anything yourself

'It has been, said that a little learning takes us away from God, but a great deal brings us back to Him.'

'Yes, I know. I could believe that. But does it bring us back to the same God?'

Sometimes religious zeal would prompt the parson to other tactics. He would rise and pour down upon her the wrath of the Church, thundering of the sin of blasphemy and the damnation that awaited the unbeliever, and Eve would sit still, stunned and crushed, white and silent. Mr. Fletcher appeared at his best in those moments; his strong figure full of an unconscious dignity, his resonant voice, his flashing eyes, all combining to make a picture of the beautiful and the terrible. But at the end, when he beheld his handiwork, his passion reacted upon himself, and only by the fiercest effort of will could he refrain from taking the girl in his arms and again offering her the support of his own unquestioning faith.

That his faith was unquestioning, there could be no doubt. Argument, irony, plain reasoning, glanced from that impervious shield and left no mark. Eve, looking at him incredulously, fancied often that he had not heard, but he showed all the outward signs of listening attentively. On the subject of his own beliefs he refused to argue, and when he spoke it was with the voice and in the exalted language of the priest. As for the girl's smattering of science and her logic, a few words sufficed in most instances to demolish them.

'The whole of your reasoning—all knowledge, in fact—depends on the correctness of certain primitive conceptions, as to which proof is impossible. We have established a number of relations, which have apparently held for some time past and hold now, but we cannot argue from the past into the future. Religion is on a different basis. It strikes direct from God to the soul of man. Reasoning cannot take us to it—on the contrary, it must lead us from it. If my religion were capable of being reasoned I should cease to believe in it.'

But though crushed for the time being, the girl returned again and again to the conflict. 'It must be terribly boring for you,' she said; 'and I am really grateful, but there seems to be a strain of what Mrs. Gird calls "horse sense" in me—perhaps you would call it by a harsher name. At any rate, my will has absolutely no power over my beliefs.'

And Mr. Fletcher, recognising that in these discussions lay his only chance of continued intercourse with the girl, suffered and even invited the boredom.

It was symptomatic of Eve's unsettled state of mind that she should argue.on the one side with Geoffrey Hernshaw and on the other with Mr. Fletcher, and it was a natural consequence of such action that the two men felt the conflict to be a personal matter. In the girl's arguments they frequently recognised each other's challenge, and at such moments both men alike drew back with repugnance from the conflict. Not on that sacred battle-ground would they fight for intellectual suprema- cy. And in actual intercourse they refused either to fight or be friends. Their meetings were naturally frequent, for Mr. Fletcher rarely passed the house without calling in, and two or three times a week he would be present at the dinner or tea table. They addressed one another only when not to do so would attract attention, and on other occasions their avoidance of a meeting was marked by precautions so elaborate that they sometimes drew the notice of others. Major Milward had, indeed, on one occasion been startled to observe both men turn back when in the act of approaching him from different points, and Sandy once deep- ly offended the dignity of the parson by suggesting with preternatural solemnity that they should resort to the concealment of a tree trunk while the storekeeper went by.

It has already been said that the religious revival which had given Mr. Fletcher such a hold on the attention of the district had lapsed consid- erably from its original fervour, and it may be added that the parson's enthusiasm in the making of converts had waned also. Man, be his pro- fession what it may, is incapable of sustaining two passions at a white- heat, and Mr. Fletcher, strong as were his convictions, was no exception to this rule. The movement had lapsed partly because its originator had allowed it to do so. It was probably true, as Mrs. Gird had once plainly told him, that not even an archangel could effect the permanent con- version of the county, but a good deal less than an archangel might have held its attention longer. Thus the meetings on the beach, at first held daily, had dwindled to two a week, and it was only on the Sunday after- noons, and not invariably then, that Eve was present to take part.

But while the one passion faded the other grew, finally assuming pro- portions alarming even to its victim. For who could say whether the vis- itation were of God or the devil? Were his thoughts turned overwhelmingly in the one direction in order that this brand might be snatched from the burning? Or—thought to be hurried over rapidly—was he not rather on the verge of a pit that should engulf his soul past hope?

It was while this self-conflict raged at its height that he came from the sunlight into the darkened room, and recognising his visitor, stood like a man turned to stone.

For he knew that he had reached the dividing of the ways, that the choice, whether for good or evil, was to be set before him, past his power to refuse. Not to all men, never twice to any man, is given that deliberate selection of his earthly fate, and a man may well pause, stricken into stillness by the supreme character of the issues that confront him. The accumulations of habit and heredity are responsible for the life-drift of the majority of mankind; only to one strong nature here and there does Destiny hand the keys of his future, thrusting upon him, will he nill he, the blood-guiltiness or honour of his days.

Mr. Wickener came forward, holding out his hand in friendly greeting. 'You have not forgotten me,' he asked,—' Wickener?'

'By no means,' Mr. Fletcher returned. 'But I am astonished to see you. Pray be seated. Or, rather, come into my study; it is a little more—cheerful there.'

In the study the diffused daylight came in unchecked, and the two men looked steadily at one another before they sat down.

'It is a long cry from Kensington to River-mouth,' Mr. Wickener said lightly, 'and you are naturally surprised to see me dropping in like this; but life is full of similar coincidences.'

'Is this a coincidence?' Mr. Fletcher asked doubtfully.

'So far as concerns you, yes. It is only a day or two ago that I dropped on the idea that you were—yourself, so to speak, and I came over at once.'

Mr. Fletcher bowed, but said nothing.

There was a little electrically charged silence; then Wickener brushed away the papers on the table before him and leant forward.

'It is no coincidence in Hernshaw's case, however,'

Mr. Fletcher lifted a paper-knife, looked absently at the handle, and laid it down again. His lips moved, then closed in a sharp line; but he did not look up, nor did he speak.

'A restful spot this,' the other said, leaning back with a weary smile. 'It is a pity that human passions must come to disturb its serenity. By the way, you agree with me on the necessity?'

'Pardon me—'

'Now, Fletcher, I speak to you as a man. I have not travelled twelve thousand miles to obtain the advice of a priest. You were saying—'

The clergyman shrugged his shoulders and returned to the examination of the paper-knife.

'And I understand that Wairangi is a spot even more restful. An oasis in this brutal world, where one might well hope that the past should die and be forgotten.'

'You have seen Hernshaw?'

'I have. We exchanged recognitions on the road. It struck me he was looking well—improved. No doubt the climate is admirable. There is a marked increase in robustness about yourself.'

Mr. Fletcher made an impatient movement with his hand. 'Come to the point,' he said. 'I presume you are not here to congratulate us on our improved appearance; and my time is not absolutely valueless.'

'This *is* the point. You know the affair between Hernshaw and myself. As I have already mentioned, I have not travelled twelve thousand miles for nothing. The scenery of this remote spot is magnificent, but I am not here to admire it; the people are hospitable, but I am not here to take advantage of them; I have come, vulgarly speaking, for vengeance.'

'What do you propose to do?'

'Now you come to the point indeed. It is on that very question that I desire to consult you.'

'Me! By what right do you propose to consult me?'

'By the right that you dare not stand by and see the woman you love wedded to a scoundrel.'

'No doubt your information as to my sentiments has been carefully verified,' Mr. Fletcher said drily.

'Do you deny its correctness?' Wickener retorted, and the clergyman was silent.

'We have advanced thus far then,' Wickener went on, returning to his previous placidity of manner. 'It remains now to discuss the affair in detail. I have gathered that the young lady in this case is good-looking and an heiress—circumstances likely to appeal to a man of Hernshaw's stamp—and he is consequently deeply enamoured. Also I am informed that the prospects of a successful termination to his suit are hopeful, and altogether the moment appears to be propitious for the striking of a decisive blow. As to whose shall be the actual hand that cuts him down I am indifferent, and if it will advantage you in any way to be the instrument of vengeance, so be it; the hand shall be yours.'

'Wickener, how dare you!'

'I dare,' said Mr. Wickener calmly, 'for two reasons. In the interests of justice—one; in the interests of a fair and innocent lady—two. Who so fitted as the servant of God to administer the one; who more suited than the lover to safeguard the other?'

'No, no, Wickener! Never! What assurance have I that this man has done you a wrong—what assurance have *you?*'

'The confession of the woman who was once my wife. This is an exacting world, but a man needs no more than that. He could do, indeed, with less. There was my two years' absence in China; there was the confidence I reposed in him: these provided the opportunities. As for the guilt, the evidence was plain, damnably plain; then the man makes a bolt for the Antipodes, the woman confesses.'

'All this might be capable of explanation. Wickener, if I had reason to think you were wrong; if I had reason to believe this man innocent of the thing you lay at his door—what then?'

'I should say that your reason misled you,' Mr. Wickener replied, smiling. 'Come, my dear fellow, we are wasting time. Be sure I did not start on an errand of this kind without convincing proofs of his guilt. If you can blot out the past, you can make him innocent; short of that, he stands as vile a thing as God ever made and the devil guided. Even as it is, action may be too late. The girl may marry him in spite of all. For love women do desperate things no less than men. But now, at this instant, the game is in our hands. The man for some reason has hesitated—still hesitates, but in a few hours it may be too late or vastly more difficult. Now is the hour.'

Mr. Fletcher half rose to his feet, then settled himself again in his chair. His face was set in hard, untranslatable lines, as under the control of a fierce effort of will. His eyes were dark and sombre, and in their depths glowed momentarily the lightning flashes of encountering emotions, the spirits of good and evil at war for his soul.

For a long while neither man moved: a complete stillness held the little room. The slumberous drone of the bar, dull, unceasing, remote, seemed but to accentuate the silence: to throw it forward, to give to it a mystic and imperishable entity as of another Presence. Wickener watched his companion with glittering eyes, and slowly at last, and as it seemed fiercely, the other turned and looked at him.

'What do you propose?' the minister asked hoarsely.

Wickener moistened his lips and drew forward to the table. 'Go to her and tell her the story as you know it. From you it will meet with implicit credence, while from myself it might encounter doubt and mis-belief. There is the complete proposal.'

'Very well, I will do it.'

Mr. Wickener leant back and looked thoughtfully at his companion. 'It is the simplest way,' he said. 'The task is not one that a man would covet—to destroy faith in a fellow-creature, to shatter the roseate bubble of dawning love—but I do not delegate the task for that reason, but solely that the work may be immediate and complete. I thank you for your compliance, but as I have said, a minister of God is the most fit-ting—'

Mr. Fletcher raised his hand with a fierce imperativeness. 'I have stated my willingness to comply with your wishes,' he said sternly; 'we will not discuss the reasons that have actuated me.'

Mr. Wickener bowed. 'Then,' he said, rising, 'I need no longer occupy your valuable time.'

Mr. Fletcher rose absently with deeply introspective eyes.

'I take it you will not delay?' his visitor said, pausing in the doorway.

The minister looked at him without understanding, then, conscious-ness returning, he turned away. 'No, I shall not delay,' he said.

Out on the dazzling beach, Mr. Wickener came to a standstill and gazed about him somewhat wearily. Pine and Mallow were gone, but there was a large group of people opposite the hotel, and others were to be seen hastening towards it from the various houses. An air of ex-citement prevailed and bursts of laughter and cheering issued from the crowd. Speculating on the reason for this abrupt transformation in the sleepy little township, Mr. Wickener was moving forward to make inquiries, when he was startled by a loud clash of cymbals close behind him, and the Maori band, bare-footed and in rags, their eyes rolling, marched past to the stirring strain of'The Soldiers of the Queen.'

Great news had come to hand. A New Zealand contingent, after heroic forced marches, had seized Pretoria. The British army, with the baggage, was believed to be somewhere in the immediate neighbourhood.

CHAPTER XXII

STRIKING THE BLOW

THE boys on the station were getting the big shed ready for a dance, for it was Christmas Eve. The wool, gum, and lumber had been shifted out the day before, and buckets of hot lime, boiled with chopped hide, brushed on the roof and walls. The shed had a solid floor of narrow planks, well laid on heavy blocks, and was spacious enough to accommodate the largest band of dancers likely to be drawn together in the district. The whitening and scrubbing being over, a stable-lad was busy suspending large kerosene lamps from the rafters, while another young man, under the direction of Eve, was engaged in looping up garlands of 'waiwaikoko' or owl's-foot moss, together with branches of Christmas tree, aflame with their blood-red flowers. An air of mirth prevailed in the building; jests and laughter passed from lip to lip, and echoed from the walls of the hollow shell. Geoffrey stood by Eve, now holding her in conversation, now encouraging the man on the ladder to renewed efforts.

'It's all very fine, Mr. Hernshaw,' said the latter at last; 'but when you've got to prop the stuff up with your head and hammer it in with your teeth, you can't get an artistic effect every time.'

'You're doing first-rate,' replied Geoffrey. 'That's magnificent if you can manage to keep it like that—don't spare the nails.' Then he resumed his low-toned conversation with Eve.

A large heap of greenery was piled in the centre of the room, and a number of well-dressed Maori girls were rapidly twisting it into garlands. The floor had been powdered with ground rice and was already becoming slippery from the constant trampling of the workers as they moved to and fro. Also, Charlie Welch and Jack Wilson, the best dancers of the station, locked in each other's arms, were waltzing slowly and elegantly round the building, and had being doing so without intermission for the last twenty minutes. When they passed the girls they addressed one another languishingly in ladylike tones. Occasionally one of them would back his companion solemnly down the room and pound him heavily against the wall; then, with a fresh grip, they would circle gracefully and largely for a further five minutes.

'Look at those two,' said Eve, her eyes twinkling.

Geoffrey watched the couple benevolently for a few moments, then he turned to the girl, the blood quickening in his veins:

'The first waltz and the last, and how many in between?'

'I shall have to dance with every one so far as I am able; and I have other duties to perform. All you have to do is look about for pretty partners.'

'I can be happy only with one.'

The dancers circled slowly by. Miss Welch was understood to say that her 'Ma' was wondering at her and that she really must stop.

Eve gave a little sunny laugh at their absurdities, and the gentlemen, encouraged by the sound, stepped out and waltzed blindly into Major Milward, who, coming in at the door, saved his cigar from destruction only by a characteristic alertness.

The young men drew back in horror, but the Major never turned a hair. 'Ha!' he said, 'busy? Mr. Hernshaw, can you spare a few moments?'

'Certainly,' said Geoffrey, and at once accompanied his employer to the office.

The two young men looked reproachfully at one another, to an accompaniment of tittering from the girls.

'Why couldn't you look where you were going?' Miss Welch inquired in deep masculine tones.

'Ah, well!' said Jack Wilson, recovering himself, 'the boss took it in good part, so it's all right. We'll have to get those sheep in; they want two up at the house. I'll give you a race to the stables.'

At the stable they provided themselves with horses, and opening the yard gate, took the dry, slippery hills at a rush, the dogs scouring ahead of them. The speed and dash of their horsemanship recalled to their minds the thoughts which at that time engrossed the youth of New Zealand, and they began speaking of the latest reported exploit of their countrymen in South Africa.

'Our chaps are doing great things over there,' Charlie Welch began.

'They are that. I reckon old Kruger's feeling pretty sick now. You mark my word, the boys 'll nab him sure as eggs.'

'Shouldn't wonder. That Captain Milward's a holy terror. You can't beat the New Zealanders; they're just on top the whole time. The Boers can't shake 'em off.'

'And they're good men too, the Boers,' Jack reflected. 'If our boys can beat them they can lick anything.'

Mr. Welch signified his assent. 'What beats me,' he said, 'is the cheek of our chaps. They don't take more account of a Boer than they would of a bullock. The way that they seized this Pretoria fair lays me over. Here was the place fair bristling with guns, a reg'lar Gibraltar, so they say, and Boers inside thick as fleas in a bush whare. Then our chaps come along. "Surrender!" says they. "Surrender be damned!" says Kruger; " who are you?" " First New Zealand Mounteds," says our boys, grinning a bit. Then Kruger turns to Steyn, De Wet, and them. " It's all up, chaps," he says. " Get along out of the back; these men have got to come in." And in they did, right enough.'

'They're a rare lot,' Mr. Wilson agreed enthusiastically. 'The British army wouldn't be much without *them.*'

'You bet it wouldn't. Not but what it must be a bit encouraging to know that there's a couple of hundred thousand men close behind you, even though they may know more about piano tunes than straight shooting,' Mr. Welch allowed magnanimously.

Geoffrey was a little surprised at Major Mil-ward's request, because of late that gentleman had shown a tendency to avoid private inter-course with him. His daily visits to the store were hurried, and, whether by accident or design, it usually happened that Sandy was present at the time. This change in manner had followed on the return of the ledger, accompanied by a list of the outstanding debts, and the persons from whom they were due. Major Milward had glanced through the list at the time, paused sharply, and closing the book gone away without remark. He had not since alluded to the subject and, indeed, manifested some uneasiness when the conversation seemed to trend in that direction. Now, however, he had the paper in his hand, and as he seated himself at the desk, he passed it to Geoffrey with instructions to apply for payment of the various amounts.

'I see you have struck out some accounts,' Geoffrey said, running his eye down the list.

The Major was reading the correspondence before him and did not immediately reply. 'Eh? Yes, that is so. There are one or two that it would be useless to apply for, and others that should not have been included—"Trust that in consideration of this payment you will_____"'

'There is one here, sir,' Geoffrey said quietly, 'which can hardly be included in the former category.'

'Then no doubt it belongs to the latter, my boy —to the latter. Yes.'

'Will you allow me to discuss that point, sir?'

'No, I will not,' said the Major sharply. 'Kindly comply with my instructions.'

Geoffrey was silent, and the Major, frowning portentously, completed the examination of the letters. 'H'm! Nothing here.' He rose to his feet, glanced at the young man, whose eyes were still intent on the paper, and walking to the window gazed out along the river.

There was nothing to see beyond the blue water and a strip of sandy beach, with a solitary black-coated horseman advancing along it, and after a moment spent in identifying the figure, the Major turned back to the room.

'Well,' he said irritably but not unkindly, 'I suppose you are entitled to have your say if you must.'

'I was made aware of the facts by an accident and with no intention of prying into what does not concern me,' Geoffrey began.

'Exactly—it does not concern you.'

'I must think that a father's debts are the concern of his son.'

'This was no debt; it was a gift.'

'As it happened. Originally, I think, the ledger proves otherwise.'

'You are persistent, Mr. Hernshaw,' the Major said somewhat stiffly.

'Not impertinently so, I hope, sir. No one could be more fully conscious of your generosity than I am, but I would ask you to allow me to remove this blot from my father's good name.'

Major Milward shrugged his shoulders and paced up and down the little office, evidently a prey to strong feelings. His was a fine, deep-chested figure for all his great age, and Geoffrey, watching him with kindly eyes, did not wonder at the love and honour in which the county held him.

'There never was a woman for whom I had a greater respect than Mrs. Hernshaw,' the Major said abruptly at last, and in his tones there was the ring of something greater unsaid. 'Robert, I think, would understand the reluctance I feel in reopening that page of the account book after all these years. But you have put your case so forcibly that I do not well see how I can dispute your right to do as you please.' The Major paused and looked frowningly out of the window. 'And,' he resumed briskly at last, 'there is another matter we had better clear up while we are about it. I have been in correspondence with your uncle for some time past—since before you came here, in fact; and he has finally made me a proposal I am half disposed to consider.'

Geoffrey, suddenly enlightened as to the origin and intention of many chance remarks dropped by his employer during the past few months, which had hitherto puzzled him not a little, looked with interest at Major Milward as he returned and seated himself at the table.

'Your uncle, in the first place, asked me to acquaint him with your movements and assist you in any way I might find possible so long as you were determined to stay in the country. His general idea was that I should take an interest in you, and I did so gladly. I was able to assure him that life was supportable even here, and that a man might do worse, from an educational point of view, than pass a few years in a British colony. Finding that you had no desire to return home, I suggested that he should make an effort to establish you here in such a manner as would give you a chance of earning a good income, and among other more or less feasible propositions, he has proposed to buy an interest for you in Wairangi.' The Major paused and smiled drily. 'Now, Wairangi's not exactly short of capital,' he resumed; 'there may be a matter of a hundred pounds or so that I can't squeeze into it any way I try, but I've been thinking the thing over, and yes, there are points about it I rather like.'

Geoffrey's thoughts leapt quickly ahead, and his heart beat more rapidly.

'It's getting fully time,' the Major went on, 'that I stepped aside and let the next generation have a try, and that being admitted, the only point to consider is the terms on which the next generation are to come in. All my sons, except Sandy, are amply provided for elsewhere, and to him the homestead will fall naturally, and with the homestead goes the business as a matter of course. It has grown into a good business and will go on growing, and I have always found it various enough to be interesting. It could employ all the activities of two masters, and so my idea, in the rough, is that Mr. Hernshaw should buy you a half share, and that you and Sandy should run the business in common.'

'It would cost a good deal of money, I suppose? 'Geoffrey said.

'It would cost money, but the money's worth would be there. The goodwill would be only trifling, because the business depends mainly on the brains and determination that are put into it, and those you would have to provide yourselves. The secret in business is to let no man pass you, and to achieve that you must keep moving. But, yes, it means money—money in timber, money in sheep, money in gum, and money ready to go in if required; but I gather your uncle is fully aware of what is needed and is prepared to find it. I have mentioned the matter to Sandy and he raises no obstacles; now the question is, How does it strike you?'

'It is very good of you, Major Milward, to consider it.'

'Not at all. This—if it is anything—is a business deal, and in that light you have to look at it. I may be more kindly disposed towards you than to those who have gone before you, and it's not every man, certainly, to whom I would make such an offer, but I propose to sell at full value and if possible a trifle over.'

Geoffrey felt a little foolish.

'Well,' said the Major, rising,'there is no hurry. Turn the thing over, and let me know when your mind is made up. Thrash it out with Sandy, if you like, or take the books and go into it for yourself. Draw out a balance sheet, and see what the profit has been under the present management for the last four or five years—that will give you an idea and me too. You might have to thank me for advice now and again, but for the rest, it would be, as I say, a business deal, even though your uncle were indisposed to find the whole amount and I had to lend you a part of it myself.'

The Major turned suddenly at the sound of a step in the store beyond, and Eve stood in the door way. Her face was cold and white, with but a spot of colour in either cheek; her eyes shone with an unnatural brilliance. She looked only at her father, though her attitude indicated subtly a knowledge of the other man's presence. Geoffrey, watching her in startled silence, was conscious of a chill of apprehension at his heart.

'Father, Mr. Fletcher is waiting in the house to see you.'

'Fletcher! Tut, tut! I thought the boys had set fire to the shed with their pranks'; and vastly relieved, Major Milward accompanied his daughter to the beach.

Geoffrey, every vestige of interest in the late conversation struck from his mind, followed them to the doorway. Major Milward had his arm round the girl's waist, and was looking at her smilingly. Suddenly he loosed his hold and they both came to a standstill. There was a sharp exclamation from the man, a low-toned reply from the girl; a moment of silence and they resumed their way to the house, Major Milward talking eagerly, the girl moving forward with downcast face. They passed through the gateway and disappeared.

CHAPTER XXIII

THE NIGHT OF THE DANCE

HIS mind in a whirl, the young man turned back into the office and closed the door. The instinct of disaster was upon him, though he would have found it difficult to define its exact origin. Less than half an hour ago he had seemed to read for the first time surrender in the girl's eyes. Her voice had held a lingering tenderness. She had shown him that she understood the uncompleted speech, the questioning glance. Her eyes had fallen in embarrassment; once they had dwelt on his for seconds, wherein his blood was tuned to music. There was a sweet homeliness in her manner, that self-revelation which is only for our nearest and dearest. And surely the thought of the coming night was in her mind as in his. The dances they were to have together; the talks, punctuated with tenser silences; the question he was to ask her. Then the dreamy delirium that followed her consent, for consent she would; in the intimacy of the morning he had read his answer in her eyes—the first love-kiss down on the sands, or in the scented garden; the times their eyes would meet thereafter, their hands go out to one another in passing. Heaven! Was it not to be after all? What had happened? He rose to his feet in keen nervous distress and walked aimlessly about the room. She had never once looked at him. There had been something deadly in her manner. Why? He heard his name called from the other side of the beach, and made his way back to the shed. The man at the decorations had finished the work of suspending garlands round the walls, and wanted to know what next.

'Where is Miss Milward?' Geoffrey asked.

'Went away with Mr. Fletcher somewhere. What price some stuff round the tie beams?'

'Very well; please yourself. Did she say how soon she would be back?'

'And I was thinking of putting pohutukawa[1] along the ridge pole,' continued the young man, intent on his work. 'It ought to look pretty well in the lamplight. Eh? No, she didn't say.'

'Very well; keep it away from the lamps. But Miss Milward will be

---

[1] The Christmas tree.

back directly, no doubt.'

The decorator seized his ladder, and rousing the stable-boy to fresh activity resumed work.

Geoffrey stood idly by, his face heavy with thought. Occasionally the man on the ladder shouted to him, desiring an opinion as to the effect he was creating and, receiving mechanical replies. There is a morbid activity of the senses attends a troubled mind. Geoffrey was unpleasantly conscious of the heavy, sickly odour of green leaves, the acrid smell that dwells in the dense bush, where the light is dim and a deathly stillness prevails. He turned to the doorway and looked absently along the beach. A horseman was receding in the direction of Rivermouth, a black spot in the golden blaze. What had happened? Suddenly the white gate at the end of the avenue opened and Eve appeared. She came forward a few yards, her eyes on the ground, her step slow and listless. Presently she looked up and espied him. For a moment she seemed to stand irresolute, then, turning abruptly, went back the way she had come. The avoidance was too pointed to allow of any possibility of mistake. His dreams of happiness for that day were dispelled as completely as if they had never existed. He crossed the beach to the store, his mind rent by anger, disgust, and despair. Anger for the man who had wrought this evil; disgust with himself that he had not long since put it out of any man's power to harm him; despair at the unforeseen results. On the table, in a pencil of sunlight, lay the list of debtors, an easy prey to the hand of a wrathful man. Geoffrey took up his pen, and setting his mouth grimly, began to write. The first demands were short and business-like, and such as none but sensitive debtors could object to, but as the list decreased and Geoffrey warmed to his work, the requests for payment took on an abrupt savage-ness calculated to raise blisters, and only stopping short of direct insult by an ingenious and narrow margin. The gong sounded for lunch disregarded, and when ten minutes later a native girl came to look for the storekeeper, he sent her back with the information that he was busy and had already lunched.

In the afternoon Sandy came in and sat down on the other side of the table. Geoffrey looked up, frowned, and went on with his work. Presently Sandy lifted one of the sheets, read it through, read it again, coughed drily, and started on another. His interest appeared to deepen as he read, and he went steadily through the remainder, his eyes gradually widening. There was, in fact, a variety in the compositions, which spoke of literary talent of a high order.

'I say,' he said at last, surprised out of his silence, 'Hogg will never stand this.'

'Let him pay up, then, damn him! 'was the savage retort. 'He's been owing the money long enough.'

Now Sandy had never on any previous occasion heard the storekeeper swear, and recognising that something had gone wrong, he refrained from pressing the point. What Hogg thought was, after all, a matter of indifference to him.

'Has the boss said anything about our going into partnership?' he asked presently.

'He has; but I doubt if it will come to anything.'

'You are not in a particularly amiable mood this afternoon,' Sandy observed, offended.

'I'm not, old chap,' Geoffrey said, raising a pair of savage but curiously friendly eyes; 'and if you don't mind, you might let me work it off a bit— alone.'

Sandy rose with alacrity and went off with the intention of making inquiries.

Geoffrey locked the door after him. The desire of the wounded creature to be alone is as old as life itself. In the course of half an hour the last demand was finished and sealed; it was a triumph of invective in polite English, and as the young man read it through it seemed to do him good. One task remained to be performed. Geoffrey looked again at the list, and jotted down the amount of his father's account, then he got out his cheque-book from a private drawer. He had received official information from his bankers that they were prepared to honour his cheque for £1000, and for the first time he intended to take advantage of the information. For a moment he sat irresolute, gnawing the end of his pen, half inclined to include interest on the loan; but even in his then perverted state of mind the act appeared little short of an insult, and he refrained. On a separate sheet of paper he wrote the words: 'With Geoffrey and Robert Hernshaw's gratitude and thanks,' and folding it away with the cheque, he addressed the envelope to Major Milward and slipped it into his pocket. That also helped to rehabilitate him, and he unlocked the door and stepped out on to the beach.

The sun had set, and from the high mystery of the central heavens night was rushing down as with the flash and shadow of enfolding wings. The light of remote orbs broke here and there through the shimmering obscurity, and over the sand-hills hung the evening star, ruddy and large as an orange. The peaceful homestead, in its setting of lawns and groves, shone out vivid and clean cut as a cameo in the last white light. Then, as he gazed, the sharp lines trembled and faded into obscurity, there was a darkling as of a great shadow in the side-seen sky, the river heaped itself and breathed lingeringly on the sands, and with the whisper of the landward breeze from the ocean came the deep note of the bar, full of a mysterious threatening. Then the darkness.

Geoffrey sat down on a stranded log and breathed in the cool night air. From the shed across the beach poured a sudden path of light, and through the wide-open doorways he could see the hands sweeping out the last of the debris. This was followed by a fresh powdering with rice; then the party trooped out and went away together in the direction of the men's quarters.

The dinner-gong had sounded some time since, and presently a shadow flitted down the beach, tried the store door, and flitted back again. It was not the woman for whom his soul thirsted. He wanted Eve for five minutes—for one, that he might tell her this thing was a black and hideous lie. For though he asked himself what had happened, he knew without the asking, and he knew that he had brought it on himself. Curses on the sense of delicacy that had held him silent when he had the opportunity to speak. He might have known that that man's presence boded him no good; that the first blow would count for all. But he would see Eve that night; whatever obstacle intervened, he would see her and speak with her.

Full of this resolution he rose and made his way up to the house. Through the uncurtained windows he could see the party assembled at the dinner-table. There were many guests—girls and young and old men—but Mr. Fletcher was not among them. Eve sat facing him, and Geoffrey, who knew her only as the simple young mistress of Wairangi, stood still, fascinated, in a sense appalled, at her magnificent beauty. She wore a ball-dress of cream silk, which had only once previously seen the light—at Government House, Auckland. Diamonds gleamed in her hair and at her throat. Her bare arms and neck had the delicacy and grace and roundness of a young child's. Her face was dazzling, daring in its animation, and her cheeks glowed with the roses of youth and health. He watched her with a sinking heart. Could she be so gay and condemn him without a word? Yet if it were so, he had no right to com-

185

plain. If they were lovers it was in thought only, and for that his mad scruples were responsible. Twice as he watched he saw her eyes turn suddenly to the opening door, and then by the lover's instinct he knew that if condemned he was not forgotten. She was expecting his advent, and though it might be with dread, that somehow was a consolation. He reached his room without encountering any one, and proceeded to dress for the dance. Dress suits were not *de rigueur,* but there was one in his trunk and he put it on. He had common-sense enough to perceive that it might advantage him to look his best.

The first dance was over when, an hour later, he entered the building, and the musicians were already beginning to tune their instruments for the first waltz. He made his way through the crowd at the door and up the room, where the couples were already beginning to arrange themselves, but saw nothing of Eve, until suddenly he came upon her, face to face. She was on the arm of a young man whom he recognised as Raymond, the ex-storekeeper, and they were evidently on the point of joining the dance.

'Hullo, Hernshaw!' said Raymond civilly. 'Hurry up and get a partner.'

But Eve looked straight before her and said nothing.

Geoffrey muttered some reply and passed on down the hall out on to the beach. Rage and jealousy and, worst of all, self-contempt tore at his heart-strings. She did this with her eyes open; such refinement of cruelty was in the heart of a fair woman. Suddenly a girl hurried past him in the darkness, and urged by a sudden impulse, he followed her.

'Miss Mallow! One moment!'

Mabel turned and peered up at him. 'Oh, it's Mr. Hernshaw!' she said, laughing.

'Whither away so fast? I was looking for you. I want to ask you a question.'

'Well? 'the girl said encouragingly.

'Will you favour me with this dance?'

'How mysterious you are! But I'm engaged to somebody else.'

Geoffrey took her hand and drew it through his arm. 'It would be too old-fashioned to dance with *him* then,' he said. 'The correct thing is to engage yourself to one person and dance with another. Come along.'

Mabel went with him, nothing loath, and they were soon circling round the room with the rest. Once or twice they were in Eve's vicinity, but the latter quickly desisted; and when he next saw her she was sitting beside Mr. Fletcher, whose objection to dancing apparently did not preclude him attending the function as an eye-witness.

Mabel was enjoying the dance, and showed no disposition to release her partner, and presently an immense distaste possessed him. What an infernal idiot he was! Would the wretched musicians never stop? All the time he continued conversing with the girl, answering her chatter, whispering daring compliments into her ear, and watching with cold curiosity the play of emotion in her eyelids in response to perilous questions. He knew he was acting the part of a monster and a madman; but while his heart hung heavy in his breast, his brain seemed fired with a fatal exhilaration beyond his power to control.

The dance ended at last, and in response to his partner's suggestion he led her out into the open air. Fairy lamps were suspended amongst the shrubs in the garden, and the orange orchard glowed with a multiplicity of coloured lights.

'Oh, we must go up there!' Mabel said, enchanted, and Geoffrey led the way to a seat among the fragrant trees. The Pacific breeze had died away, and the night air breathed warm and languorous across the heated sands. It was a night for love, and the reflection struck bitterly to the heart of the man, stilling his brain to silence. Mabel rattled on, her words empty as the wind, her tones full of a subtle challenge, but the man replied only in monosyllables. What was he doing sitting by the side of this girl, for whom he cared nothing, when the one woman of the world was slipping from his grasp?

'Why are you so silent? What are you thinking about?'

'Of you,' he replied idly.

'Tell me,' she said coaxingly.

A man with a cigarette came quickly up the path and paused in front of them. 'This is our dance, I think?' he said.

Mabel rose hurriedly. 'You have not asked me for another,' she whispered.

'Then tell me which it is to be.'

'The last waltz before supper.'

Geoffrey bowed, and the girl disappeared down the path with her cavalier. He heard her low laugh in the distance. Hateful sound! And this was the night to which in the morning he had looked forward with such intensity of longing!

He rose after awhile and wandered down to the beach and on to the doorway of the shed. A group of smokers blocked the entrance; now and then he caught a glimpse of a mad whirl of figures within. Presently a hand closed on his arm and he was drawn back to the beach.

'Come and have a drink, old chap,' said Sandy; 'you look bored.'

Geoffrey hesitated, then, yielding to the pressure of his companion's arm, went with him up to the house.

Major Milward was in his element. All the old identities of the county, rich and poor alike, were present. Withered old men with rosy cheeks, whose eyes many a time had looked squarely into the face of death— men whose memories went back to the beginning of things when the authority of the Maori chieftain was a stronger law than the Queen's. Grizzled, tongue-tied giants who knew only the cult of bush and river, but knew that with the intimacy of an instinct. Little wizened sailor men, with huge broad-chested sons already well past middle age, whalers or deserted men-o-war's-men, it may be, whose talk was of the *Eliza Jane* or the *Rose* of Bristol and of stirring adventures in low latitudes, even yet only partially explored. Frail, stooping veterans, talking familiarly of university boat-races away back in the 'forties, and cackling in high-pitched voices over jokes that had been dead and buried for a couple of generations. There was the burly form of John Manders, descended from the great missionary family, and owning twenty thousand acres of the richest land in the North country. There was Captain Russell, that prince of half-castes, dark, handsome, portly, held in honour by both races from the North Cape to the Bluff. There, again, his round old face wreathed in smiles, was little Tom Welch, the butt and boon companion of all ages, who had made and squandered at least three fortunes, and had not a vice in his composition, nor a regret.

'All the tribes,' Sandy said. 'God bless 'em!'

Major Milward, his blue eyes beaming, a spark of bright colour in his cheek, was pressing a liquid hospitality on his guests, passing from group to group, two or three hands on his shoulder at once to detain him. 'Was it '57 or '58?' 'I say, Milward, you remember that night in? Here's Milward, he will tell you. It was a small convoy; they could have cut us up to a man, for the ambush was well planned. But it happened the Reverend John was riding along there a mile or so ahead, and the chief—Honi it was—came out to speak to him. " An ambush! " said Manders, when he understood what they were about; " but there is only a handful of them, and it's murder, not war. The Maori is too brave a man to commit murder." Honi scratched his ear. " That not the pakeha way? " he asked. "That the good war, I think." But Manders assured him differently, and the end of it was that the Maoris came out and let the convoy through. And the commanding officer got his supplies, and in a few days he had finished the job. But the parson was wrong and Honi was right for all that—the ambush was good war.'

'What are you boys doing here?' the Major asked, returning to the table where the liquors were set out. 'Drink up, and come back in thirty years' time when you are properly seasoned.'

'Ay, it's a tough crowd this,' said Tom Welch, nodding his cheerful old face. 'We could tell 'em things that would make their hair curl, eh, Major? Don't seem to know this young 'un,' he added, looking at Geoffrey.

'You remember the Hernshaws of Rukawahia, Tom? This is the eldest son.'

'Ay, ay, I mind them. He favours the father more than the mother. Yon was a man that couldn't catch on to the life. Some can't, while others take to it as natural as a duck to the water. Uncommon clever man yon, but no grip in him for a place like this. Ay, ay, and this is the son. Lay hold with two hands, lad, and you'll do all right.'

Geoffrey smiled amiably, but the words set him thinking, and his thoughts were hardly pleasant. He lifted a whisky bottle and began to pour cautiously just as some one, pressing from behind, jerked his arm, with the result that the glass was half filled.

Sandy laughed and passed him the water-jug. 'Drink it up, he said; 'it will do you good.'

Geoffrey complied with a dull feeling that he had lost his will-power and was open to the suggestion of the first man who chose to direct him. He ran his eye observantly over the crowd around him, and was struck by a curious resemblance in the diverse faces, a resemblance which was not of feature or complexion but of type. These were the heads and bodies of strong and resolute men— men who laid hold with two hands, men whose deep chests spoke of mighty organs and the power to achieve great desires by the force of great vitalities.

The liquor sent its exhilaration through his veins with the speed of a lightning flash. Here, then, was the keynote to success. To demand forcibly, to take strongly with both hands, to hold resolutely in the face of all obstacles. Woe to the man who, in this new land, struggling with the giant forces of nature, should stand to count the cost or ask himself what he desired. Woe to him to whom a succession of obstacles brought not fresh lust of battle but the apathy of despair. And the stronger course was after all the simpler. To move forward undeviat-ingly to the desired end, suffering no hindrance from without or within. And if with no success, at least with the consciousness of a good fight well fought, and without that curse of self-reproach which for ever dogs the footsteps of the weak.

The last waltz before supper was about to begin as Geoffrey again entered the dancing-room. Through the crowd of moving figures he caught sight of Eve, still sitting with Mr. Fletcher, who was regarding her with smiling eyes. An impulse came upon him to put his fate clearly to the touch, here under the public gaze. He would ask her to dance, he would force her to speak to him, to give him a direct yes or no. Full of this idea, he was making his way slowly through the crowd when he felt the light touch of a hand on his arm, and Mabel Mallow stood beside him.

'How late you are! 'she said reproachfully. 'Did you think I would follow the fashion when it tells against yourself?'

'If I had found you in the arms of another it would be no more than I deserve,' he returned, inwardly fuming at the dilatoriness of the other men.

But Mabel, to do her justice, had refused several eligible partners, and she was bent on exacting payment for her abnegation.

'Why are you not dancing?' she asked as he swept with her down the room.

'How have I merited this unkindness?'

'Well, now, of course, but you have not been here since the first waltz. Was it so dreadful?'

'It was divine. Your eyes are as observant as they are beautiful.'

'You mustn't say things like that. Why don't you dance with Miss Milward?'

'Would you prefer to sit down?'

Mabel raised her glorious brown eyes and looked at him steadily.

'I believe you two have quarrelled,' she said.

'You are as clever as you are lovely,' he replied, smiling.

'Then you have? What a pity! And at Christmas-time too. Why don't you kiss and be friends?'

'May I class myself among the number of your friends, dear lady?'

'You would not be so daring if you were in earnest,' Mabel replied composedly. 'But yes, you may, if you will go to her and say, "Forget and forgive."'

'You are a strange girl.'

'I know what it is to be as miserable as you two are now.'

'Is it so evident?'

Not to others, perhaps, but to me, yes. What do you say?'

'I say nothing now, not even that you are beautiful'

'No, because for the first time you are beginning to think so. Shall we stop?'

He led her from the room and in the wake of the couples who were moving up to the house. The supper-room was already crowded. Geoffrey attended to his partner's wants and stood by her in silence, his eyes scanning the room.

'Go away now,' Mabel whispered, 'and do as I have told you. There is time for happiness yet.'

He went obediently, and presently, finding the heat oppressive, passed out into the hall. The oil-lamp had burnt down, and the place was almost in darkness. He threw himself on a divan and listened to the clamour of voices in the room where the veterans were assembled. Presently Sandy came out, his face flushed but as solemn as ever, and sat down beside him.

'It's a fact the new generation can't live with the old,' he said; 'but I shall be astonished if some of the old boys don't have heads on them in the morning.'

'They do seem to be celebrating a little.'

'The water-jug's been dry in there for quite half an hour, but they haven't found it out yet, and they keep on pouring all the same. Come in and watch, it's dead funny.'

'Oh, it's all right here!'

The curtain at the end of the hall lifted, and a white figure came out into the dim light.

'Well, Evie?' said Sandy. 'How goes it? Come and sit down.'

But Geoffrey started to his feet and placed himself before her. 'Miss Milward—Eve,' he said in low passionate tones, 'will you not speak to me? What have I done to deserve this?'

The girl drew herself to her full height, her eyes flashing dangerously. 'Kindly let me pass!'

He stepped aside at once, his face whitening, and she moved on into the supper-room.

Sandy rose and laid his hand on the other's arm. 'I'm sorry, old chap,' he said, 'and I don't pretend to understand anything about it—but hang the girls anyway! Come and have a drink.'

Geoffrey looked at him dazedly.

'If you feel it like that, why did you let her go? I would not have interfered between you. And the curse of it is, she has engaged herself to Fletcher; they are to be married in March.'

'My God, no!'

'But it's a fact. I had it from the old man's lips, and he is no more pleased than I am. But, good heavens, if it's like that with you, what haVe you been doing? You have had the game in your own hands for months past. Look here! Well, come and have a whisky.'

But Geoffrey turned without speaking and went out through the merry crowd on the verandah down on to the beach.

And some hours later Eve sat white and trembling in the privacy of her own room, and asked herself despairingly what she had done.

'Do you neglect the torture of anxiety I must suffer until my wife's whereabouts are discovered?'

'No doubt you are feeling disappointed,' the Major returned cheerfully, as he struck the bell on his table; 'but none the less I am confident you will see the advisability of returning to Rivermouth. At present I am disposed to think a reconcilement between husband and wife is the best solution to this disgraceful affair, but a very little might cause me to alter my opinion. Sandy, will you see that Mr. Fletcher has a horse?'

When Sandy returned from his errand he found his father pacing the room in agitation.

'Jack Wilson knows something about it, father,' he said. 'He is outside. Shall I tell him to come in?'

Major Milward gave his assent, and listened in silence while the shepherd stumbled through his story. 'Very well,' he said, as the youth concluded, 'you may go. See that Mr. Wilson is paid off tonight,' he added, turning to his son.

Sandy winked cautiously at the lad as he closed the door upon him, but he was too wise to seek to change his father's purpose just then.

'It is almost certain she has gone to the Girds,' he said; 'but the Maoris say the fire has crossed the road beyond M'Gregor's, and it is doubtful whether she could get through. Anyway, supposing the Girds have not been burnt out themselves, they could only be got at on foot by a bush track from behind.'

'Then she must be brought back,' said his father. 'Take the best horses and riders on the station and go and fetch her.' He paused suddenly, a deepening look of anxiety on his face. 'Where is Geoffrey Hernshaw?' he asked.

'Left last night for the settlement.' Sandy's eye, roaming uneasily, fell on the whip lying in the corner, and he picked it up and returned it to the rack.

Major Milward watched his actions with unseeing eyes. 'Sandy, on the table there you will find a torn letter; take it and read it.'

Sandy obeyed. When the two men looked at one another again the resemblance between them was pronounced.

'Whatever happens they must be kept apart.'

There was no consent in the son's face.

Major Milward's brows contracted. 'Whatever happens,' he repeated slowly, 'they must not be allowed to meet.'

Sandy shook himself as though to be rid of some evil influence. 'So be it,' he said solemnly.

'Then go; bring her back; promise her anything; but do not return without her.'

Sandy turned with alacrity and hastened to the rear of the house. At the back-door he found Jack Wilson awaiting him, his face overspread with gloom.

'Cheer up, Wilson,' he said. 'Get in the horses quick and lively.'

'I've got them in already, Mr. Milward—Seabird and Hohoro and The Lance and Wardog.'

'Where are the boys?'

'Waiting in the stockyard.'

'Half a minute while I put on my spurs.'

Sandy darted into the harness-room, and a few moments later joined the others in the stockyard. In a twinkling the four men were in the saddles. The stable-boy threw open the gate, and with a clatter on the cobbles and a thud on the turf the horses swept forward on the chase— round the rough cattle-tracks on the hills, down with a plunge on to the hard sand of the beach, and away in a tireless gallop to the looming portals of the forest.

The sickly pallor of the sun's rays had thickened into an orange-coloured mist as they entered the bush. Mile after mile of the journey was traversed at a gallop, the gloom of the atmosphere deepening with the miles; but still, beyond the density of the air and the pungent scent in their nostrils, they came upon no sign of the great fire. Once they overtook a bullock team drawing a huge kauri log destined for some settler's homestead, and paused to make inquiries. The native drivers had seen no wahine[1] answering to Sandy's description, but they had come up by the coast road and the lady would probably be a long way ahead. At M'Gregor's store a party of native bush-fallers were at work extending and burning the clearing, the storekeeper watching them from the verandah, occasionally turning his eyes to look anxiously along the road or up into the brassy skies. He shouted out and pointed

---

[1] Woman.

as they drew near, and Sandy wheeled his horse to the verandah, the others reining in some distance ahead.

'You can't get through,' said M'Gregor; 'the mail man turned back an hour ago and has gone down to Jessup's landing.'

'How far along is it?'

'About four miles where it touches the road. The worst of it's in the dip before you rise to Girds' bush. The mail man crossed the bridge, but his horse wouldn't face the hell on the other side. The bridge 'll be gone by this. Were you wanting to make the settlement?'

Sandy nodded. 'Did the mail man see any one about? 'he asked.

'No; but the natives say that a young woman went through about twenty minutes before he did. They called out to warn her, but she took no notice. Some of them were saying it was Miss Milward,' M'Gregor added, laughing.

Sandy's mouth had hardened a little when he joined the others. 'Straight ahead, boys,' he said curtly, and again the whole party broke into a gallop.

Round the sharp bends of the winding road, up hill and down, clattering across culverts and bridges, with ever the brazen streak of the sky above, the yellow streak of the road beneath, and the dense green walls of the forest towering on either hand. And now the obscurity began to take on a tinge of grayness, thickening into a ghostly fog, through which horse and rider loomed gigantic and ill-defined. The sweating horses grew restive, eyeing the flying wall of greenery with suspicious eyes, their ears thrown back, shying for no perceptible reason from one side of the road to the other. Hitherto the atmosphere had had the transparency of stained glass, but as they approached the scene of the conflagration it became an opaque screen, ever withdrawing itself as the horses plunged forward. But at last it withdrew no farther. It began to move, to turn as on an axis, to roll forward and blot out bush and road and sky alike. The riders drew rein in the heart of the smoke cloud, with the deafening uproar of the burning forest in their ears. Then slowly forward again, the frightened horses rearing and snorting, turning savagely to bite at the urging spurs. And so to the brink of the gully, to a view of the great terror itself, to a seething pit of smoke and flame.

'Is the bridge there?' asked some one.

'No, nor the road.'

Sandy dismounted and handed the reins to Wilson. 'Take the horses back out of this,' he said, 'and run up some kind of shelter for the night. Where's the tucker?'

'Charlie Welch has it.'

'Hand it over to Wilson, Welch. Stay, you had better keep a snack or two in case we get bushed. That's it. Welch is coming with me, boys; he is the best bushman in the crowd, I think.'

Jack Wilson nodded, but he looked supremely disappointed. 'Are you going to try the bush, Mr. Milward?' he asked.

'Yes, it should be two miles to Gird's as the crow flies, but there won't be much flying about it to-night, if we get through at all before dark.'

'You might be able to take to the road a bit farther on.'

'We'll try that, and if all goes well come straight back; but if not, make yourselves as comfortable as you can. Let me see . . . matches . . . knife . . . tobacco. That a tomahawk, Charlie? Thoughtful boy. Well, which way?'

'Keep to the creek,' said Welch, assuming the lead with the confidence of the expert; 'it crosses the road again half a mile up.'

With a cheery good-bye the two plunged into the rolling smoke of the gully.

Then the long night of the waiters began. A night full of strange sounds, of spectral lights, of false alarms, of sleepy reconnoitrings, with the enemy ever drawing nearer, now almost imperceptibly, now with fierce irresistible bounds.

And once out of the darkness of the homeward trail there burst into the light of the camp fire the figure of a galloping horseman—man and horse coal-black and of gigantic stature. The watchers sprang to their feet with arresting cries, lost, as was the sound of the hoof-beats, in the fearful pandemonium of noises. Lost? Or had their passage indeed been soundless? What living man would ride thus recklessly into the jaws of hell?

'Did you recognise him?' the elder man asked, with a curious shake in his voice.

Jack Wilson shook his head.

'Mark Gird. There was not a man of his inches in the county, and he rode just so. Many a time before he was struck down I've seen him on his black horse, riding for home. Ay, on this very road; and I've seen the far-ahead look in his eyes same as I see it there to-night.'

'You're balmy, Stephen.'

'He was struck sudden,' continued Stephen, unheeding—' full of meat and strength, and he died hard. But I reckon he's a whole man to-night, and he ain't forgot the old trail and the hut in the bush.'

'Bound for home?' Wilson whispered, overawed by the other's conviction.

The old bushman seated himself and spat thoughtfully into the fire. 'It's a bad business,' he said, 'and there's worse ahead. You bet, we're not coming through this without a price. For years we've been going along that quiet that we've most forgot what sudden death is like, but the bush is out for its utu[1] now, and I wish to God the little lass was safe at home in her bed.'

'Drop it,' said Wilson fiercely, starting to his feet and kicking the fire into a blaze. 'I don't believe it was Mark Gird, nor in your utu either.'

'What should a shepherd know about the bush?' returned Stephen contemptuously. 'I'm talking about what I know. There's a spirit in these forests same as in a man. It ain't the new chum that comes slashing at the bush without knowledge and takin' risks that would make his flesh creep if he knew of them that pays the price. It's the man that has mastered the trade, or the man that never tried to learn it, and it's on such as them that the blow's goin' to fall now.'

In such conversation, broken by intervals of slumber, the darkness wore itself away, and in the gray of the dawn Wilson awoke to find some one standing over him. Of a sudden the whole restless, disjointed, uncanny night he had lived through seemed inspired with meaning.

'What is it, Mr. Milward?' he cried, starting to his feet.

'Get your horse and ride back to the station as quickly as you can. She never got through.'

---

[1] Properly 'uto,' an expiatory payment, vengeance.

CHAPTER XXXI

THE FIRE IN THE SETTLEMENT

Although Geoffrey Hernshaw had steeled himself to the point of enduring events with an impassive countenance, it is not improbable that he was glad of the plausible excuse to absent himself from the wedding which was to be found in the continually arriving reports of disaster from the settlement. The sympathetic captain of the steam-launch which carried subsidiary mail streams from a dozen points on the river had offered him transport to the creek, promising, moreover, to stand by for any settlers who having lost their homes and possessions desired to seek refuge in the county township.

Although it was after ten o'clock when the boat arrived at its destination, a gleam of gum torches on the little ramshackle wharf showed that their coming was not unexpected, and many were the blessings rained down on the head of the skipper who had not deserted them in their hour of need.

'Is that you, Geoffrey?' asked a shy, pleasant voice, as the young man ceased from assisting in the task of getting a large family and some miscellaneous bundles safely stowed on the deck of the little craft. The voice was so pleasant, and such a friendly turn was given to his Christian name, that Geoffrey's sore heart was touched even while he wondered.

'Why, of course, Lena! How stupid of me not to guess! Where's Robert? Good heavens! have you been burnt out too?'

'No, no; we're all safe. The fire went on and left us; but Robert hadn't had any sleep for ages, what with fighting the fire for ourselves and other people. He was just worn out, poor boy; so after tea I got him to take off his boots for three minutes, and he's been asleep ever since.'

'And what are you going to do here?'

'You have just done it for me. Those were my brothers and sisters you carried on to the boat, and that was my mother you took the bundles from.'

'Is that so? I thought there was something angelic in the faces of those youngsters, and this shows how a good action may be its own reward.'

The bustle on the wharf ceased presently; the last bundle, animate or inanimate, was put aboard. The captain stood stretching his legs by the gangway, chatting with the men-folk on their experiences, and regretting that he could not spare a few hours to run up and give them a hand. Snatches of their conversation floated to Geoffrey and Lena as they stood on the land end of the wharf, waiting the departure of the boat.

'Mark Gird hadn't been dead three hours. . . .' 'Well, anyway, it's a strange thing that all the years he lay dying there was not a serious . . .'—'Don't know how the idea got going, but the bushmen believed in it. . . .'—'One death since; yes, but that was fire. . .' —'Well, it may be nonsense, but the feeling comes over you at times and you can't get rid of it.'

'I should have mentioned your loss, Lena. It was terrible, but it was heroic. No man could meet a more honourable end than to die a great death in the cause of humanity.'

Lena put out her hand and pressed her brother-in-law's fingers, at once gratefully and restralningly. 'Please say no more, Geoffrey,' she said; 'God alone knows the secrets of that dreadful night'; and quick to grasp a hidden meaning in her words, Geoffrey was silent.

The little group stirred and parted. The captain stepped across the gangway, blew his whistle, and amid a chorus of good-byes the black hull slipped away into the darkness.

Lena shook her torch into brighter flame and turned towards the track.

'What a terrible thing life is!' she said, with a seriousness that contrasted strangely with her sweet face and few years; 'and yet every now and then you seem to see the finger of God intervening, as though to prevent it from being worse. Is it as He would have it? or has He also to wrestle with a Power nearly as great as Himself?'

'Men have thought so, Lena; they have founded their religions on that hypothesis. But come, this is only the night, and to-morrow the sun will shine again. Give me the torch. Did the fire get down here?'

'No; the wind was off the water. But all the lovely bush between the road and Bald Hill Do you remember?'

'Yes, indeed.'

'Ah! but you had only known it a few years. There is nothing left but the black trunks. Doesn't it seem sad? And I had known it all my life.'

'Where else did it go?'

'It began just beyond Mr. Beckwith's. You can hardly see where the house stood now. Then it spread to Flotter's, and they lost everything too. It missed Green's place, except the bush near the front; but it crossed the road there, and spread right along in front of us. You never saw such a sight; and if the wind hadn't been in our favour, and the house so far back from the road, it must have shrivelled up where it stood. The fence was alight in a dozen places at once, and at last we had simply to let it burn and run for our lives, the heat was so terrible. After that the fire seemed just to leap through the settlement. It crossed back to the river-side and burnt out the Finnertys and Robinsons. Mrs. Robinson saved herself and the Finnerty children in the cattle-tank, and now the men are going about the settlement with their arms round one another's neck, the best friends in the world. It made a clean sweep of everything right down to Gird's bush, and there for the moment it stopped.'

Lena stopped also, and pushing open the charred and twisted remnant of the picket gate, led her brother-in-law toward the house. At scattered points around fires gleamed, where fallen logs— long since buried in vegetation—were being slowly consumed. Under the close-drawn screen of the night monstrous smoke wreaths crawled, fading spectrally as they receded from the glowing arch of conflagration in the west. At intervals a clot of flame showed above the tree-tops, the sky lightening and darkening like a winking eye.

Leading the way softly into the house, Lena turned up the lamp and indicated a seat on the sofa. 'I will just go and have a peep at my boy,' she whispered, 'then we can tell one another all the news.'

When she returned she brought some sheets and hung them on a chair before the fire. 'He hasn't moved,' she said. 'He was just dying for a sleep. He has done wonders, and the settlers have said such nice things to me about him.'

'Robert is not one to spare himself,' Geoffrey said.

Lena busied herself in preparing food for her guest, then with house-wifely care she turned the sheets, and at last came and sat down beside him.

Geoffrey had watched her movements with contented eyes, and a re-laxing of the tense self-repression under which for months he had exist-ed. The grace and beauty of the young wife were delightful to witness; but it was her kindness, her thoughtful-ness for others, her complete self-unconsciousness which warmed his heart towards her. So, though in his acute distress of mind he had desire neither for food nor speech, he accepted both from his brother's wife with a pathetic gratitude.

'I thought it very likely you would come through to-day,' Lena said, as she took her seat, 'and so I tidied your room in readiness.'

'Yet I received Robert's note and knew that you at least were all right.'

'It was not on account of what was happening here that I expected you,' Lena said wistfully.

Geoffrey shrank as from the touching of a raw wound — even that tender sympathy was as yet unbearable. 'You were telling me about the Girds,' he said quickly.

'Mark Gird is dead—did you know? He died on Tuesday night. Dr. Webber was there from the township and told us on Wednesday morning. The fire was burning then, and whether any one went to see poor Mrs. Gird or not I don't know. And after that no one could get there by the track, because the fire was all round.'

'I thought you told me it stopped at Gird's bush?'

'Yes; but if you remember, their section only begins half-way down the track, and the strange thing is, that it stopped dead short there when there was nothing to prevent it going on.'

'They say that bush fires do behave in that unaccountable way at times, crossing apparently impossible gaps, and checking at nothing at all.'

'Well, everybody thinks this is particularly strange,' said Lena; 'and they are saying that the fire will not cross the boundary so long as Mr. Gird's body remains there.'

Geoffrey smiled at her earnestness. 'That is framing a theory to account for facts with a vengeance,' he said. 'And has no one been through to the house yet?'

'Oh yes! Robert and some others were there this morning. You can get through now quite easily. The body is to be brought out to-morrow evening. I am going there in the morning myself. Poor Mrs. Gird!' added Lena, her eyes brightening with unshed tears. 'It seems so cruel that she who was always ready to help others should in her own trouble have been left quite alone.'

'That appears to have been unavoidable, and I hardly think she would have had it otherwise could she have chosen. There are some people to whom it is difficult to offer an acceptable sympathy, and I doubt if I should have found a word to say to Mrs. Gird.'

'Well, I don't think the men said much. They took up some planks with them and made a coffin, and they decorated the outhouse with palm leaves and fern fronds and put a sprig of kowhai over the door, and left him alone. Mrs. Gird made them some tea, and asked after every one, and seemed quite cheerful, Robert said.'

Geoffrey was silent awhile. 'Where is the fire now?' he asked at length.

'Where isn't it?' returned Lena. 'It has gone right along the road and crossed at half a dozen places into the Big Bush. Then it is working back towards the upper settlement on this side, and unless it is checked somewhere they will have to fire the beautiful bush behind the school-house to save the building. Robert would have been there now if I hadn't persuaded him to take a few minutes' rest.' Lena looked smilingly at her brother-in-law.

'Happy Robert!' said he.

'Now it is your turn to tell me the news,' said Lena, lowering her eyes. 'We hear that Wairangi is so full that people are camping out on the beach.'

'That is so far true that the natives have a camp under the Christmas trees.'

'And Eve will be married to-morrow?'

'Yes.'

Lena stroked her hands nervously. Her old childish awe of her husband's brother was not quite extinct, but the worship of one man gives a woman confidence in dealing with others. 'We hoped it would never come off,' she said at last; 'we hoped you would prevent it.'

'Ah, Lena, it is not every woman who is kind as well as lovely!'

'Why didn't you marry her, Geoffrey?' his sister-in-law asked coaxingly.

'Did I have the opportunity?'

'Did you not? What was it came between you at the last?'

'Madness, false report, lying, pride, — all the deadly things that lie in wait for happiness.'

'Tell me.'

'Some day, perhaps.'

'Tell me now.'

He looked into the fair, sympathetic face and found it irresistible. And after the first effort, once the gates of reserve were fairly broken down, the task proved less difficult than he had anticipated. He told his story with a certain plainness and an absence of comment from his tones which was perhaps remarkable enough. Shades of anger and bitterness there may have been, but a quick intelligence is a stern disciplinarian, and from the taint of self-pity the tale was wholly free. For all emotion his voice betrayed he might have been relating the story of another man. Yet the bare facts were sufficiently unkind, and Lena's tender heart was moved to pity.

'What a cruel thing!' she exclaimed, gazing at him with tearful eyes. 'And oh, Geoffrey, the pity of it if nothing can be done to put it right!'

'Nothing can be done.'

'Do you think Mr. Fletcher really believed it was true, or did he only make use of it for his own purposes?'

'He had my assurance that it was false. Many months ago, shortly after the rumour first reached me, he gave me reason to think that he had heard the story and believed it. I wrote to him at once, requesting the thing should be put in plain words, and challenging an investigation of the facts. He never replied.'

Lena sat looking at the lamp, the expression of her face changing momentarily. Presently she gave a little shiver. 'I was once very unkind to Robert for a long while,' she said. 'I thought it would be best for him to give me up, but I made him miserable, and ah, how miserable I made myself! How my heart did ache! How hard and terrible the world seemed then! Do you think she may be suffering like that?'

'God forbid!' Geoffrey said fervently. 'But ask yourself, Lena,' he added a moment later, 'whether it is likely. You loved Robert, but I have no assurance that she ever cared for me. Could she have done this thing if she had? Look into your own heart and answer me.'

'Yes,' said Lena after a pause,' it is possible. In a moment of insane jealousy a woman could do that.'

'And stand to it?'

'She could be held to it.'

'Even supposing the thing had been true, why should she be jealous of the past?'

'Why should one be jealous of the future, of the present—why at all?'

'Yes, that was well said. After all, there is no justice in demanding that her feelings should be different from my own in the same circumstances.'

He was silent after that, and Lena, searching vainly through the maze for a loophole of escape, was silent also.

The following day the brothers were up before daylight. Early as they were, Lena had the fire burning and breakfast ready for them when they appeared; and after breakfast, as it was possible they might not find time to return in the middle of the day, she cut them some lunch with her own housewifely hands. More was to depend on this precaution than any of the three at that time imagined.

Through the long morning hours and until midway in the afternoon the fierce conflict raged round the upper settlement. Not only were the school-house and newly erected Wesleyan church in danger, but also the homes of a dozen settlers, who, ere the day was well advanced, found themselves surrounded by a zone of fire. The danger to most of them lay in the conflagration spreading through the dry grass, and more than half the available labour had to be devoted to thrashing out the insidious, all but invisible menace from this source. For the rest there was the herculean task of holding the monster in check in the bush itself. A track was selected cutting through the arm of bush which projected into the settlement, and from this point the undergrowth was fired and again thrashed out. No water was available had it been possible to use it, and the only weapons of the defenders were branches of young tea-tree continually renewed. The phenomenally dry season had withered the undergrowth to the point when it was only necessary to drop a lighted match to arouse a conflagration. A hundred times it seemed that the fires of their own making must break away from them and become their masters in place of their servants; but, scorched and suffocating, with labouring breasts and aching arms, the band stood heroically to its work, and in the end the victory was theirs. The mighty conflagration sweeping up towards them suffered a sudden check. For awhile it licked at the lofty foliage and sought to sweep over what it could no longer undermine, but in half an hour the danger had passed and the settlement was saved.

Geoffrey stood alone, hot and exhausted, hearing to right and left the triumphant cries of the settlers. Already with the cessation of toil the exhilaration of the last few hours was dying away. He heard advancing footsteps and moved onward through the fire-blackened trees in the direction of the road. He could condole with them in their despair, but in their triumph he desired no partnership. Soon their voices faded away and he was alone. He looked at his watch and noted that it was past three o'clock. By this time Eve would be married, probably have begun her wedding journey. He glanced at his soiled rough clothing and blackened hands, contrasting them with the doubtless immaculate person and attire of the bridegroom.

'Damn him!' he muttered savagely.

Now and then his steps took him through a little green jungle, left miraculously like an oasis in the general desert. Whither he was going or why he had no idea, a torturing unrest possessed and drove him forward. Yet afterwards when they came to track his path through the ashes it was seen that he had moved with a strange directness to a certain point on the road. Before that point was reached he was in the midst of the burning forest, not unconscious of danger nor actually indifferent to it, seeing the fires closing in on his tracks and, as it were, pushing him forward. Yet when he came to the road he had but to descend the cutting and step across to comparative safety. He stood looking about him. To the left a huge tree had fallen across the way and was crackling and blazing merrily; to the right his view was cut off by a sharp bend in the road, round which volumes of smoke were rolling. He stepped down and began to make his way across. Nothing was visible in the hollow round the bend, but a deep roaring sound showed that in that direction the fire had gained a good hold. He paused a moment to consider his course. The road to the settlement ran under the burning tree and was clearly impassable. It would be needful to enter the bush and strike the road farther along. Suddenly he turned his head quickly and looked into the rolling smoke.

Was it possible that amid the continuous uproar he detected the sound of galloping hoofs? Yes—there was no mistaking that frantic clatter, momentarily growing nearer, thundering out of the darkness to meet him. He stepped quickly aside as horse and rider burst through the smother of smoke, swept past him and reined up abruptly in the clearer atmosphere between him and the fallen tree.

He could see the whites of the horse's eyes as it reared and wheeled. He had time also to note the perfect seat of the rider ere she turned to look at him.

Then, like a man who nears the end of a dream and fears awakening, Geoffrey Hernshaw moved towards her.

CHAPTER XXXII

TOGETHER

Eve was on her feet by the time he reached her. Her face was deathly pale. 'Is the road impassable?' she asked at once.

'For the horse, quite.' Geoffrey possessed himself of the reins of the plunging animal despite a movement on the girl's part to resist the attention.

'And it is not possible to turn back? Then what is to be done with the horse?'

Geoffrey looked round and shrugged his shoulders. 'Freedom is the only chance for him, Miss Milward.'

'I was married this morning,' she said quickly.

Geoffrey removed the saddle and bridle and turned the horse loose. He made no comment, nor did he look at her as he said brusquely, 'Where do you wish to go?'

'I was on my way to Mrs. Gird's, but if that is impossible_____'

'Mrs. Gird's is as possible as anywhere else from here. Wherever we go we have only the alternatives of the bush or the fire. You shall say which it is to be.'

'How did you get here yourself?'

Geoffrey pointed up the bank, 'Return that way, however, is no more possible than it is by the way you have come.'

The girl stood silent. The horse after snuffing the wind had entered the bush and was breaking his way noisily through the undergrowth.

'Show me the way then,' she said at last.

He took a step forward and paused. 'There is no way, and I know the direction no better than yourself. It is best you should understand that clearly. The bush is thick and rough, and there may be difficulty in getting through.'

'You have said there is no alternative.'

'I was wrong—there is one. We can stay here on the chance that the fire will burn itself out before it reaches us. When there is a certainty that it will not we can take to the bush.'

'By that time we shall probably be in darkness.'

'Yes, that is inevitable.'

'Then let us go now while we have the day-light.'

Geoffrey turned and led the way into the jungle. For all his set face there was the glow of an Indian summer in his heart. To him and not to her husband was given the blessed privilege to help her in her hour of need, and if the moments of their companionship were destined to be few, they should at least be unforgettable while life lasted. Yet he moved forward in silence, only occasionally pausing to hold aside some obstacle from her path or to assure himself that she was close behind him.

At first the bush was intersected by cattle tracks running in all directions, most of them formed during the winter when the soft roads were all but impassable, and by taking advantage of these he hoped either to strike the road or to arrive in the vicinity of the Girds' section. But in this idea he had reckoned without the fire, which, having crossed the road at several intervening points, was slowly eating its way into the dark unvisited depths. Time after time they were forced from the direct course and pushed farther back into the forest.

Not every man born in a bush country becomes a good bushman, and to many a long-time dweller in cities has it fallen in time of need to demonstrate that the faculty of direction is as much a gift as that of mathematics. But Geoffrey Hernshaw was not of these, nor did he possess the long experience which might serve in the absence of the finer quality. So long as they kept to the tracks, even though they were those of mere beasts, their case was not hopeless, but in the confidence that he moved in the right direction, and tempted, as many a poor victim has been before him, by a stretch of country easier than the track seemed to afford, he made the fatal mistake of attempting to break fresh ground in the jungle. Then, as it were a net spread for their feet, the great mysterious forest closed silently upon them.

It was long ere they discovered it, and meanwhile their progress increased in difficulties and deviations. At first the girl resisted the proffered assistance of her companion. She had pinned up her riding-habit, and though suffering more inconvenience than the man, her physical strength and experience in many a bush ramble served her now in good stead. Yet his assistance was at times inevitable. Twice with trembling fingers he extricated her skirt from the spines of the tataramoa[1] ; once she gave him an icy cold hand in stepping from one moss-grown trunk to another; and once she allowed him to lift her down a steep rock in a ravine, and then he was aware of the rapid beating of her heart and the extreme pallor of her face.

'Is it peace between us, Eve, at last?' he asked.

'Yes,' she said, and stood still, looking at him with strange eyes.

When all is said as to the mistakes of those first few hours, there remains the distraction of their thoughts to account it may be for everything.

The inevitable moment arrived at last. With great difficulty they ascended the other side of the ravine, only to find a bush denser and gloomier than that they had quitted. Geoffrey looked thoughtfully around him—at the matted growths, the darkening sky.

'I confess I am at fault here,' he said lightly enough.

Eve looked neither to the right nor the left, she stood patiently waiting, her face absolutely expressionless.

'What is your idea of our course?' he asked suddenly.

'Between those two palm-trees,' she replied at once.

'Really? I should have thought exactly the opposite.'

'Go on then,' she said.

No, no. We have had enough of my bushman-ship.'

He turned in the direction she had indicated and began to force a slow passage through the dense growths. The ground rose gradually, and in the end culminated in a ridge whence a glimpse of the surrounding country was obtainable. It was no more than a glimpse, a few acres of tree tops, a narrow ribbon of darkening sky, with a segment of lurid cloud low down on the horizon. Not a leaf stirred, not a bird sang, an appalling loneliness held the scene. Even as they gazed a star twinkled forth, then another. Night was setting out his lamps in the ocean of space.

Whatever thoughts may have passed through the man's mind in the moments of gazing, they found no expression in his voice.

---

[1] A species of bramble.

'Do you wish to go on?'

'It is impossible to go on.

'Then—what?'

'There is nothing to be done but wait for the daylight.'

For the first time her voice showed signs of unsteadiness, and he turned quickly towards her; she was still gazing at the remote cloud.

'The night will be long and probably cold,'he said in matter-of-fact tones. 'If you will sit down, I will light a fire and find you some protection.'

She obeyed in silence, and he busied himself In collecting firewood, of which an abundance lay. scattered around the little opening. Soon from that island in the ocean of vegetation there arose a slender pillar of smoke that brandished itself against the stars and was lost in the growing darkness. Through the heights above went a faint whisper like the sweep of a garment. Remote at first, scarcely perceptible to the ear, it grew rapidly in volume, the leaves turned themselves softly in the air, vibrating expectantly. Swiftly accumulating, the river of melody swept onward until the surrounding forest rocked and danced with a weird frenzy in the embrace of the first wind of night. A few minutes later a second gust followed, and after a further interval a third, then all was still.

'Will you come to the fire?'

Even in the shelter of the forest the night air struck chill. The girl rose with a shiver and followed him. He had cut some palm leaves and plaited them into a sort of screen, against which he had piled a heap of dry fern fronds.

'That is the best I can do,' he said. 'I am afraid you will suffer some inconvenience, but no more than can be avoided. The screen is on the weather-side. I will see that the fire does not go down during the night.'

She looked at his preparations but made no motion to avail herself of them.

'It is unfortunate,' he added after a moment, 'that my companionship should be forced upon you, Mrs. Fletcher, but I will endeavour to remind you of it as little as possible.'

Had he been watching her where she stood in the red of the firelight he would have seen her wring her hands with a despairing gesture, but still no word escaped her.

'I have brought you an incredible distance in the wrong direction,' he went on with the same biting calm; 'probably it would be impossible to convince you that I have not done so intentionally —nevertheless, such is the fact.'

Then she raised her eyes and looked at him— looked at him long and reproachfully. 'Hate me if you must,' she said in a low voice; '1 have earned your hatred, but do not think it needs your cruelty to make me suffer.'

He drew back sharply, as a man withdraws who finds himself unexpectedly on the verge of a precipice. When he again approached the fire her figure was almost indistinguishable among the fern.

'Eve,' he called softly.

The girl moved and sat up.

'I had forgotten I have some food in my pocket. Are you hungry?'

'No, but I could drink.'

He unstrapped his water-bottle and, kneeling down, held it up between her and the light. 'There is not much,' he said; 'and if we are many hours in the bush to-morrow, you may need it more than you do now. Does that seem cruel?'

'Then give me just a mouthful.'

He complied and watched her as she eagerly drained the small metal cup. 'Now another,' he suggested.

Eve declined resolutely, and passed him the little vessel. The hands that held it were icy cold, and he possessed himself of them and held them with some force between his own.

'Why are you like this? The night is not so cold. Are you in pain—in fear? Tell me.'

Slowly, yet forcibly, she extricated her hands one after the other from his grasp; but her manner showed no resentment—hardly, indeed, feeling of any kind.

'Have you no speech for me?' he asked bitterly. 'Is our separation such that even circumstances like these are unable to span it?'

Still she was silent.

He rose and stood looking down. A log on the fire fell in, suffusing her face with light. 'Is it in your mind that some sort of explanation is due between us?' he asked.

'Yes,' she said.

'Will it come before we part?'

'If you insist.'

'And if we never part?'

She looked up, and in her eyes was the same unreadable expression he had seen in them in the ravine hours before. That was all the answer she gave him; nor was there any further interchange of speech between them until the morning.

For Geoffrey the night was spent in attending to the fire, his labours broken by brief snatches of rest that never lapsed into complete unconsciousness. He had tasted no food since the early morning, and hunger conspired with cold and anxiety of mind to keep him waking. That they were now aware of the direction in which the settlement lay counted for little; for if they had been unable to strike the road when close to it, what chance had they of doing so when separated by two or three miles of untracked forest? Little, indeed! yet the attempt must be made and persevered in—must be made, too, possibly without water, and with very inadequate supplies of food. The absence of water constituted, indeed, the greatest threat. During the fight with the fire, 'water' had been the chief cry of the workers; and he knew that the forcing of a passage through the bush was a task little, if any, less arduous. How was it possible the girl could endure such hardships?

Yet with the coming of the light these gloomier anticipations vanished, and the thought of the long and intimate companionship with the woman he loved which was destined to be his filled his mind with a great unreasoned happiness.

In the first gray light Eve sat up. A tinge of colour had returned to her cheeks, and a greater serenity seemed to dwell in her eyes.

Geoffrey produced his supplies and began quietly to explain the situation. 'Fortunately,' he concluded, 'Lena has generous ideas as to what constitutes a mid-day snack, so things are not quite so bad as they might be. The liquid department, however, is in other case, and there is where the shoe is likely to pinch before long.'

Eve listened in silence. 'Very well,' she said, when he had concluded; 'if you will divide one of the sandwiches between us, we will eat it before we start. As for the water, we will take it when we must.'

'I'm afraid you have not been listening very attentively,' he returned quietly. 'I endeavoured to explain beyond possibility of mistake that these things were for you, wholly and solely, and that I have no idea, immediate or remote, of sharing in them.'

'Then put them away,' said the girl, her eyes flashing. 'Before I descend to a vileness like that, may I die a thousand deaths.'

'But you cannot surely be serious? Consider our probable disparity in powers of endurance. There can be no fair partnership where one person is called upon to endure more than the other.'

She rose to her feet. 'Are you ready?' she asked finally.

He looked at her in perplexed reflection. There was a semblance of the old sunny smile he knew so well lurking in the depths of her eyes, and that more than anything convinced him that it was useless to continue the argument.

Before starting again on their journey, Geoffrey examined the scene long and carefully. 'If we can reach that big kauri,' he said presently, indicating a tree a quarter of a mile away, 'and then keep to the side of the hill, every step must take us in the direction of the settlement. I can see no better landmark than that.'

For upwards of two hours they searched the bush in vain, and long ere those two hours elapsed their sense of direction was again obscured. Trees of every other description there were in countless numbers, but of kauris apparently none.

'We have been keeping too close in,' Geoffrey decided at last. 'We must try farther afield.' And they pushed on with the idea of widening their circle of explorations. The third hour was nearly spent before their search was rewarded.

'I see it!' Eve cried suddenly; 'there below you.' And in a few moments they stood by the huge tawny barrel of the King of the Woods.

He stood, as is the manner of his kind, in royal isolation from the remainder of the forest; so magnificent in his suggestions of strength and eternal youth that, for a moment, the pair stood still, forgetful of self, in that mute reverence which the mighty works of Nature must for ever arouse in the heart of man.

'It is lower down the hill than I thought,' Geoffrey said at last. 'However, our course should be simple; we have only to keep to the same level, and the trend of the spur must bring us to the road.'

'If only we could find some water!' Eve said, seating herself under the tree.

Already the demands on the bottle had drained it of its contents, and every creek they had so far come to had been dry. Geoffrey looked at her uneasily and then down the slope.

'There should be water in the gorge,' he said. 'I can try while you sit here and rest yourself.'

The girl sprang at once to her feet. 'If there is water, we will rest beside it—together.'

What evil lurked in the words to cloud his eyes with cold suspicion? 'Are you in fear that I will desert you?' he asked.

For a moment her eyes blazed passionately, then she turned away with cold indifference. 'Go, then,' she said.

But in an instant he was at her side, had snatched her hand and carried it to his lips. 'God forgive me! God forgive me! But try to conceive the miracle your presence here is to me. For months I have lain under the lash of your scorn. I, who would have died to save you an instant's suffering. Eve! Eve! there is not a drop of blood in my body that does not worship you. Life and death have no torments that can blot out the love I feel for you. Look up, my dear one, look up and tell me, however it may have been in the past, that now and for ever you trust me.'

The face she raised to his glowed with an indescribable radiance. 'Now and for ever!' she said, and gave him her other hand.

So for awhile they stood in all but perfect understanding. And over them the kauri spread his leafy screen. Rooted in the centuries, he had watched through a thousand generations of man the fleeting shadows on the forest floor. And still they came and went.

The journey to the bottom of the gorge was made together, and together with the subsequent ascent, it proved the most arduous task they had yet encountered. Every foot of the way was a struggle with the dense vegetation that rioted in these dark and humid depths, where even the fiercest sun-ray was powerless to penetrate. Tangles of supple-jack, declivities of bare rock, fallen trees buried in filmy ferns blocked their way at every turn. And when at length they reached the pit of the gorge, where only the shade-loving palm had the heart to grow luxuriantly, they found that the long drought had penetrated even here, and the bed of the creek was dry.

Then, exhausted, they sat down on the rocks, which in the winter time were covered by a foaming torrent, and looked despairingly at one another.

CHAPTER XXXIII

IN THE HEART OF THE BUSH

WATER! What melody breathed in that hitherto unheeded sound! What enchantment in the thing itself! Its coolness, tastelessness—sweeter in imagination than the perfumed wines of Spain. The incomparable quality of it; the delicious flow, quenching the electric stammer of the fevered blood, allaying, satisfying. As a thing to be seen; in diamond dews at rest in the pure cold bosoms of flowers; in leaping cascades, glancing with a fearful magnificence in dusky glens; in the broad, full river, moving glassily, without a murmur. As a thing to be heard; the withdrawing roar of the breakers; the continuous thunder of the rolling bar; the ponderous tread of the cataract; the splash of a body plunging into the elastic depths.

He looked up suddenly from his reverie. In the division of the water he had found it possible to deceive her. Now in his suffering the terrible fear came over him that his abstinence might react to her injury. The thought whipped him to his feet.

'Water is surely to be found somewhere about here,' he said. 'Let us go a little way along the channel and explore.'

And, as though the bush sought to play with its victims, they came presently to the thing they sought. The water lay in a pool at the foot of an abrupt descent, where the winter cataract had worn deep into the rocks. It was both abundant and pure, and when, an hour later, they quitted the brink of the pool they did so with strength and courage renewed.

By this the sun had reached his highest altitude. The heat on the hillside was like that of a hothouse, and reaching the tree at length, they were glad to sit down and rest before the final stage of their journey was attempted.

Then again the struggle began. For hours it was impossible to estimate their progress, no opening, even of a hand's-breadth, permitting them a view of the country they were traversing. So far as was possible where insuperable obstacles to a straight course were for ever occurring they kept to one level, but after awhile, beyond an occasional slight undulation, the suggestion that they were on a hillside vanished, and thenceforward it was but a blind burrowing through the growths. Deeper and deeper they penetrated into the primeval solitudes, where no man had come perchance since the beginning of the world. Nothing they had yet seen equalled in grandeur and beauty the scene they now invaded. Everywhere huge trunks of hoary antiquity rose like ponderous pillars of masonry into the obscurity of the forest roof. Monstrous plants of strange growth and in unnumbered variety choked the earth and wrestled with one another in a fierce battle for life. Overhead, mosses and epiphytes, vines and climbing ferns draped the branches, and lianas and the rugged cables of the rata bound the woods together in a grip of steel. Now and then they burst into a tiny glade sacred to some majestic tree, the record of whose years might serve for the lives not of men but of races. At other times, less fortunate, they came on tangles of bush-lawyer, against whose ferocious claws no strength or agility might avail, and again and again they were driven away in search of easier country.

So in the hopeless struggle the day wore itself away, and again in the mysterious murmur of the leaves they read the signal of approaching darkness.

Late in the afternoon they had been seduced by easy stages into a country of unsurpassable difficulty and gloom. The vast trees still remained, blotting out the sky in a dense interlacing of foliage, but the place of the varied undergrowth had now been taken by one plant—the supple-jack. Casting its black canes from tree to tree, scrambling across the ground, turning and twisting snake-like on itself, this hellish vine added the final touch of horror to the scene. The dead sooty blackness that had displaced the vivid green of fern tree and palm, the distorted and suffocating saplings seeking to break upwards from that pit of terrors, the hideous fungoid growths like huge cancers on the trees, the chill air, the ominous rattling of the canes—formed together a scene in which the imagination of a Dante would have revelled.

Despite the care with which he had guarded it, Geoffrey's knife had been dragged from its sheath and lost in the scramble, and this loss now added greatly to their difficulties. At every step the canes had to be forced apart and the body adapted to the opening thus provided. Almost fainting with fatigue, the girl endured this final torment in heroic silence, while the man, his eyes dark with sullen rage at his powerlessness, spent himself in her service till every nerve in his body vibrated discordantly.

Once, frantic at the sight of her sufferings, he opened his clenched lips and railed at himself, cursing the day he was born, accusing himself of bringing this misery of torture upon her; but the touch of her hand on his stilled the evil mood, and for a grateful moment he held her fast in his arms.

'We will try no more,' he said at last. 'When we get out of this hell—if we ever do—we will stay still and wait. And if we wait for death, better so than that we should struggle forward to meet it.'

And as though there were a charm in the words to break momentarily the net that held them, presently the maze opened into a little fern-covered glade, set about with lofty trees, kahikatea and totara and rata, with at their feet the glancing foliage of palms and the tender green of clustered tree-ferns. Scattered about the centre were the last white decaying remnants of the foretime giant tenant of the opening, and a mound such as is raised by man to mark the resting-place of his mighty dead covered his immemorial dust. Whether it were merely the contrast with the Inferno from which they had emerged, or that there actually was something in the peace and loveliness of the scene to inspire delight, the two looked around them and at one another with smiling eyes.

'But that water is probably wanting this is an ideal camping ground,' Geoffrey said. 'Surely the good spirits of the forest must have spread it for us in the midst of the desert.'

'It looks like a cemetery,' Eve said suddenly. 'Look at the white things like stones among the green fern.' Her eyes still retained their smiling expression.

'A cemetery it is. Here lies the dust of one who flourished probably in the days of Solomon, and whose resting-place is sacred even in the fight for existence which is being waged here.'

In the reaction from the severe labours of the day all thought of the terrors that awaited them passed from their minds, and inspired with fresh energy, they set about their preparations for the night. From the palm trees Geoffrey tore the leaves by brute force, and, Eve plaiting them together, a protection was soon formed against the heavy night dews. The approaching darkness rendered it impossible that anything more elaborate should be attempted that night, and the remainder of the brief twilight was devoted to the collection of fuel and the building of a fire. The tree ferns under which the shelter had been erected formed with their trunks, to which the spent fronds still clung, a species of rough hut, and by piling other fronds against these a certain amount of comfort was secured. Their water-bottle was more than half-full, and three sandwiches remained from the store Lena had cut for Geoffrey. Thus the second night began.

The sky above the opening was of a perfect clear darkness, deep also with a depth that passed infinitely beyond the stars. Sirius blazed, the binary star in Orion darted his rich colours through the trembling leaves, the Pleiades emitted soft beams as of lamp-lighted pearl, the 'most ancient heavens' were 'fresh and strong.'

'Can you read the stars?' Eve asked at last. 'Do they tell you anything of where we are?'

'I know the constellations,' he replied, following the direction of her gaze; 'but where they should be at this time of the year or at this moment of time I have no idea.'

'But if we watched their motions, should we not be able to distinguish the points of the compass?'

'Yes, within limits. But to make a further attempt to get out would be suicidal. Could you endure another day such as this has been? Our mistake was in ever leaving the spot where we camped last night.'

'Do you think they are searching for us?'

'That depends on how much is known of your movements.'

She reflected a moment. 'And what is our chance supposing a search party is out?'

'It was good yesterday, not so good to-day; tomorrow, if we move, it may vanish altogether.'

Eve looked thoughtfully into the fire. 'What brought you to the place where we met?' she asked suddenly.

He checked the words that framed themselves on his lips. 'Fate,' he said briefly.'

'To save me?'

'Perhaps.'

'Why, then—when it was too late?'

'Was there something before—something from which you desired to be saved?'

'Yes.'

'Yet you chose between us—with your eyes open.'

'No!' she said passionately,—' no! He blindfolded me; he lied away my reason. It seemed incredible that a man should love God and serve the devil. Every instinct of righteousness urged and compelled me to believe him.'

'Could I have broken down a belief so founded?'

'You could have tried.'

'Did I not try?'

'You should have help me by force,—you should have compelled me to listen—to believe. If you had killed me for my obstinacy I should have died worshipping you.'

'Eve!'

'I loved you—I loved only you. Every hour which brought me nearer to him was an agony— yet you stood by.'

'Eve! Eve! was the fault mine? Could I guess at a love that went masked in hatred? What made you disbelieve in the end?'

'I learnt that he knew the charge was false; that he had known it all the time. But then—I was his wife.'

'God help us!' he said hoarsely.

'Has the law no mercy for us?'

'None.'

'Is there any mercy in life?'

He was silent.

'In death?'

He took her hand and raised it to his lips, but still no word escaped him.

'Geoffrey,' she said softly, 'even now, in the darkness, where no hope shows itself, and the shadows of eternity thicken around us, where life stands threatening on one hand, and death on the other, I believe that God exists, and that He has not forgotten us. Was it a blind chance that led me without volition from that man to you—that fated we should meet at the one point on the road where no choice was left to us? Then take my promise, since God has brought us thus together, that though I may not now be yours, at least no law nor force shall make me his. And if that be so in life, much more will it be so in death when evil shall no longer have power against us.'

Still he kissed her hand in silence.

'Speak to me,' she said. 'Tell me what is in your mind.'

He raised himself slowly from the shadows at her feet, and in his eyes, as they caught the firelight, she saw only the dulness of despair.

'What shall I say?' he said. 'How clumsy a thing is life if death be needed to repair its mischiefs. Yet each of us must believe according to his nature, and only death can prove who is right. If all that tremendous to-morrow shall be for us a silence, even as the tremendous yesterday is a silence, where then shall be the recompense for what life denies us? Hope, faith—what are they but shadows compared with the substance we shall have missed. Can I reconcile myself to die now, with the knowledge that you love me still beating in my blood? No, no; give me life with its chances, even though it part us for ever, rather than the risk of sleep and forgetfulness.'

Orion passed out of sight. The Southern Cross, slowly turning in the black sky, appeared at the edge of the opening, leading up the glittering lights of Argo, the stars of the Centaur thrown off from its points like the spokes of a jewelled wheel. The night grew chill. He rose suddenly, and going out into the opening busied himself in replenishing the waning fire. When he returned, the girl had retired farther into the shelter, and after a moment he lay down in the fern at her feet.

The night passed for him, as had the last, in a weird mingling of dreams and waking anxieties, and at the first sign of daylight he rose stiff and unrefreshed.

During the darkness he had formed the idea of endeavouring to obtain a view of the country from one of the surrounding trees, and he now walked round the glade until he had found one suitable for the purpose. The strong lianas in which it was draped rendered the ascent of the lofty barrel possible, though by no means easy, and in his exhausted condition he found it necessary to rest for awhile in the fork before proceeding farther. Then branch after branch was scaled, until at a giddy altitude he was able to rise to his feet and look around him. In all directions rolled the billows of that great ocean of verdure; nowhere from horizon to horizon was a break or opening of any kind apparent. Beautiful was the scene, but terrible in its suggestion of loneliness; no bird sang, no breeze blew, no cloud was visible in all the expanse of sky. Black were the woods, save where at intervals a towering summit caught the beams of the rising sun and rayed them forth in sparkles of yellow fire.

He gazed awhile, then began a cautious descent to the ground. Far below him he could see Eve, standing motionless in the opening watching his passage from bough to bough. Her form drew his eyes like a magnet, till in his divided attention his foot slipped, and he was saved from falling only by a miracle. That warning was sufficient, and he looked at her no more till he reached the ground. Then he found her white and trembling.

'Why did you do that?' she said passionately.

He endeavoured to smile away her fears. 'It is a fact I am a bit out of practice, but it was necessary that we should endeavour to find out where we were.'

'What does it matter where we are?' she returned in the same tone. 'What does anything matter now, if only_____' She checked the words on her lips and turned away.

He was at her side in a moment and had taken her hand. 'If only what?' he asked.

'We are together.'

'To me—nothing,' he said.

After their frugal breakfast he turned to the shelter and suggested improvements with the object of more perfectly excluding the cold night air. 'Some more nikau[1] and a few fern fronds,' he said cheerfully, 'should render it quite habitable.'

'Is it worth while?' the girl asked.

The question fell like a stone into a still pool.

'It shall be,' he said, and went resolutely to the work.

In an hour's time all the interstices between the stems had been plugged with stakes and rushes, and a large heap of dry bracken gathered for the floor of the hut. The collection of fuel was the next task, and when this had been sufficiently attended to, Geoffrey expressed his intention of making a search for water.

---

[1] Palm leaves.

'I will not go beyond the reach of your voice,' he said; 'and if you feel anxious as to my whereabouts, cooey to me and I will answer you.'

After some demur the girl consented, and he made his way into the forest.

A two hours' scramble proved profitless of results. Only slight undulations deflected the land from a dead level, and apparently neither creek nor spring existed. The part of the forest to which they had attained presented indeed some of the features of a skilfully constructed trap. Solid miles of cane-bound trunks surrounded them, offering here and there tortuous passages like blind rat-holes in the wall. The kiwi alone, the hair-feathered representative of a genus of wingless birds, appeared to possess the key of the jungle. These creatures, as they subsequently discovered, abounded, becoming visible at twilight, uttering their weird notes throughout the night, but frustrating any efforts at capture by their unceasing vigilance and rapidity of movement. The season for berries was not yet, but at one spot Geoffrey found a number of large purple drupes, with which he filled his pockets. There was not a sixteenth of an inch of rind on the woody kernels, but they were not unpalatable. At another bush, laden with black, grape-like berries, he looked askance, but subsequently returned and marked the spot with some care. Why he did so was not clear to his mind, yet he was aware of some significance in the action. The labours of the morning, from the perilous ascent of the tree to this culminating struggle through the canes, combined with privation of food and sleep, had clouded his mind, and only the magnetism of the girl's voice drew him with many dull pauses from the chill gloom to the warm sunshine of the glade.

'Then it is to be without water,' Eve said quietly when he had reported his failure.

'We may have better luck next time. The water we have will not last over to-day however we economise it. Then comes to-morrow and to-morrow.' He stood looking drowsily down upon her.

'Drink now,' she said pityingly. 'You look utterly exhausted.'

'What—I! No. I have been feeding on the fruits of the forest. " And He bringeth forth His fruits in due season." 'He let the berries rain into her lap.

'I have often eaten these,' Eve said speculatively, 'but is there life in them?'

'Surely—an abundance. Where was life more vigorous than it is here? Life, life everywhere, and for us—no life at all.'

Eve looked up, startled at the dull voice, and met the gaze of a pair of smiling, drowsy eyes. Even as she looked the man swayed on his feet.

She sprang up in concern, and catching his hand sought to lead him into the shelter. He raised the hand to his lips, but the lids of his eyes fell lower.

'Geoffrey! Geoffrey! Did you have no sleep last night? Ah, how cruel I have been to you! And you on the cold ground! Geoffrey.' She put her arms round him.

'Sleep!' he said thickly. 'No, not for ages. Yes, I will come with you. Gently, my darling, or the boat will upset. Could I sleep while you were cruel? But now that you are—kind—see, I will kiss your feet.'

He made a motion to stoop, and in the attempt sank into the couch of fern, her arms still round him. For a few seconds he held her, then the weary muscles relaxed, and she was free to release herself if she chose.

In the darkness he awoke refreshed and with a clear mind. The fire burnt cheerfully, but the wind had veered into the south, and an Arctic chill was in the air. For moments he lay still, endeavouring to recall the events of the day, but for him one-half of them had no existence. He remembered dimly returning from the bush; that was the last fact which could be definitely separated from his dreams. The cold air bit into his limbs, causing him to change his position.

From the other side of the shelter came the sound of frequent movements, now slight rustlings, now louder, as of one tossing from side to side. He lay still listening, his heart beating painfully. There was a long-drawn sigh.

'Eve,' he called softly.

'Yes.'

'Is it the cold? Let me put my coat over you.'

'Come then,' she said after a silence.

He moved to her, and she drew him down, encircling his neck with her arm. 'Would you kill yourself to save me pain?' she whispered.

'A thousand times.'

Her lips sought his. 'Will love endure through the torments? Will he be with us there, when the trouble is done and we stand at the gates of death?'

'Even then.'

'Lie down beside me. Put your arms round me. Oh, my beloved, whom I have tortured and killed! I would give you life if I could—life and love if it were possible. But for us there is only love in death.'

Outside the fire roared, eating into the heart of the night. The shadow of its drifting smoke swept across the spectral flare, moving upwards, aslant, in endless procession over trunk and bough. The deep monotoned ko-ko of the abounding morepork came with a profound significance, breaking the silence as it were the opening of a tragic door.

CHAPTER XXXIV

THE TOLL IS PAID

AT a spot four miles back in the forest a huge column of flame and smoke roared upwards into the midnight sky, and round it—seated, squatting, or stretched out full length on the ground—an army of rescuers waited impatiently for the dawn. For at last the trail had been found.

On a mound, their backs against the broad barrel of a tree, sat three men, while a third—a native—lay half asleep at their feet. There was no sleep, however, in the eyes of Mr. Wickener or Robert or Sandy Milward, and in their restless movements, snatches of eager speech, and ever-recurrent watching of the stars, was to be read such a state of mental anxiety and suspense as might well keep slumber at a distance.

'Twenty past one,' said Mr. Wickener, referring to his watch,—'say four hours.'

'It will never pass if you keep counting it like that,' Robert said.

'Makit te watch te stop,' Pine grunted; 'dat te best.'

'You sleep on, Pine,' Mr. Wickener said, looking down, upon him. 'I'm going to make you a rich man.'

The Englishman had made the same promise several times already, but he still uttered it as though it had just occurred to him, and appeared to derive satisfaction from the repetition.

Pine sat up, yawned dismally, and passed an eye over the constellations. 'If no fire,' he said, 'dat good, dat te easy; but fire—ah, makit te biggy search! No fire here, no fire any more. All ri' now.'

'How old do you reckon the trail is?' Sandy asked.

Pine put his hand in his shirt and pulled out a fragment of black cane. 'Dat not te rongy time,' he said. 'I 'pose tree, four days.'

'And you are certain they are together?'

'If Iwi, she not makit te cut like dat. Dis te strong cut. If Geoffrey, he makit one cut, he not cut all te same he cut down te bush; dat acause Iwi come arong ahind.'

'You lie down and go to sleep, Pine,' said Mr. Wickener approvingly.

'You save yourself up for to-morrow.'

'Go on with what you were saying about Stephen, Sandy,' Robert said.

'Yes; where was I? I told you I left him and Jack Wilson to look after the horses. When I got back the next morning I sent Wilson on to the station, and took Stephen with me. The fire had burnt itself out, and we walked along the road as far as the creek where the bridge used to be. The road falls steeply there on both sides, and the first thing we saw as we looked down was the carcass of a horse, still bridled, but lying all doubled up with its back broken. It was not a pretty sight—death has no dignity in an animal—but Stephen paled as though he had seen a ghost and caught me by the arm. "I wouldn't go nigh it if I were you, Mr. Milward," he said. "That's Mark Gird's horse." But I had seen something else, partly hidden by the water and the charred piles, and that put what he was saying out of my head. I knew the horse in fact the moment I saw it, and I guessed the rest. When we had got him out, and it was no easy task, Stephen told me of what occurred the night before. It appears that when Fletcher rode through the pair of them sprang up to stop him, but he took no notice; and from this, and the circumstance that he was riding a black horse, they seem to have made up their minds that he was Mark Gird's ghost.'

'There's a good few of them tarred with that brush,' said Mr. Wickener, his eyes travelling round the camp.

Sandy nodded. 'But this is what I was going to tell you. Stephen had been terribly despondent up to that time, so much so that I believe if I had proposed to give up the search as hopeless he would have thought it a perfectly natural suggestion and acquiesced. But the discovery of Fletcher's dead body made all the difference. "There's the mark of the bush there, Mr. Milward," he said. " There's no askin' pardons about the bush; it's just life and death. That man never knew what happened to him any more'n Andersen did. The thoughts he were thinkin' when he galloped on to the creek he's thinkin' still; fur his neck were snapped on the piles before he come to the water, and what he got in his brain were fixed there time everlastin'." '

'That's not a pretty idea,' said Wickener, 'unless_____' and he fell silent.

'What *was* he thinking just then?' Robert wondered.

'It was understood that he was to wait events. I saw him on the road to Rivermouth. He must have come back after dark and been making for

Gird's when they saw him. An hour earlier he would have seen the danger, but the fire had passed on and left the gully in darkness. He never pulled up on the rise; he rode with a loose rein down the slope. What was he thinking? *He was thinking the bridge was there.'*

The others were silent.

'We laid him out on the bank,' Sandy resumed after awhile, 'and the natives came down with an ox-waggon and took him away into the township. But the effect of it all was that Stephen cheered up and began to look about him. He had counted the chances according to his bush philosophy, and they were all in our favour. 'The bush strikes hard,' he said; 'but it don't strike often, and I reckon the price is about paid. 'Twere meant—well, never mind how 'twere meant—this chap took up the bill when he hit the creek, and there won't be no more'n the three graves yet awhile.'

Wickener rose quickly to his feet and paced restlessly up and down. 'If only one possessed that primitive capacity of belief,' he said. 'For me it would suffice to feel assured that the sun will rise again.'

'Faith is an impressive thing,' Sandy said musingly. 'No man, however incredulous he may be, is entirely proof against its influence. I believe they are alive. I believe that within a week we shall be able to begin to forget. But that is only so with me because I have clung to Stephen as a drowning man clings to an oar.'

'I could believe in the daylight but not now. This place is too tremendous for me.'

Wickener reseated himself with a groan, and a silence fell on the group.

So the protracted minutes drew their unforgettable trail across the minds of the watchers and building up the hours brought finally the first faint indications of dawn. Long before this the camp was astir, and a new spirit of hopefulness had dispersed the gloomy forebodings of the darker hours.

Hitherto the search, spread across a wide tract of country, had been conducted in isolated groups of two or three individuals, the difficulty of their task being greatly increased by the fires which had ravaged the country in the neighbourhood of the road; but now the discovery of a trail and the necessity that it should not be crossed called for a different order of advance. Where all were eager for work, howsoever severe, it was no grateful task to apportion to the voluntary workers the share of prominence they should take in the rescue, but at length the various parties were organised and the plan of campaign propounded. The leaders, on whom lay the delicate task of following the trail, consisted of the party on the mound, together with Charlie Welch, Stephen, the bushman, and three natives, of whom Pine, as the discoverer of the first clue, was tacitly acknowledged captain. An hour after their departure an advance was to be made by the second party, and after a further interval the third. It was hoped in this manner to avoid any overrunning of the trail, while provision could also be made for the return journey by a direct, and having regard to possible encumbrances, more practicable route. Thus in the first dim light of the morning the memorable journey began.

'Show them the stuff you are made of, Pine,' said Mr. Wickener, laying his hand on his *protege's* shoulder. 'We've got to reach them to-night, and you are the boy to do it.'

But Pine drew himself erect, and shaking from his person the detaining hand of the white man, regarded him with the offended dignity of the savage. Then he spoke in a low swift voice in his own liquid tongue and turned away.

'What does he say?'

Sandy looked embarrassed. 'He says you are to keep behind. He has no time to talk with children.'

'That so?' said Mr. Wickener good-temperedly. 'Well, you can never tell the depth of the sea till you put down a line'; and he fell back to the rear.

The natives moved forward, now rapidly, again only after long deliberation, and as they moved the men behind blazed the track with their axes. The dew had not ceased to rain from the foliage when they came to the spot where Geoffrey and Eve had built their first fire. The joy with which the party regarded the gray ashes was, however, short-lived, for there was a long and heartbreaking suspense, and the second party was already in sight before the advance could be continued. It was not the absence of a trail, but the number of them which caused the delay, and it was in the solution of the problem these trails afforded that Pine again covered himself with glory. Yet while his companions scoured the forest he squatted on his heels near the white men, his eyes fixed on the scene, only occasionally deigning to cast a brief reply in his own language to the questions Sandy put to him. Even Mr. Wickener began to lose faith in the oracle. 'This will never do, Mr. Milward,' he said; 'if the natives can't manage it, we should consider the desirability of passing the command over to Stephen.'

'Wait awhile. I see the importance of what he has in his mind. They were looking for something, and if we can discover what it was, we shall get a clue to the direction they took.'

'Water,' said Robert.

Sandy shook his head. 'I suggested that, but he says no; they were looking for a tree, but____'

His words died away, for Pine, with one swift movement, was on his feet, his eyes scanning intently every inch of the scene. For twenty seconds he stood there, then, with a loud cry, plunged down the hillside.

The white men followed pell-mell. In a few minutes the whole party stood under the shade of a kauri, listening to the talk of the Maoris, who were assembled in the centre.

'I don't want to be a nuisance,' said Wickener; 'only tell me if it is good news or bad.'

'Good,' said Sandy. 'Pine knew that they were looking for the kauri; what puzzled him was why they didn't find it.'

'And why didn't they?'

'Because they found this one instead'

'What was the object of finding it?'

'It was their landmark. They did the right thing. If they had found it they would have been on the right side of the spur, and every step of a straight course must have brought them nearer the road; but they struck the wrong tree and went up between the hills instead of outside them.'

'That's a miraculous piece of reasoning,' the Englishman said incredulously.

'Well, it is capable of proof. If we pick up the trail here, and if we find it running along the hillside, the thing is demonstrated.'

And in a few minutes the trail was picked up. The first announcement was to the effect that the unfortunates had descended to the bottom of the ravine for water and had returned by the same track. Then came the discovery of a fragment of lace clinging to a thorn bush, at which tender evidence that the trail they followed could be no other than the one they sought, such a ringing cheer went up from the whole party as had never been heard in that forest before.

Then all day long, with only brief interruptions, the natives led them slowly but confidently ever deeper on and on into the silent forest. The sun reached his highest altitude and began to descend, the gloom of the woods deepened, the vegetation increased in density, but the trail ran on—here, a severed cane or a broken frond; there, a torn fragment of moss or a crushed fern; at times well defined, at times a thing of inference, at times vanishing away altogether, to be rediscovered only by that obscure blending of reason and instinct which is the miraculous faculty of the savage. But slow, with an agonising slowness, was the journey. So delayed and cautious that again and again, tortured beyond endurance, the white men cried out to go on at all hazards.

'Taihoa' (wait), said the guides, when they deigned to take notice at all. Their brows were knitted in hard lines over piercing eyeballs that nothing escaped. The sweat of their exertions poured down their faces disregarded. They never flinched; they took no risks. Step by step, every step in the right direction, they led the army of resouers like a huge snake through the forest. Now and then a gun was fired, rousing perhaps a solitary pigeon or a noisy troop of parrots and bringing down a rain of dust from the foliage, but no response came, and the bush sank immediately back into its original stillness.

At length they reached and penetrated into that huge thicket of supple-jacks where Geoffrey's most heroic effort had been made, and at the same moment, as though there were a blight on the place to wither the hopes of the rescuers, the sun sank below the ranges and the light began to wane rapidly. Presently there was a halt. There had been many such, and every man stood still, possessing himself of what patience he might. A minute went by—ten minutes. Still no movement. Man after man dropped down by the wayside to discuss the situation with his neighbour. Was it the end of the journey? No, or the guns would have announced it. Then a disquieting rumour crept backwards. The trail was lost. The light ahead was insufficient for the trackers. It would be necessary to form a fresh camp. Nothing more could be done till the morning. Those behind might close up with the advance party.

So to the building of the camp fire, the getting ready of food, the preparations for the long night.

'Can nothing be done?' asked Mr. Wickener, not for the first time, his face drawn and haggard.

'We can keep the guns going,' Sandy replied; 'that will encourage them if they are within hearing. Nothing more.'

With the advent of darkness and cessation from toil Pine's English returned to him. Again he sat at the feet of the white men, following their conversation with the simple admiration of a child, and showing himself, in strange contrast to the *hauteur* of the daytime, a creature of 310 reserves.

Mr. Wickener, grateful for the opportunity, plied him with eager questions.

'How do you account for the trail disappearing?'

'I tink p'raps Geoffrey lose te knife. One time he makit plenty cut, nex' time he makit no cut. I look—he not come back—so I tink.'

'But you will be able to go on.'

'Dis te hard bush. No fern in dis bush. Only te dry stick. Dat te very hard trail.'

'But you will be able to go on.'

'I tink dey makit camp not far. Too mutty te biggy work; no kai (food), no water, p'raps so. If dey go on—ah I we no find; dey die.'

'That's what it amounts to then,' said the Englishman, turning to the others; 'we shall either find them close at hand or not at all.'

No one answered him, and a long silence fell on the group.

Round the camp fire the low-toned murmur of conversation died away at point after point as the men lay back and settled themselves to sleep. Only the sharp crackle of the blazing branches broke the quietude of the night. Here and there the trunk of a tree stood forth, gleaming redly in the firelight, a dead branch projected itself like a flame overhead, the leaves of a sapling glittered and darkened, but the background remained of an inky impenetrable blackness. Suddenly an owl squealed loudly from the thickets. Pine glanced quickly over his shoulder and drew nearer to his companions.

'Dis te bad bush,' he said. 'Te Maoris not come here; too many plenty what you call ghostes in dis bush. My mates very 'fraid men, dey no likit te stop, dey tell me clear out te best; but I tell no, dat te bad ting, dat make all our hapu[1] ashamed for long time—so dey not talk it any more.'

Sandy put out a hand and clasped the dusky paw of the native. 'You are a man, Pine,' he said.

'I tink it more ghostes come when run away den when stop here,' Pine explained easily. 'You tink plenty roun' dis place?'

'Did you ever see one?'

The native nodded. 'My mother's father he very ol' man when he die, more'n one hund'ed years. Two, tree monts ago I come down te bush to his kainga[2] when te moon shinin' pretty roud, and I see te ol' man on his horse, I call out to him, and he rook back over'm shoulder, but he go arong jus' same. I make my horse te trot, he trot too; I garrop, he garrop too. When I purrup, he purrup and rook back rike before. Dat make me very 'fraid, so I turn and garrop te other way; but when I rook back, I see him come after me rike he terriber angry, and dat te worse kind. So I purrup and he turn roun', and I go after him arong out te bush. But when I come to Waiomo I not see him any more, but prenty many light der and te biggy tangi, and dey tell me te ol' man been dead—one hours.'

No one commented on Pine's story, but Stephen, who had been an interested listener, opened his lips to say: 'There's them kind o' ghosts and there's the kind that ain't never been nothing else but ghosts, and they're harder to see and the meanin' hangs to them thicker. I mind the night before Jim Biglow was killed, as was the best bushman, barrin' only Mark Gird, inside the county pegs, that I sat within a few yards of one and never seen 'un. Me and Jim had gone up to the back of Wairiri to mark a spar for the barque *Eliza*, that lay inside the bar with only one stick standin', and what with one thing and another, not knowin' the lay of that country too well, and the kauri bein' most all cut out of it, we got a bit farther than we intended and had to camp out for the night. It was a middlin' cold night, and we kep' a good fire goin' the first part of it; but somewhere about the small hours Jim woke me with a clutch of the arm, and I see as it had burnt down till there weren't no mor'n a pile of red embers with a flame or two runnin' over'm now and again. " There's something here besides ourselves," says Jim, trembling like. " Look dead across the fire agen that kauri we marked and tell me what

---

[1] Tribe.

[2] Dwelling-place.

291

you see." "I don't see nothin', Jim," I says, " barrin' a bit o' scrub." " Why, where's your eyes, Steve?" he says. " The blarsted thing's lookin' dead at us and 'is eyes is like live coals." Well, I looked this way and that way, but I couldn't make nought of it more'n a bit o' scrub. We got up and went over, and sure enough there was nothin' there, but when we got back Jim see it again plain as ever, and he never left off seein' it that night. Well, in the mornin' we come down together till we struck the track, and there I left him, havin' something to do up in the township and Jim wantin' to make the river. Well, gents, he never got there. There was a big wind blowin' that day, and when we come to look for'n, we found'n on the track with a branch across his chest that would have broken the back of an elephant. An' I reckon,' concluded Stephen, 'if I had seen that thing same as he seen it, that they'd have pulled more'n one of us out when they come to get the jacks under that tree.'

No one spoke, and in the silence that followed the morepork squealed again, and away in the supplejacks the black canes rattled without reason.

Pine looked round him with bulging eyes.

'Any other gentleman like to oblige with a humorous story?' Mr. Wickener asked.

'Hark!' said Robert suddenly.

Away in the supple-jacks the canes were rattling again, this time continuously for nearly a minute, then complete silence.

'Kiwis,' said Sandy, his hand falling by force of habit on his gun. He handled it a moment, then, picking it up, set the butt on the ground between his knees and drew the trigger.

A spurt of flame, a ringing report, answered by many echoes, hushing away at length into silence;then again, distinctly audible, nearer at hand, the rattle of the canes.

Every man rose as by one accord to his feet. Round the camp-fire the sleepers stirred and sat up one by one. Into every countenance crept an intense expectancy.

Silence again, this time prolonged until strained attention relaxed and a little fire of speech crackled from lip to lip.

'Kiwis.'

'Wild dogs hunting them more likely.'

'There is one story,' said Wickener in a low voice, 'of a man who—but it reached me second hand_____'

'Hush! What was that?'

Men were rising to their feet in all directions, urged by an uncontrollable impulse of hope. Every eye was bent fixedly on a spot in the blackness whence the rattling again proceeded. A moment of listening, then some one voiced the hope in an excited 'Yes.' And as though there were a charm in the word to loosen the spell that held it, the camp broke suddenly into action. From a bundle near the fire a dozen hands grasped the native gum torches, and thrusting them into the flames, cast the glittering light in the direction of the sounds.

Was it man or beast that came crawling thus toilsomely through the tangled vines and panted as it came? Was it human or animal that seeing them drew gaspingly to its feet and pointed wildly back the way it had come?

Yes, yes, poor soul, we understand you. And even as you thus urge us, the slash-hooks are at work which shall never cease until they have brought rescue to her also. But first feel the grip of these human hands that have snatched you thus alive from the jaws of a dreadful death. First moisten those parched lips that have lost for the moment the trick of speech and stumble dumbly against one another. We know what you would say and we lose no time. We know that you cannot have come far, and in every direction the rescuers are cutting through the jungle.

No talk of waiting for the dawn now, as in the flare of the torches each little party hewed its own way through the thickets. No heartbreaking delays absorbed in the re-discovery of a lost trail, but every man for himself, and as rapidly as the nature of the ground permitted.

'There is an opening here,' said Sandy Milward, stepping from the dense tangle into uninterrupted starlight. A torch burst through at the same moment a few yards to the right, a second indicated itself flickeringly behind the foliage at the end of the glade.

'Give me the light, Mr. Wickener; I think this is the end of our journey.'

A few steps brought them unexpectedly in front of the shelter, and by one impulse both men stood still.

'Go on,' said Wickener hoarsely.

Sandy stood motionless. The hand holding the torch began to tremble and droop earthwards.

The Englishman caught it suddenly from his weakening grasp and shook it into vigorous flame. His own face was deathly.

'Go now, Mr. Milward,' he said.

And Sandy nerved himself and went.

A long minute passed. From the skirts of the opening the torches straggled up singly or in pairs, every moment adding to the group. A word or two sufficed to convey the intelligence to each newcomer, but for the rest they waited in silence. At last a shadow came forward to the front of the shelter.

'Is it all right?' asked a voice.

'All right.'

There was a deep breath.

'Don't make a row,' some one cried just in time.

There was a quick shuffling of feet—a laugh. The lights scattered, came together again farther away, grew gradually dimmer, and finally went out, one by one, among the trees.

Long before dawn the whole camp had been transferred to the glade, and a great fire of logs crackled before the shelter. Then their anxiety relieved, their task accomplished, a great drowsiness overcame the workers, and man by man they dropped down where they stood and fell asleep. Only in the shelter where the two rescued ones turned tortur-ously back on to the highway of life was there a waking eye in the camp.

The morning came dimly through a dense fog, causing Sandy to defer the return journey until the sun should have dispersed the vapours. But meantime word must be sent through to Major Milward, and who more entitled to the honour of carrying the good news than Pine.

Stand up then, Pine, bearer of glad tidings, ragged and unwashed as you are, and take this pencilled scrawl, which shall be more precious to the receiver than all the gold of Waihi.

Pine tightened the strap at his waist and looked anxiously at Mr. Wickener. 'You make me te rich man? 'he asked.

Mr. Wickener smiled; every one smiled, but there was no malice in their amusement.

'I have said it,' the Englishman replied; 'and I say it again now.'

Pine regarded him with undisturbed seriousness. 'Dat good,' he said. 'I see you again by'm-by.'

With a rattle of the canes he was gone.

And some hours later, when the heavy mist had lifted and the golden sunlight filtered through the leaves, the whole party followed in his wake.

CHAPTER XXXV

MAJOR MILWARD PLAYS A GAME OF CHESS

AND after the darkness—light.

'Put a match to the lamp, Sandy. I hear them at the gate.'

There was a tremor of eagerness in the Major's voice. He took a step irresolutely and stood still.

'Quick! I hear her voice. That's better.'

Steps sounded on the shelled walk, then on the verandah. A murmur of speech, girls' and men's commingled; a subdued laugh, with a note of gladness in it; a man's voice, pleasant, protesting, and in the open windows, against the background of the falling night, Eve, smiling and radiant.

'Welcome, my child; welcome to you both.'

With one swift movement her arms were round his neck, her glad tears moistened his cheek. 'Father, father, how glad I am to be home!'

'Home has been empty a long time, my dear,— a long time.'

'Yes, I have counted the months, all of them; but it shall not be empty any more. Wait.'

She undid the fastenings of her cloak and hat and threw them recklessly from her. 'Now,' she said, 'Jove me. Yes, you may shake hands with Geoffrey. He's quite well, thank you. No; you are not going to talk with him yet. Now!' And the Major, nothing loath, allowed himself to be pushed into a chair and entirely obscured from the view of the rest of the company.

'How nice and kind you look, darling, and how well!'

'I am well, but I've not been kind; I've been a wretch. Life has been practically unsupportable to every one on the station for twelve months. I've interfered in everything. I have found fault with every one. The sight of me now inspires terror wherever I go. Even Sandy examines me carefully before he calls my attention to the weather.'

'Have any of the hands left?'

'No.'

'Are any of them going to leave?'

'Not that I am aware of.'

'Then I don't believe a word of it.'

'Are you happy, Eve?'

She whispered long into his ear. 'There!' she said aloud in conclusion.

'Let me welcome you also, Evie,' said Sandy, looking down upon her.

She sprang up with a little cry of self-reproach and kissing him on both cheeks, looked guiltily round the room.

'I am so excited that I do not know what I am doing. I did kiss you, Robert,' ticking him off with a little nod; 'and you, Lena.'

The contentment in her eyes was a wonderful thing to see.

'How beautiful you look!' Lena said, with a shy impulsiveness.

'It's a case of the pot and the kettle,' said Sandy. At which, and the smiling attention the remark called down upon her, Lena drew back blushing.

'Where's this immortal baby, Robert?' his brother asked, and Eve, with shining eyes, drew nearer to her sister-in-law.

'The intention was to produce him at supper-time,' Sandy said, and appeared surprised when both ladies turned their backs on him.

'Take me to him, Lena?'

'I suppose they do think things like that about us in England, Geoffrey?' Sandy said, recovering himself as the door closed.

'Not quite so much so now since the waking up the war gave them. The English Geographical Society has definitely announced that New Zealand is not a suburb of Melbourne, and it is hoped in the course of time that a boundary may be agreed upon between this country and New South Wales. There is a fair idea of the monstrous creatures which people our forests—in fact, the only animal the British public find difficulty in accepting is the telephone. Tell them of a sanguinary encounter between a moa and a tuatara, and they listen with bated breath; conclude by ringing up the doctor, and they smile incredulously. But what I am pining for is local news. Tell me something with the colour of the country in it to make me feel that at last I am at home.'

Major Milward nodded approval. 'That has a good sound,' he said. 'Sandy, see that there is sufficient champagne on the table. We will drink a toast by and by to the country of our children— the Fairest Land in the World.'

'What will satisfy your craving?' Sandy asked. 'Business has been good; timber and wool both top prices. The firm of Milward and Hernshaw has made a satisfactory profit for the year. Or is it the people? Mrs. Gird will be here directly. She has the native school across the river and is proving a huge success, though the authorities hesitated a long time before they gave the appointment to a woman. Raymond is here too; we sent him across in the yacht to fetch her. By the way, I wrote you that we bought Hogg out bag and baggage, so Raymond is our man again.'

'Go on,' said Geoffrey, as Sandy paused.

'Let me see. The Mallows? Mabel is married to a new chum from England—terrible swell fellow, but a decent chap too. Winnie's single still. Old man Mallow spoke to me the other day of his own accord—I was never more surprised in my life. Pine—you'll be interested in Pine; he has a wooden house and a flock of sheep and lives like a pakeha. I took our local member through Waiomo a month or two back, and he was greatly impressed with Pine's opulence. Pine took him over the estate and pointed out the objects of interest. " You appear to have an extensive property, Mr. Pine," said the member. " That so," said Pine. "All a land you see roun' here belong a me. All a land you can't see belong a my wife."'

'That's characteristic,' said Geoffrey, laughing.

'There's something about Pine,' continued Sandy, 'that fetches you. Howell was telling me that he once gave him offence by refusing him credit. I think that was the reason. But, any way, shortly after Pine came into funds he walked into the shop and bought four pairs of boots, planking down the cash like a white man. " You makit a pretty fair poot, Howell," he said patronisingly on concluding business. " Come and have glass wine." And that was how he took his revenge.'

'You can never tell what depth of water you are in with the natives,' said Major Milward. 'Did you go into Derbyshire again before you left, Geoffrey?'

'Yes, sir. We have about ten cases of mementoes for you from various branches of the family. Sir John Milward gave Eve a grand piano, and he sent you a walking-stick.'

'The rascal,' said the Major.

'There's the boat,' said Sandy, as shouts sounded in the direction of the water. 'That completes our little party.'

There was a streak or two of gray in Mrs. Gird's hair, but her eyes were as bright as ever as she held out her two hands to Geoffrey.

'Welcome home,' she said. 'I see the word written in your face.'

'It is written in his heart,' said Eve, looking up at her husband, her arm round the elder woman.

'Did you write it there, my dear? But you need not answer me. Whoever wrote it spelled it, I notice, with three letters.'

'How are the lovely boys?' Geoffrey asked.

'Here they come,' said their mother.

There was a shrill clamour in the hall, subdued to whispers at the door; the handle turned softly, and Mark and Rowland came demurely forward to shake hands with Geoffrey and suffer themselves to be kissed by his wife. Then, of one accord, they made for the master of the house.

'Wasn't Columbus the greatest sailor in the world, Major Milward? Mark says____'

'He was a great sailor,' interrupted Mark; 'but he wasn't the greatest, was he, Major Milward? You told me who the greatest sailor was, didn't you, sir? But I have forgotten his name, and even mother doesn't know.'

'Tut, tut!' said Mrs. Gird. 'What's this?'

Major Milward took the lads between his knees. 'Mark is perhaps right, Rowland,' he said; 'and we will give honour to a brave man whatever his colour. The name you have forgotten, my boy, is Ui-te-rangio-ra. He lived some considerable time before Alfred the Great sat on the throne of England. He was the mightiest navigator of those times; he was perhaps the mightiest navigator the world has ever known. His vessel was a canoe; he had no compass other than his knowledge of the stars, yet in a voyage of four thousand miles he discovered New Zealand. Nor was that his longest voyage, for all his life he was a sailor, and it is claimed for him that he visited every island in the Southern world.'

It was a happy and merry party that sat down to the supper-table, and full of brightness were the faces that drank in brimming glasses the toast of the Fairest Land in the World.

'Now,' said the Major, rising with alacrity, 'set out the chessmen, Sandy. Mr. Raymond and I will play a game of chess.'

'Only one, father,' said Eve.

'Just one, my dear.'

'And win it,' she whispered. 'You must win it, dear, for my sake.'

She looked hesitatingly at the others who were all crowding together on the sofa and, taking a low stool, sat down at her father's feet.

Rowland and Mark occupied a chair jointly on his other hand. Now and then Sandy or Geoffrey came and looked down over Raymond's shoulder, but it was plain that the storekeeper had no backers.

Whenever the Major secured a piece, the boys nudged one another gleefully; when he suffered reverse, a tragic gloom overspread their features.

'Mate,' said the Major at last, and Eve drew a long breath of relief.

'Two games out of three, sir?#8217;

'Certainly, if you wish it, Raymond.'

The men were set out again and the battle recommenced. This time fortune dealt less favourably with the master of the house, and it was shortly evident that he was in trouble.

'Your move, sir, I think.'

'I am aware of it, Mr. Raymond.'

'Mate,' said the storekeeper.

'Ye-es, I cannot understand how the king's rook comes to be where it is. It must have been shifted inadvertently.' And Major Milward glared fixedly at the board,

'On the contrary, you gave four minutes' deliberation to that move.'

'oh, pardon me_____

'I saw you move it.'

'Game each,' said Sandy cheerfully. 'Now for the conqueror.'

The play this time was more deliberate. Raymond's mouth was set doggedly; he was plainly putting forth all his powers. Nor was the Major less determined. The eyes under his shaggy brows glittered with the light of battle, yet occasionally his hand trembled; for after all he was an old man. When his opponent's move was long delayed, he leant back with polite resignation, but his eyes never left the board. As the opportunity offered, Eve possessed herself of his hand and held it between her own or pressed it against her cheek. Her face was full of distress.

Sandy brought occasional reports to the party on the sofa.

'Old man got his queen jammed; have to sacrifice something.' Then more hopefully Wairangi holding strong position on left front. Enemy retiring disconcerted.'

Geoffrey watched his wife's face with anxiety.

'Happy man,' said Mrs. Gird, following the direction of his gaze. 'Would you change one line of it if you could'

Sandy crossed the room excitedly. 'Raymond hopelessly fogged,' he reported. 'Come and see.' And the whole party trooped over to the table.

Major Milward was leaning back watching the other's intent face, a bright spot of colour in his cheeks, a light of victory in his eyes.

Raymond put out his hand to move, hesitated, drew it back and sat up. 'I resign,' he said.

Mark immediately knocked Rowland off the chair and fell upon him.

Eve sprang to her feet, and throwing her arms round her father's neck, kissed him rapturously. 'You clever man,' she cried. 'You brilliant general.' Then she turned with rosy compunction to the storekeeper. 'I did so want father to win to-night, Mr. Raymond.'

'It might have simplified matters if you had mentioned the fact at the beginning,' said Sandy drily.

The storekeeper looked round the assembled company, and gathered for the first time that the match had been of interest to all of them.

'If I had guessed your feelings, Mrs. Hernshaw,' he said, 'I might have declined to play, but it would not have occurred to me to offer Major Milward the insult of playing less than my best.' For after all he was a university-bred man and a gentleman.

'Mr. Raymond's generosity completes my triumph,' said the Major, rising to his feet. 'But come, it is late. The oil in the lamp is nearly burnt away. I have not enjoyed a game of chess so much since—since'—(the failing lamp flickered and cast a momentary shadow)—' since a game I played with Governor Brown in '57. And I beat him two games out of three.'

301